Finch's Arms

Laz Newton

Burton Mayers Books

www.BurtonMayersBooks.com

To walking – the quiet companion.

Author's Note

What sparked the idea? One particularly windy evening, I was out on the porch trying to light a cigarette while holding a glass of wine and wrestling my hair out of my mouth. The glass smashed, the wine was lost, and my hair singed. I looked up to the heavens and cursed the human form.

Finch's Arms

Laz Newton

CHAPTER 1

Danny Finch throws his room door open, and the trapped heat hits him like a train.

Fancy taking your shoes off in a place like that, thinks Danny, hurling his rucksack over the bed. He slogs over to the kitchenette sink and runs the cold tap.

His hand is cut on that fleshy pad beneath the thumb. But it's alright. It's stopped bleeding now. Luckily the glass didn't cut too deep. He angles his hand under the steady stream of water, and rinses off the sun-dried blood that began its journey down his wrist and inner forearm less than an hour ago.

Leaving the tap running, Danny dislodges his ponytail from his sweaty neck and moves it aside. He lowers his head in the sink and lets the water cool his burning neck.

He pushes the already open window above the sink as far as the safety restrictor hinge will allow, a couple of inches if that, and gets annoyed. He swears and boots the kickboard under the sink, and it falls onto the split, outdated, patterned lino.

He leaves it.

He's pissed off.

He's pissed off and highly irritable on day three of an abnormally humid heatwave, unprecedented for early June. He's pissed off after cutting his hand, it's his right one as well. He's pissed off after having to trudge up four flights of stairs to his stale, stuffy room up in the eaves and he's pissed off there's no air. He's pissed off about the lino and even more pissed off that his room *has* lino. He's pissed off that he's thirty-nine and still renting a room at all. He's pissed off that he went for an afterwork drink. He wouldn't be feeling so wound up if he hadn't have got talked into going. He's pissed off that he can't remember where the plasters are, he knows he's seen them around somewhere.

He's pissed off that he's him.

After much left-handed slamming of kitchen drawers, the plasters still haven't surfaced. He goes out to the shower room along the landing and tries the cabinet above the toilet, which is where his search ends because they're not in there either. He gives up, and using great restraint, stops himself from slamming the magnetically hinged, mirrored cabinet door shut, and closes it gently. He's had quite enough adventures with broken glass for one day.

Re-entering his room, he falls back on his unmade bed, landing his face in the direct sunlight blazing through the skylight window, just above him, and in hand's reach on the slanted ceiling that he bangs his head on nearly every day. He pulls the skylight's black shutter blind down and strips down to his boxer shorts.

Letting out a deep sigh charged with regret, he thinks back to what happened earlier in the pub.

Work drinks, in one of those chains where you can have a pint with your fry-up, where everyone barges their way in at the bar eager for their mass-market offering of low-priced food and drink. Danny didn't want to go. He never does, and nobody was expecting him to, but a couple of the new packers on Danny's section who had been joking around with him about his hairnet – everyone with long hair must wear a hairnet in the bakery – managed to twist his arm.

It was Danny's round. The place was rammed. There were no trays, and Danny didn't fancy taking two trips in the heat, across the garden lawn littered with half-empty mayonnaise sachets and cigarette butts, then all the way from the heaving bar to their table right at the back, so he thought he'd chance it and carried out all four pints in one trip.

And he was off to a flying start, keeping a firm grip on two of the pints, one in each hand, with the other two held in by his sides and secured with his elbows, until he alighted the first step leading back to the garden, and the pints slipped out and smashed against the sandstone.

While everyone was clapping and cheering in keeping with good old British pub etiquette, a topless man of around fifty with a pierced eyebrow started getting a bit bolshy with Danny, told him to pick up all the glass immediately before someone gets hurt. 'My kids play in this pub,' he said.

Then the awful scream, from a woman who had taken her shoes off, coming up the stone steps. The ball of her foot felt the full force of a particularly nasty shard of glass in the surrounding area.

'Pick all that glass up, *clever bollocks*, before someone else gets hurt. You've got one pair of hands, you know, and if you don't pick it up, I'll rip 'em off and make sure you have none.'

'And that's my cue to leave,' said Danny, turning unsteadily on the steps after having been in there since five, drinking in the sun.

When he hit the floor, the two pint glasses he was still holding smashed, and, as tradition dictated, everyone clapped. That's how Danny cut his hand. When he tried to push himself back up, he landed his hand straight on a piece of glass.

Sucking the blood from his hand, Danny bolted through the gate and caught the 109-bus home.

That's where Danny is now. Home. In his hot box of a room, miserably regretting ever having gone for a drink and vowing to never be so easily persuaded again.

Fancy taking your shoes off in a place like that though.

A bluebottle flies in through the kitchenette window and briefly lands on his forehead, further increasing his irritable state.

'*You've only got one pair of hands. Why didn't you take two trips, clever bollocks?*' he sneers, lying back, stewing as he stares at his cut hand. This isn't the first time Danny's rather cavalier attitude towards carrying potentially

3

dangerous items has gotten him into trouble, and what transpired in the pub brings a particularly dark time in Danny's past back to mind.

His mother's face. Maddened and red. Christmas Day, 1996. It was one of the coldest winters on record.

The bluebottle lands on the back of his hand.

'Get off,' he snaps, freeing it to buzz lackadaisically about his room before catapulting into the window. *The heat is even slowing down the most hyperactive of insects*, thinks Danny in brief distraction.

Such an awful day – the day his mother gave him one hell of a backhander with her freckled hand across his face. A powerful blow for such a tiny woman.

'Turn it down,' she's saying to him, 'turn it down for God's sakes.'

His mother's face. He'd never seen her like that before.

Top of the Pops Christmas Day Special, blasting out from the old, chunky, cathode-ray set. The Mariah Carey poster on his bedroom wall. The framed photo of his father on the mantlepiece: a man he has no real memory of. The smell of brandy on his mother's breath, always shouting, always stressed.

'Such a sweet thing you were back then,' she's saying. 'Hard to believe it looking at you now.'

A chicken instead of a turkey. It was just the three of them that year.

'*Turn it down.*'

SLAP.

Mairead, his mother, screaming in his face. The teenage Danny, gangly and long, so tall for only thirteen. Flat footed and always frowning. Misguided and moody. Awful in the mornings.

Mariah Carey sitting on Santa's knee. Gramps sitting up at the table. Vacant. Staring, always staring through the patio doors.

'Remember this one Gramps?' But Gramps can't hear. Danny turning up the volume, gently coaxing him up from the table with both hands, floating him over to the television. Skin like filo pastry. Thick, rigid, blue veins underneath.

'Tommy?'

'No Gramps. It's Danny. I'm *Danny*.'

'You're not my Tommy.' Gramps looking up at Danny with eyes pale and misty, distant, and lost, like he's in the grip of a menacing stranger. Gramps, throwing down Danny's hands, shuffling back to the table. Early onset dementia. Soiled sheets. Good days. Bad days. New meds, so many meds.

Nintendo 64. Sega Mega Drive. X-Files poster. Gillian Anderson. Pulp Fiction. *The truth is out there...* Sonic the Hedgehog. *All I want for Christmas – is yoo-ooooou...* Hiding away in his bedroom. Gramps has soiled his sheets again. Tempers frayed, frazzled and fried. Doctors' appointments, so much carting about.

'Would you turn that damn thing down for Christ's sake, Daniel?!'

The back of her freckled hand.

Gravy boat. Pigs in blankets.

'Stuffing Daniel, take it through. Come on now, stop mucking about. Take it through, before it gets cold.'

Bare knuckles against boiling bone china. Gravy. Stuffing. Not enough hands. Hold it, Danny, *hold it. Ow, ow, ow, ow, ow, ow, ow.* It starts to slip – *ow, ow, ow, ow, ow.* Pouring on Gramps' exposed bald head. Gramps slumped over, asleep at the table. Gravy boat slipping. *Hot, hot, hot.* Molten lava cascading. Gramps' head like a blanched tomato with its skin peeled away, coming away so easily in your hand.

'I'm Brenda, your new foster mum. I'm going to be looking after you for a while, Daniel.'

'It's Danny. I'm Danny.'

Filo pastry. Thick blue veins. Molten lava. Bubbling. Burning knuckles. Not enough hands – ow, ow, ow, ow.

'Daniel – hurry up.'

'Alright, alright. I've only got one pair of hands, you know.'

Cascading. Pouring. Burning knuckles. Filo pastry. Eyes, pale and misty. That blood curdling scream. His mother wiping Gramps' head with a cloth and the skin coming away, so easily, peeling away. Gramps on a stretcher. Hot liquid death.

His mother. Maddened and red.

'The shock alone will kill him! Why didn't you take two trips, you *stupid* boy? Stupid, like your father!'

'I've only got one pair of hands, you know!'

'How *dare* you.'

Danny's right cheek stinging like hell.

Gramps died three days later.

Danny goes over to the kitchenette sink to splash his face with water. His shoulders bounce as he leans against the sink sobbing.

'It was an accident,' he mouths. 'An accident.'

CHAPTER 2

After possibly one of the most uncomfortable night's sleep Danny has ever had, he is woken up by the sound of kids kicking a can about down on the street below.

It's day four of the heatwave and his duvet is drenched with sweat, yet he's freezing cold. Something's wrong. A fever, a summer flu perhaps. The sides of his ribcage are itchy and sore.

He looks down at his sides under the duvet. They're red raw and covered with tiny bumps. Scratched to ribbons. The cut on his right hand is stinging where it has opened from all the unconscious scratching. Something must have bitten him in the night, and from the look of things, he suspects that it's something bigger than a gnat. A mosquito maybe, brought over with the heatwave. Mosquitos can survive in the British Isles; Danny saw a documentary about them not long ago.

But unable to resist any longer, Danny gives in to the burning, insatiable urge to scratch both sides at once, and the pain of his cut hand becomes secondary. He wonders whether he's having an allergic reaction to whatever it was that bit him, or if he could be experiencing the early stages of Malaria. He'd do an internet search for symptoms if he could only stop scratching for a moment. He looks ahead at his digital radio over by the sink for the time. It's gone noon, he can't believe it's this late. Pulling his sodden duvet up snug around his neck, he continues to scratch at his sides underneath like some crazed ape.

Danny's now so thirsty that his tongue is sticking to the roof of his mouth. And he's so cold the less than two-meter distance to the sink seems unfathomable.

But he makes it, and drinks straight from the faucet until he's unable to stand a moment longer swaddled in his sweat soaked duvet. Switching the radio on for company, he shuffles back over to his bed and curls up in a sticky, shivery ball, wondering what the hell is wrong with him.

A soothing female voice talks on the radio, but the pressure in his head is preventing him from being able to focus on what she's saying. But still, he finds it a comfort all the same.

'*I never intended on joining the Royal Air Force – not at all, really. I had always been driven towards a very different career path, but it was after studying medicine, that I realised – all I wanted to do was join the military…*'

Scratching his sides, unable to stop himself, he wonders if it could be a rash or maybe hives. Whatever it is, it's spreading.

'*Your father, Lieutenant Matthew Bishop – he served as a navigator, didn't he? Out in Germany, wasn't it?*

'*Yes, dad was stationed at Munich, but shortly after, he sadly lost his life and I think it was that influence on my life at such a young age that kind of turned me against ever joining up – but it was always my faith that got me through and I suppose, my walk with God that helped me.*'

'*And now for Helen's final Sunday hymn – her father's favourite hymn: 'When the Roll is Called Up Yonder' and this is particularly wonderful. You're listening to – Sunday Worship…*'

The full swell of a church organ blasts out from the radio sending his heavy head reeling. He covers it with the duvet wishing he had the strength to make it back over to the sink so he could turn the volume down.

'*And that was this week's Sunday Worship. Tune in next Sunday where we will be speaking to the Bishop of Clogher and…*'

It's funny. Danny could have sworn he just heard "Sunday Worship" which he knows can't be right. He's never been so ill that he's hallucinated before. The realisation frightens him. Could it be malaria, after all?

'*Thank you for listening to this week's Sunday Worship...*'

There, he heard it again.

For a moment, he stops scratching, and with his left hand, reaches for his phone. Bleary-eyed, he checks today's date and sees "Sunday" in the bottom right-hand corner of his SmartScreen.

'No. It can't be…'

But it is. Saturday has gone, which means Danny's had almost forty hours' sleep – as disjointed and uncomfortable as it was.

A sharp, sudden pain shoots down one side. *'Jesus,'* he moans. With eyes watering, he looks under the duvet and sees a plum-sized, plum-coloured blister or papule, pink and yellow fluid swirling around inside – a nauseating sight. The plum looks like it might burst at any moment, and with Monday morning's six-am start at the bakery looming, there's no way he's going in. Not like this. The sickly sweet, yeasty aroma is filling his nostrils just thinking about the place. *All that ripe wheat and batter. All those muffins. Vanilla pastries. Cupcakes and buttery, crisping croissants.*

He queasily turns over, careful not to pop the painful, purple blister.

All those sugared donuts. Sweet plum focaccia. Plum turnovers. Plum jam cookies. Spiced plum custard cake.

Lurching over the bed, Danny projectile vomits on the floor.

'Oh God. Help me.'

Gathering enough strength to yank his work t-shirt down from the headboard, where it's been hanging since Friday, he wipes his mouth with it and then covers the pile of sick, before finally succumbing to a deep sleep.

It's six-pm by the time Danny wakes up. The radio's still on and the itching sensation has been replaced with an intense stabbing pain – so bad, that he's sure that *thing* must have burst. Plucking up the courage, he checks beneath the duvet.

It's worse than he thought. It's still there, only bigger, and there's one on the other side now too. They're the size of clementines, at least, and there's a putrid smell. 'Oh God.' There's no way he can go in like this, no way.

Wincing in trepidation, Danny tries to act out some of

the movements needed on a typical day's shift: packing lemon slices into a box; taking a tray of sour dough loaves down from the top shelf; keeping his arms down flush by his sides to make way for innumerable racking trolleys speeding though from dispatch. Making a noise not dissimilar to that of an injured animal, he resigns himself to his fate – he's going to have to call in sick. Normally, such a thing fills him with dread, but right now, he's in too much pain to care.

With his arms outstretched and as far away from his sides as possible, very much aware of a malodorous smell, he hauls himself up and switches off the radio – an exhausting excursion, which leaves him hunched over on the end of his bed, staring down at the dizzying lino for a few moments before he is able to make the call.

Gerry, his boss, finally picks up.

'Danny?' Gerry answers loudly over the mechanical din of the bread grinder. A call on a Sunday from Danny can only mean one thing. 'Wait a minute. Let me go outside,' says Gerry walking out to dispatch where it's quieter.

'Don't tell me. You're sick again. Am I right?'

'Gerry, I…' Danny's voice cracks. '…I feel shocking. Something's wrong with me.'

'Oh dear. What was it this time? Dodgy curry? Reheated rice? Or was it the oysters again, *hmmm*?'

Danny's pulled more than his fair share of "sick days" this past month alone and Gerry's not buying it.

'I've thrown up, Gerry. I'm shaking all over.'

'Well, that's a hangover for you, Danny. No need to ham it up so much. I heard about the, err, work drinks. You're lucky you weren't barred.'

'Something's happening to me.' Danny looks down at his painful clementines. 'Gerry. I'm scared. I think I've got an infection or something. There's a smell.'

'God, Jesus, Danny, *please*. Spare me the details. Get yourself down the GUM clinic. I don't want to know.'

'Please. Gerry…'

'Look, whatever it is, I'm sure you'll make yet another miraculous recovery.'

The corner of the duvet brushes over his left clementine, causing him to yelp with pain.

'Good Danny, *very* good that was, but I ain't buying it. You got that?'

'Gerry please. You don't... you don't understand...'

'Don't I?'

A racking trolley filled with freshly baked baguettes comes racing through the double swing doors. Gerry moves out of the way.

'Now you listen here, Danny. I'm getting a bit fed up with this to be quite honest, with this... this pattern. You must think I'm soft in the head or something. And maybe I am. Now look, you can have tomorrow off. Sleep off your hangover, but this time it comes out your wages.'

'But...'

Gerry hangs up.

For the past hour, Danny's been telling himself to man up and tough it out, like he did when he had a stye the size of a chickpea on his upper eyelid. He couldn't open his eye for a week, but then out of the blue, it just vanished. It was as if it had never been there at all. No scar, nothing.

And the whitlow finger. The same thing happened with that. After his finger ballooned to the size of a sausage, he woke up one day to find it reduced back down to its normal size with the whitlow gone.

And the horrendous cluster of verrucae he had on his foot, which formed into a rock-hard scab. He sounded like Fred Astair when he walked across a tiled floor. Danny truly believed it would be there forever. But then on the beach one day, he walked on the sand, had a little splash in the sea, and the whole thing fell away in one go to reveal perfectly fresh, pink healthy skin underneath. Why should this time be any different?

Danny braves another peek.

They're angrier now, fuller. The pink and yellow swirling liquid has turned to blood orange, but Danny's refusing to panic:

They'll go on their own accord; most things usually do. Probably just a couple of ingrown hairs, bad ones, I'll give you that. Just got infected, that's all. Nothing major. Nothing serious. A couple of ingrown hairs and a summer flu. Perfectly normal. Perfectly natural. Everyone gets 'em from time to time. They'll be gone by the morning. Nothing to worry about. Absolutely nothing to worry about. Cysts, that's all. A bit of pus, a bit of swelling. No big deal. A Couple of ingrown hairs, that's all…that's all…that's all…

Heavy rain pummels down against the open skylight window. Danny awakes to big, fat, unplayful dollops bouncing off his dry lips, bringing with it an earthly perfume. Breathing it in, he senses a new freshness in the air – in his head, too, and painlessly reaching across to a distant roll of thunder, he pulls down the release clamp handle on the window and shuts it.

Without looking, he feels his sides.

'Oh, thank God. Thank God.' It's over. They've gone. The smell too.

It's just like he said. 'Just like the whitlow,' he says, laughing and snorting in relief and swinging his legs round the bed. Careful not to tread on his work t-shirt, and with feet wide apart, Danny grounds himself on the floor, feeling almost human once again.

Opening the mirrored wardrobe door, he takes down a clean towel from the top and heads out to the landing for a much-needed shower.

But just outside his door, he stops and looks down at himself. *Must be seeing double. Another one of them delirium hallucinations*, he thinks to himself, rubbing his eyes. *Blurred vision that's all, a bit of paranoia, from the fever no doubt.*

But it really *was* "Sunday Worship", and he really *did* sleep through all of Saturday. No delirium hallucinations there. Re-entering his room backwards, he stops in front of the wardrobe, widens his eyes in the mirror.

A vigorous shake of the head followed by a sanity-questioning slap across the face leaves him dizzy, knocking him for six and causing his foot to squish into the t-shirt covered vomit. In the mirror, he sees two, stinging red, hand marks brandished across his numbing cheek.

Two?

Slapped by two right hands. Two right hands slapped him. *Two right hands slapped me?* Two right hands at the end of two right arms. The clementines may have gone, but not without leaving something in their place.

Four hands? Two lefts? Two rights? No, no way.

Four hands, four arms. Twenty fingers but ten of them belong to new hands. Smaller hands, more delicate than his usual pair. The arms too – puny, weird looking things, not that his usual ones are anything to write home about. Danny's no beefcake. But they do make his usual pair look comparatively impressive.

And he finds it funny for a while. Until the shock sets in, and he starts to make this pained noise – a high-pitched, almost wailing sound. He can't accept it. He won't accept it. Sprouting a second pair of arms – just like that? Locking eyes with his otherworldly reflection, he psychically commands the imposters to leave.

The landing stairs creak. The coughing and heavy breathing tells Danny that it's Murphy – his live-in landlord and the only other person desperate enough to live in the unloved, neglected excuse for a building he calls home.

While Murphy's banging about in the boiler cupboard, Danny quietly locks the door and tries to thread both pairs of arms through the sleeves of his dressing gown. He'd rather not be seen like this.

'Come *on.*' They won't fit. With a sigh, he slides his usual pair through in the customary fashion, then folds the new pair across his chest. Pulling the towelling fabric snug around his body, he cinches his waist with the belt, trying to keep his cool.

Having someone to talk to would help, as self-conscious as he is. But who? There's no girlfriend, no family. The only real friends he does have are all married with kids, got mortgages, careers. Everyone moved on, made something of their lives while Danny got left behind, permanently wedged in the nineties, with nothing to show but a couple of battered pairs of vintage Adidas Superstars and a scattering of vinyls.

'Hurry *up*,' he mutters, following Murphy's heavy tread all the way down to the ground floor.

After a mad dash for the shower, he locks the bathroom door behind him and whips off his dressing gown and boxer shorts in one motion.

And then he looks at them, tries to take it all in. These doll-like appendages with hardly any hair at all, not even under their little armpits. So pale and white when the rest of him is so swarthy and hairy. Even as a teenager, Danny had dark, glossy hair extending well below the wrist. Hairy knuckles too by the age of eighteen.

Soaping up in the shower the usual way, he makes the tricky manoeuvre of untying his ponytail, matted and knotted after three nights of sweating, tossing, and turning. Lathering his hair under the frustratingly low water-pressure, he begins working on his nether regions.

Ordinarily, he would have dropped the soap by now – or at least lost his balance when reaching for his feet. But with this extra pair, Danny finds he can steady himself against the cracked tiles of the cubicle and even catch the soap with ease before it falls.

While clipping his toenails, he unclogs the shower drain. As he rinses the conditioner from his hair, he gathers the clippings. He even squeezes in a shoulder massage while squeegeeing down the shower screen. Wrapping a towel around his waist, he gives the dripping showerhead built up with years of limescale and sediment a good scrubbing with a wooden nail brush.

But why must you look so bloody different, thinks Danny, running a comb through his wet hair and staring ahead at his little arms in the wardrobe mirror. *Maybe then it wouldn't be so bloody weird.*

Brushing new fingers over the soft, baby hairs of his new forearms, he gazes up through the skylight. A gathering rain cloud passes, and he thinks, *why now? Why me?*

Two accidents, caused by the easy mistake of carrying too much in one trip. First Gramps, and then this woman in the pub – *poor cow.* Of course, it could have been avoided, and of course, he regrets it, but not everybody learns from their mistakes.

Setting his comb aside, he wonders if his transformation might be linked to temperature extremes. After all, the incident in the pub on Friday occurred during one of the hottest days on record, while the tragic spilling of the gravy happened on one of the coldest. This polarity must have something to do with it, surely? Or was it lightening, sending a jolt of electricity through his body while he slept. Did sparks fly all over? Did somebody experiment on him in the night? Or a celestial happening, up in the heavens, where the stars aligned, and all the angels got together and decided to gift Danny with these objects of plenty? Helping hands bestowed upon him by the universe, nevertheless.

Having resumed his hair combing in a trance, Danny's been remembering the dream he once had of running a beach bar in Tenerife. With Billy Backhurst, but Billy bailed on him at the last minute, saying he'd met a girl, so the dream died. Danny didn't want to go it alone. But all this? Now? An extra pair of hands might be just what's needed to bring it back to life.

They'd certainly streamline the cocktail-making process and help him trim staffing costs. All that ice, all that straining, all that muddling – simplified. Closing his eyes,

Danny pictures himself behind a moonlit bar, effortlessly pouring piña-coladas for sun kissed holiday makers, two at a time, as soft reggae drifts through the warm night air.

Newly spirited, spraying deodorant under his armpits, an encouraging grin starts to spread on his face. By armpit number three, it's gone. His deodorant has run out.

'Great. Bloody marvellous,' he says, throwing the used can in the bin and mourning the reality that his expenditure on deodorant and hand soap has just doubled. Any notion of the beach bar is readily dismissed.

With the monetary burden of his arms sinking in, their celestial allure rapidly converts to grievance.

'A whole new wardrobe I'm gonna need now. That won't come cheap.' Not forgetting food. His calorie intake is set to increase considerably. 'With these things leeching off of me.'

The last time any food passed his lips was Friday, but with only a half-squeezed tube of tomato puree and a Jif lemon in the fridge, he's going to have to go out. He can't hide away forever, not when he has work tomorrow.

Work. Now there's a thing. It's likely that Gerry will make him work double the speed and raise his picking target to unachievable levels, taking full advantage of his new edge over his fellow packers.

Life's about to get significantly harder, supposes Danny, looking up through the skylight. *They're a curse, a punishment. Divine retribution from Gramps beyond the grave.* Danny doesn't blame him.

Hacking two extra arm holes in one of his baggiest t-shirts, Danny's craving a gummy, gelatinous menagerie of slithery, fruity, foamy based sweets that get horribly stuck in his teeth. Torment often leads him to the pick 'n' mix, so without further ado, he throws on his rucksack, and heads for the supermarket.

They're only arms. You've seen one arm you've seen them all, he thinks, breezing through the automatic doors, making a beeline for the confectionary aisle with his new arms tucked in behind his rucksack – concealing them well enough that nobody has batted an eyelid so far. And Danny knows that people these days are so glued to their smartphones, he could have sprouted two heads and still, nobody would take a blind bit of notice.

His self-consciousness subsiding, he grabs two clear plastic scoops with his right hands and holds two pink-and-white striped paper bags open with both his left and gets shovelling.

A blue and green jelly snake escapes to the floor, and noticing the aisle is empty, he quickly picks it up and bites into it, tugging it down, his bottom lip stretching to his chin. Moaning with delight, he quickly scoffs a couple more, just as a hungover man with a mop of dark, curly hair – still in yesterday's shirt and business suit – enters from the far end of the aisle.

Skimming the acrylic floor in his brown leather brogues, the man frantically searches for the toiletries aisle.

'Shit,' he says. Wrong aisle.

Deciding to make a quick exit past Danny at the pick 'n' mix, a double take causes him to momentary linger. He knows he had a lot to drink last night, but not enough to still be seeing double. Quietly, he moves back, safely obscuring himself behind a pallet of *Dolmio*, and secretly films a video on his phone.

After hitting send, he calls Heather.

'Jem. What is it? I'm busy.'

'You don't need any more strawberry laces by any chance, do you, H?' A supermarket Tannoy announces a BOGOF deal on three-ply toilet roll.

'Jem? Where are you? What are you doing?'

'Oh, just a bit of talent spotting. "Bring me something diverse" – *isn't that what you said?*'

'Why are you whispering like that? Are you in Gino's?'

'*Just watch the video I sent you.*'

Moving over to her office window, Heather surveys the

busy Mayfair high-street several floors below. 'Jem, be a darling and pick me up a cappuccino on your way up, would you? Oh, and an apricot swirl.'

'*I can't.* I'm in *South Ealing.*'

'South Ealing? What are you doing there?'

'It doesn't matter. *Just play the video, please.*'

'Ah, I get it. Colleen kicked you out again?'

'Yeah, something like that. *Just play it.*'

'But South Ealing? Why didn't you try the Grange? Or the Belvoir? I could have got you a discount. South Ealing, honestly.'

'You try finding a hotel last minute with my wife breathing down your neck.'

The slight raising of Jem's voice makes Danny turn around. Jem slips into the cereal aisle and locates a lookout behind the last remaining boxes of Rice Crispies.

'What's this you've sent me?'

'*Look, just watch it,*' pleads Jem, looking up to the ceiling and instantly regretting it – the glare of the flush mounted LED ceiling lights is the last thing his hangover needs.

'Alright, alright.'

Finally, she hits play, and after only a few seconds of watching, she is stunned into silence.

'But those – those can't be real. Surely, those can't be real. They must be fakes.'

'Diverse enough for you?'

'Well yes, this is quite a discovery.'

'Didn't I tell you? – Oh, *shit.*'

'What? What's happening?'

'It's moving. It's heading towards the baked goods aisle.'

'Well, *track it.* Follow it. Find out where it lives. Don't let it leave your sights—'

'But I haven't checked out the hotel yet. I haven't even shaved.' Colleen didn't give Jem the good grace of packing an overnight bag before booting him out last night.

'Just follow it, Jem!'

Heather pulls up the agency client base on her computer. She knows exactly who'll go for a freak like this.

~

'Funny little fellas aren't you,' says Danny, lying back on his bed, floating his new arms and hands above his head. He's been doing it long enough for them to have gone tingly from the loss of blood, and detached, as if belonging to someone else. Will the novelty ever wear off? He can't imagine it will. Such slender fingers. Such soft skin. No cuts or scrapes. No scuffs or callouses. Feminine looking really. They're going numb.

Transfixed by their delicate wrists, he shakes them out to get the blood flowing again, then slips them beneath the sheets and introduces them to a very old friend.

The intercom screeches – coitus interruptus. Danny throws on his dressing gown with the same frustration as before, and trundles down the stairs, the little fellas shielding his partial tumescence.

Probably the council complaining about the bins again, he thinks, reluctantly opening the door. But when he does, he's relieved to see a man in a shabby suit standing on the doorstep. Hot. Sweaty. *Poor guy*, he thinks, staring unenviously at him. *Door-to-door sales – it's a tough racket.*

After tracking Danny all the way to his door, Jem fell asleep on an aluminium perch seat under the bus shelter at the end of Danny's road. A phone call from Heather soon fixed that, jolting him from his slumber, his neck stiff after being wedged against the toughened safety glass for so long.

Through the hell of his hangover, he speaks:

'Thanks so much for coming to the door. I won't keep you. I'm here on behalf of—'

'Sorry. Not today, thanks.' Rather than waste time, Danny puts the man out of his misery and gestures to close the door.

But a brogued foot edges into the doorway, preventing it from closing. 'I'm not trying to sell you anything. I'm here to make you an offer.'

'Look, dress it up how you want, but I'm skint. I just had to put two bags of pick 'n' mix back in the supermarket just now.' It's true. Danny's card got declined. 'Really, you're wasting your time with the likes of me. Now, if you don't mind...'

Met with equal resistance, they grapple with the door.

'Wait. Please,' says Jem, 'I saw you. In the supermarket just now. At the pick 'n' mix. I was watching you.' Recoiling from the cocktail of last night's booze and this morning's coffee on Jem's dehydrated breath, Danny loses his grip long enough for Jem to sneak a few inches inside. 'Come on. We both know what you've got hiding under there.'

A woman pushing a buggy towards the side of Danny's building glances over with an amused smile, halting their clandestine conversation. Danny pulls his dressing gown tighter across himself.

'Come on,' says Jem once she's passed. 'Let's not do this on the doorstep, yeah?'

'Do what?'

'I liked what I saw, okay? And many more people are going to like it too. Here...' Taking out his wallet, Jem shells out the money he was intending to pay off last night's mini-bar bill with. 'That's twenty, forty, sixty, seventy, wait – look, that's ninety-five-quid. For two hours' work.'

He's a pervert, not a salesman, thinks Danny, looking down at the fanned cash.

'Go on, take it. It's yours,' says Jem, nodding earnestly. 'Go on.'

'Ninety-five quid. For two hours?'

'Sorry. That's all I've got for now.' Ninety-five pounds is more than half of what Danny makes in a week. 'But I promise you won't have to do too much. Just be admired, really. A marvel like you should be *adored*,' says Jem, edging his way further inside the doorway. 'And there'll be more to follow – if you want it.'

'Want what?' Danny tightens the belt of his dressing gown a little more.

'Shall we – go up?'

Danny casts a glance at the door to his right, hearing Murphy snoring away behind it.

'Come on, then. Quickly,' he says, ushering Jem inside, shocked at how willing he is to sell himself for a quick buck and convinced that these arms truly are a curse. Already, they have brought such vice, such humiliation. *A fitting punishment for me, eh Gramps?* The old man always did have a wicked sense of humour.

Turning on the stairs, Danny takes the money from Jem's hand. 'Let's just get this over with, okay? I'm right at the top,' he adds, pointing the way.

The temperature rises with each step of their four-storey climb.

'Two hours?' says Danny, unsticking his ponytail from his neck when they reach the top. 'That's all you want?'

'That's the gig.'

They enter his room.

'Christ, it's hot in here. Mind if I...?' says Jem, gesturing towards the end of Danny's bed.

'Sure,' says Danny, brushing off a stray sock while Jem sits and undoes another shirt button. Danny looks away.

'Now, look. I want to be as thorough as I can be with you, but there's a lot I need to cover—'

'Music? How about some music?' suggests Danny, wishing not to be "adored" in stone silence.

'Well, I suppose so, but please listen. I have something *very* exciting for you. Something big.'

'Big? How big?' says Danny, facing the sink and selecting *Sensual FM*. Janet Jackson's *That's the Way Love*

21

Goes plays.

'*Massive.*'

After a silent prayer, he disrobes and lets his dressing gown drop to the floor, then at awkward angles, presents himself, floating his arms to the music. 'Sorry,' he says, noticing the contorted expression on Jem's face. 'I'm new at this.'

'New at what?'

'*This*,' whispers Danny, softly placing all four of his hands on Jem's knees.

'No. *God no.* Stop. Please,' says Jem, shooting up like a rocket. 'Are you insane? You've got this all wrong. I don't want – *that*,' he says, ruffling his hands through his hair. 'There's been some kind of misunderstanding. That's not what I'm here for. Put your clothes back on, man.'

'Now hang on a minute,' says Danny, knotting his dressing gown belt. '*You* were the one perving over me at the pick 'n' mix. You, matey.'

'Yes – *no*. I mean, yes – but not like that. Not perving, spotting. I'm a talent scout – for now anyway. I'm here on behalf of *Complete Celebs*. I'm here representing the agency, that's all – for today at least. Here—'

Danny takes the business card from his hand and reads:

'*Complete Celebs*. One of the UK's top celebrity talent agencies. Heather Harridan?' Jem's eight o'clock shadow is suddenly confusing.

'That's not me. I'm not *her*. I'm Jem. My name is Jem.'

'As in, Gemma?'

'No. *Jem*. I work in television.'

'Talent?'

'Yes. As soon as I saw you, I was straight on to the phone to Heather who told me to follow it – *you* – follow *you* – and here we are! There hasn't been a talent as diverse as you since, well, the Victorian age. The Victorian age, Danny! And what a sight you are. Heather wants you on the books as soon as possible. She's ready to put you to work straight away.'

'Put me to work?'

Janet Jackson rolls into Chris Isaak's *Wicked Game*.

'Please. Can we lose the music?'

Danny turns it off.

'Now, I have so much to tell you, but first – please may I have some water?'

Over several glasses of water, Jem fills Danny in on his gig.

'*Isabella's*? Where all them sleazy politicians go?'

'Well, yes... or more precisely, the world-renowned private members' club hosting an exclusive birthday event. Now, stay with me...'

Isabella's, with all its unapologetic snobbery and daunting good taste.

'It's a high-class event. Think art, not sleaze. You'll hardly have to do anything at all, just walk across a stage – I think. Anyway, a black Mercedes will collect you. Listen out for two beeps of the horn. We're starting you off on a Grade-C fee, but it won't take long until you're on a Grade-A or Grade-B...'

'Grade-C?'

'Two thousand pounds – including travel. You know how cruel these London roads can be.'

'Two grand?'

'Yes. In a brown envelope. You'll receive it after the show. Your car will pick you up at five-thirty this evening...'

'This evening?'

'On the dot. A black Mercedes.' Jem heads for the door. 'Now, I think that's everything.'

'But it's Monday. Who has a birthday party on a Monday night?'

'Ah, I knew I forgot something – Kelly Ross, that's who.'

CHAPTER 3.

Kelly Ross: Essex-girl-turned-world-famous-supermodel. Spotted on Southend seafront in the early nineties, with cheekbones so sharp they cast their own shadow.

Kelly Ross: regularly papped getting blottoed on Bolly, on billionaires' boats in black bikinis. Kelly Ross, with her penchant for leather and wrinkles, holidays with counts and countesses and parties with Elton John. Kelly Ross, in that ridiculous perfume advert, seen jumping off the Eiffel Tower, then morphing into a white peacock and chasing a black stallion through the Paris night before vanishing in a puff of cigarette smoke.

Yes, that's her.

Now, Kelly's crowd is select – or so she likes to think. Artists. Luvvies. Socialites and starlets. Air kisses and grandiose displays of affection. These are the beautiful people who go by a paradoxical playbook, where disingenuity equals cool. Any expression of gratitude, no matter how slight, would be social suicide for this lot – at least for *this* season.

Kelly must keep this impossible lot satisfied, *she must*. With so many needs they can easily bore. Their eccentric lifestyles and complicated tastes have become a burden, and their lack of responsibility hers – for tonight, anyway.

But all this excessive partying takes its toll. Many of them will be exhausted – *poor darlings*. And you mustn't think of them as shallow, it's not as deep as that. If you were to try and scratch their veneer or dare to question them at all, it's unlikely you'd get an answer, and it would be cruel to expect one. They simply wouldn't understand.

Kelly currently considers herself a Dadaist, inspired by a movement that needn't be understood for it to be understood. Kelly doesn't have time for heavy reading, and besides, the less she understands, the more she seems to grasp it.

'Nonsense, it's a load of nonsense,' she said only in last month's *Harper's Bazaar*, and much of tonight's focus will be on the nonsensical. Kelly has employed the *découpé* cut-up technique to help her decide on a title for Danny's performance. As soon as her management showed her the video of him, Kelly knew she had to have him. She immediately began scribbling the first words that popped into her little head onto scraps of paper, tossing them into her Tibetan singing bowl. At exactly nine-and-a-half-minutes before the show, she will pick out three of the words and feed them to the show's moderator through an earpiece.

'I want people to go away thinking, *what the fuck was all that about?* whenever they leave my parties,' she told *British Vogue*.

Sitting tight in the foyer of *Isabella's*, Danny remains oblivious to tonight's particulars. The Victorian age – what did Jem mean by it? There hasn't been a talent as diverse as you since the "Victorian age" – that's what he said up in Danny's room.

But he said nothing about his arms – or what he can even do with them. Juggle, for instance. Or perform magic tricks. Two at a time, no less. Insane DJ scratching. Juggle while solving a Rubik's cube? Unfortunately, Danny can't do any of these things, but it would have been nice to have been asked. Manners cost nothing.

Gazing up at the ridiculously high ceiling of the Georgian mansion, Danny thinks on: *A marvel like you. That's what Jem said. Marvel. Mar-vell-ous. To marvel. At what? At me? Can you marvel at a marvel? To marvel, to ogle. To gawp, to stare.*

A red and white circus tent appears in Danny's mind, crammed with all those curious weirdos: The Bearded Lady. The Conjoined twins. The Three-Legged Man. *Step right up, step right up.* The tuba's sinister, waltzing bassline. The dissonant notes of the steam-whistle organ, striking an eerie balance between spooky and bright, as the Four-Armed Man joins the historic lineup of sideshow freaks. The biological oddity that is… Danny Finch: The Four-Armed-Freak. *Step right up. Step right up.*

It's been over twenty minutes now. Twenty minutes of restless leg-jigging while holding tightly onto the padded shoulder straps of the rucksack on his back, with his new hands tightly concealed behind, thinking how dirty the laces of his Adidas Superstars look. Yesterday's vest he's wearing doesn't look too much brighter, either. It was the only garment he could find with armholes big enough to fit both pairs of arms through. He couldn't bear cutting up any more of his t-shirts.

The approaching click of fast-paced footsteps on the marquetry floor pulls him out of his shoegazing. A paunchy man dressed in black, wearing a headset with a little mouthpiece pressed into his plump cheek, speeds through two byzantine columns.

'Are you the man with the arms?' he asks, a little breathless. Danny nods. 'Oh, thank God. You're here. I'm Nigel.'

'Nice to meet you,' says Danny, standing and awkwardly extending his usual right hand. His newer, smaller one shoots up unexpectedly.

'Sorry,' says Danny, pushing it back down. 'Automatic reflex. Still trying to work on that.'

Unnerved by this physical quirk, Nigel doesn't shake. 'No time for pleasantries I'm afraid. Let's walk and talk. This way.'

Leading Danny back through the byzantine columns setting an impressive pace, Danny quickens his step. *Nigel's fast for a porker*, he thinks, the soles of his Superstars squeaking against the high-polished floor.

After a sharp turn, they enter a vast, heavily draped room, decked out with animal-print furnishings.

'The stage set is all Pritt-Stick and staple guns. My six-year-old niece could have done better. Nothing to do with me. Just *go with the flow,*' adds Nigel, with a flourish of the hands. 'Kelly's all about the *flow,* you know. Come on. Keep up.'

They exit through two colossal wooden doors leading out into a corridor of gilt-framed mirrors. 'Carved oak,' says Nigel, smoothing his hand over the doorframe before stopping at one of the mirrors to straighten it.

'So, what does Kelly want me to do exactly? I mean, what does she want from me up there, on the stage?'

'*Hmmm?*'

'I can't dance or sing. I hope she knows that? I can't even juggle. I can't do anything.'

'The cleaning staff have really taken their eye off the ball lately,' comments Nigel, buffing a smudge off the mirror with the sleeve of his black turtleneck. 'They might be working faster, but it's certainly not *better.* Come on. It's just through here.'

Whizzing down the corridor, Danny catches glimpses of his puzzled profile in every mirror as they pass.

'Deep breath *in,*' says Nigel, filling his lungs as he braces himself for the spiral staircase. His short, stubby legs attack each step, while Danny takes two at a time.

'No lifts in this place, then?' asks Danny, already out of puff.

'Oh yes, plenty. But Kelly insists that you arrive – *à pied.* Something to do with you "finding your centre" before taking to the stage.' Hand flourish after hand flourish after hand flourish.

'Finding my centre?'

'Yes. Solid. Rooted. Stable like a tree. She would hate for you to be – *on the fritz,* as it were. Come, come. Nearly there.'

Clambering for the banister, his vest sticking with sweat, Danny feels about as *on the fritz* as he's ever felt. How Nigel can be wearing a cashmere turtleneck without breaking a sweat astonishes him, so much so that he is no longer fazed by the uncertainties of tonight's performance. And there isn't much Danny *wouldn't* do for two grand.

At last, they reach the top.

Hurrying along in Nigel's wake, Danny feigns interest in his detailed commentary on the cantilevered staircase, the elaborate plaster ceiling, and the majestic Rococo-style fireplace as they pass, doubting whether he'll ever "find his centre" in this seemingly endless journey.

'Those are real palm trees over there,' Nigel keenly points out as they breeze through the Giraffe Room. 'And that's mohair in the wallpaper, harvested from Angora goats.'

Danny reaches out a hand.

'No, no. You mustn't touch,' snaps Nigel, batting it away. 'Through here.'

Exiting through an unassuming side door, camouflaged by the hairy wallpaper, they leave the lavish world behind them.

'And this is back-of-house,' says Nigel, regretfully, closing the door behind them with an ambient thump. Exposed cables now adorn the walls, instead of transportive murals offering early views of India and Babylon. 'And be warned, there's quite a chill along here. And mind that mop and bucket down there. I don't know why housekeeping insist on leaving it there, I really don't.'

Swerving the mop and bucket, they journey through a miserably narrow, concrete corridor where Danny is grateful for the cooler air. His little arms, clammy and marked by the mesh of his rucksack after being in the same position for so long, unfold and release, while Nigel stomps ahead rubbing his woollen-sleeved arms up and down against the apparent chill.

A woman clattering a tea-trolley comes by. Pressing himself against the wall to let her pass, Danny relishes the cold concrete on his back.

Squeezing past a stack of wooden chairs, they come to an industrial door with a roller shutter mechanism. Nigel activates a button, and the corrugated metal groans and rises.

'Yin?' says Nigel, over the din of the steel slats disappearing into one another.

'Yes?' answers a female voice.

'Kelly's *court jester* has arrived. I'll leave him outside the door for you.'

Turning to face Danny, Nigel says, 'And this is where we part.' Danny extends his old right hand, managing to overcome his auto-reflex issue, but still, Nigel won't shake it and again leaves him hanging. Danny detects a glimmer of repulsion on his face. 'Must dash. Break a leg.'

And off he recedes, back down the corridor, muttering into his mouthpiece. Danny watches him until a flash of blue snatches his eye as the door opens, sending his arms straight behind his back.

'Come in, come *in*,' says a petite, smiley young woman eagerly ushering him into a spacious square room with a single bed in the corner with a half-eaten bowl of cereal on the floor beside it. 'This backstage,' she informs him, gesturing towards racks of dresses, wigs, and costumes. There's a sewing machine too, and messily stacked paints and materials on floor-to-ceiling storage shelves along the back. 'So,' she says, tying a large-pocketed apron around her tiny waist, 'you ready to be painted gold?'

'Gold? I guess so,' answers Danny flatly, apathy having set in. 'Nothing would surprise me now.'

Leading him by an old elbow over to a bulb-lit vanity mirror, Yin gently encourages his folded little arms out from behind his back. 'Don't be shy,' she says, pulling at his rucksack.

'I'm not,' he says, taking a seat in a dusky rose makeup chair, quickly slipping it off and shoving it under the dressing table.

The sudden confrontation with his reflection in the mirror makes him tense, unsure where to place his hands –

so many hands.

'You're tall,' she says, pumping the foot pedal to lower the chair.

'You be proud of what you've got,' she says, sliding off his hairband and detangling his hair with a flexible bristled brush. 'I've seen many strange things in my life.'

'Don't tell me – I'm the strangest.'

'No. There was a man in Phuket.' Yin speaks with the hairband between her teeth. 'With no arms at all, and no legs. Everyone was so cruel to him.' Danny watches her brown eyes go glassy in the mirror. 'It made me angry. I got *real* mad.'

Danny doesn't know whether she's telling him this to make him feel guilty or to make him feel better about himself, but strangely, her anecdote makes him feel a mixture of both.

'One minute,' she says, going over to the shelves. Danny watches her in the mirror while she vigorously shakes a can of gold paint. The ball-bearings rattle loudly as she comes back over.

'Close your eyes,' she tells him, standing on a stool, preparing to spray his face.

Halfway through spraying his right old arm, her phone rings, and they watch it vibrating and jittering on the dressing table.

'You gonna get that?' says Danny, his arm aching from having held it out for so long. But in a trance, she just keeps on staring at it, until something compels her to grab it and rush out of the room.

Although not intending to listen, Danny can hear her outside the door, her voice subdued and contrite, all the colour gone. And when she returns, her demeanour has changed. Sulky, almost pouty, as she traipses back over to pick up the can and give it another furious shake.

'*Cranberry soda! Cranberry soda! Cranberry soda!*' she blasts, over the racket of the ball-bearings. '*Cranberry soda!*' she fires out once more. 'Who she think she is? Queen of...

Queen of... Shiva? Fix your own drink next time. *Jeez.*'

Watching her eyes burn in the mirror, Danny thinks it best not to point out her idiomatic error. 'Ah, the boss, eh? If it's any consolation, mine's an absolute arsehole. I'm meant to be in tomorrow. Don't think I'll bother. Think I'll quit. Go abroad. Tenerife, maybe. What you reckon?'

Yin reckons nothing. Firewalled off, it's like getting blood out of a stone. Danny stops yacking and lets her finish the spray-job in peace.

Behind an oriental screen in the corner of the room, Danny changes into tonight's outfit: a black sleeveless tuxedo with a white sleeveless shirt, black bowtie, black slacks with black satin ribbons running down each outer leg.

'How you getting on?' asks Yin.

'The trousers are a bit short,' he says, stepping out and showing her his pale, hairy, ankles. 'That's the problem with being tall. And my hair – you're not gonna leave it like this, are you? It's just that I never wear it down – usually – ever – well, never.'

Slinging his tennis shoes over his shoulder by the laces, Danny follow's Yin's widening eyes down to his feet. Bringing her hand to her mouth, she gasps.

'What? What is it?'

A finger-like, hairy toe pokes out from a hole in his sock.

'Your dress shoes not in the bag I gave you? Where are your dress shoes?'

'*Dress* shoes? What, heels? I'm not wearing heels, especially not with my hair like this.'

A futile and frantic fifteen-minute search ensues, ending with Yin screaming and flinging herself on the bed.

'Where the fuck are they!'

'Oh, does it really matter all that much? They're only shoes. You know, somewhere out there is whole other dimension full of misplaced things: single socks, vanishing

31

pens, lighters, TV remotes, passports, tennis rackets, asthma inhalers—'

'Wait!' Yin sits up on the edge of the bed and brushes her hair back from her eyes. 'Last night in *The Lounge*. That's where I left them.'

'Well, that's where they are then, *silly* – hang on a second,' Danny says, glancing at the half-eaten bowl of cereal by her bed. 'This *is* your lounge, isn't it? I mean, you *do* live here, don't you?'

'Well, yes, but *The Lounge* is a... it's a... anyway, it's shut, that's what it is. And only Shiva has the keys, but she's not back until – Oh, *God*. What are we going to do? They want you down in the party room in five minutes.'

They try to think. The ripe odour of Danny's tennis shoes fills the void.

'Black are they then, these shoes?' he says, flexing his toe.

'I don't even know. I never took them out of the box.'

'They're bound to be, and look – my socks are black. No one will notice. I guarantee. It's my arms they'll be gawping at.'

Swimming the breaststroke with his golden arms, Danny manages to bring the tiniest of smiles to Yin's face. 'See, *silly*. Let's go!'

'Go straight through,' says Yin, nudging Danny towards the grand archway of the party room: a room filled with hundreds of weighted down, pink and gold, helium balloons. 'All the way. *Go on*,' she says, with a shove, and Danny is swallowed by the sea of balloons.

Heading a pearlescent orb out of his path, freeing it from its tether, it starts to drift towards the ceiling. But before it escapes, he grabs it by its silver ribbon and continues to swim through.

'Yin?' he calls back, emerging out into an expansive dining area where the ceiling soars high above. The foyer now seems like nothing more than a hobbit hole in comparison. 'Yin! Come on in. The water's lovely.'

But she's gone.

Bored with the balloon, he releases it, letting it float to the ceiling, where silk flowers crowd the edges in a soft, tangled bloom. He watches its lazy ascent, mouth half-open in a lopsided grin, until it bounces gently off the ceiling.

Winding his way through the rows of uniformly laid out dining tables, he comes upon the centrepiece for tonight's dining arrangement: a carousel horse, rearing back on a twisting golden pole – though, on closer inspection, he realises it's not a horse at all, but a unicorn.

The floor beneath him is sparkly and black, irresistibly slick, and with no one around, he glides about on it in his socks, skating and taking running starts, before finishing with his *grand finale* – an agonising knee skid.

Rubbing his knees with his little hands, he picks up the nearest place card off the table with his usual right and reads the name. 'Maribel Laurent? Never heard of him.' *Ms.* Laurent, as it happens, is the editor of *French Vogue*. He sets the card back down and reaches for another.

A sudden hand clap echoes through a loudspeaker, followed by the sound of rigging being pulled. The lighting grid comes on to reveal a stage. The curtain pulls up.

'Shut the mids,' a voice dripping with theatrical flair orders over the loudspeaker – but nothing happens. 'The mids. *The mids*!' it insists again, and the lights dim. A spotlight finds Danny standing between the tables. 'Well then, *ducky*. Don't just stand there like a misplaced umbrella – open up!'

Concealing his exposed toe with his other foot, Danny holds up his arms and steps out from between the tables.

'Heavens, don't look no scared. You're not under arrest!' booms the voice, accompanied by a dreadful screech of feedback. 'The *shoes*. You're not wearing any. Where are the *shoes*?'

The diction of the voice reminds Danny of the time

he'd forgotten his plimsoles in P.E. and he was forced to do gymnastics in his bare feet earning him the unfortunate moniker of 'monkey boy', a label that haunted him throughout his entire school career.

'Whose idea was this then? Was it yours?'

'Idea? Who, me, sir? No, sir. I... I don't know.'

'You don't *know*? Well, was it Kelly's?'

With the slightest of shoulder shrugs, Danny feigns innocence; he's no grass.

'Say no more, say no more. The girl came to her senses in the end, and that's all that matters. Vermillion Winklepickers would *never* have worked. Absolutely *ghastly* things. No, no, this works much better. And I love the sense of humour with the toe.'

'Sense of humour?'

'Yes, yes, this will work just fine. Closer *ducky*, closer.'

Danny shuffles forward.

'That's it, that's it. All the way. Up the stairs. That's it. Splendid, s*plendid*.'

Standing centre-stage, Danny now sees what Nigel was getting at. A bunch of disenchanted sixth formers could have knocked something better up in no time. A rusty red, torn leather armchair sits stage-left, while two green hosepipes, adorned with googly eyes stuck on with glitter-glue and with forked tongues made from fuzzy felt, lie strewn on the floor stage right, recognisable as snakes, at a stretch.

'Sit down, ducky.'

Spying a free space on the floor, Danny squats down.

'On the chair, ducky. On the chair! *That's it.* Now, sit tight while the ART is brought on. Find your centre. That's it. *Splendid.*'

Numerous stagehands bring on the ART: a Greek column, mocked up out of MDF; a female mannequin, naked, with no arms – some kind of statement about *him*, perhaps? Cardboard boxes. A Three-foot vase. Toby jugs, table lamps, and a kiddies' *Big Yellow Teapot* toy. Marbles.

Clocks. A load of old toot with no end in sight, until the *pièce-de-résistance* is wheeled on: an enormous Perspex wine glass and wine bottle, fit for a giant.

A few years' back, Kelly was involved in a drink-driving scandal. She crashed head on into a Blockbuster Video in Kensington. It was a funny business because instead of damaging her image, she exploded, becoming more "rock-and-roll" than ever, gaining more contracts in those past few years than in her entire career previous. And even though she was three times over the legal limit, the whole thing blew over surprisingly quickly. Kelly even brought out a line of t-shirts: white, featuring a single-line, Picasso-style drawing of a wine glass on the front as some kind of memento. Everyone was wearing them: Mick Jagger. Felicity Kendall. Joanna Lumley.

'Now, let's try the *sss-snake,* shall we? Monty will show you. Monty?'

Monty, one of the stagehands, careens on stage and scoops up one of the amateur looking snakes. Aiming it high over the giant wineglass, he presses a button on its head, and a steady stream of blue-coloured water shoots from its mouth, filling the glass with a pleasing, acoustic splash.

'See, ducky. There's nothing to it. Your turn. That's it. *Splendid.* Very *good*, ducky. Very good *indeed.* Back in the chair. Quickly. That's it. *Lovely.* Now, brace yourself. Hold on tight.'

'Why? What's this thing gonna do?' Danny says, digging his fingernails into the soft, worn leather.

'Ready? And – *lift.*'

Propelled by a hydraulic scissor-lift mechanism and flanked by green silk, the chair begins to rise. It's a rather crude mechanism that wobbles and jerks until it shakily reaches its ascent of ten feet before coming back down.

'A trifle on the bouncy side wouldn't you say Monty? – *Monty*?'

35

And that's all Danny gets in the way of a rehearsal. The rest is up to him, and after a small cup of water and a quick toilet break, Danny is back in the chair listening to Kelly's guests take their seats from behind the curtain.

While the lighting crew carries out another spotlight check, Danny peeks around the side of the curtain.

A woman, on the front row, maybe fifty, is wearing a black leotard, with lilac hair, orange tights, and high-heeled leather boots. Next to her, a man in a top hat, monochrome stripy drainpipes, and six-inch stackers. Next to him, a man in a leather bolero jacket, with nothing but two nipple piercings underneath.

But seeing no sign of Yin, he resumes his seat.

The spotlight sweeps from stage-left to stage-right, illuminating his golden limbs, which glisten, speckled with diamonds. Pre-show jitters set in, followed by post-show – he expects there'll be plenty of mingling afterwards, and looking down at his vulnerable big toe, a wave of panic hits: his beloved *Superstars*. He must have dropped them when he was battling his way out of the balloons. And with all those stilettos and stackers clacking around down there, his feet will get mangled without them. He'll ask Monty after the show. *Good old Monty – he'll know.*

The curtain still down, Kelly's guests cough, rustle, and whisper in their seats. The noise simmers down to a low murmur, until only a solitary sneeze echoes from the back row. Wait. Something's happening...

'*Ladies and gentlemen, toys and twirls,*' cuts a rich voice, belonging to a moustached Ringmaster on stilts, wearing a bright red tailcoat, striding through the crowd and speaking into a headset microphone. The spotlight follows him as he stilt-walks over to the carousel unicorn.

'*So – you thought a night out, eh? Run away to the circus? Little Kelly must have talked you into it.*'

Energised laughter spreads through the room, petering out into a mumble. As someone clears their throat, a bright beam of light projects out, shining over to Kelly, sitting up on the bar with her glossy legs swinging over its edge. She raises her coupe glass high, first to the Ringmaster, then to the crowd, who clap and blow kisses her way. Danny anxiously picks at the broken leather of the armchair, wondering what's going on.

'*She's a bit of looker as well, eh?*'

Wolf-whistles. Whooping. The crowd's excitement fills the air.

'*Well, what is it you want then? To twist the facts? Contort the fictions? To catch your breath and be knocked for six?*'

The Ringmaster's thunderous voice halts.

A crash of cymbals.

The spotlight traverses over to a tiny female figure in electric blue sequins, holding up two giant cymbals above her head.

'*Are you ready to scratch the veneer of the weird and wonderful? Are you ready to be thrilled by the perilous stunts of the Gerrymandering Fungal Tart?*'

From behind the curtain, Danny's face screws. 'Fungal what?' These words violate his causal reasoning. Whatever it is, it must be him. Armless mannequins? Big Yellow Teapots? And now this?

'*To marvel at a feat of coordination never seen on planet Earth. Well, rabies and plentiful – I give you – the Gerrymandering Fungal… Tart!*'

The curtain lifts to rapturous applause. Another wild crash from the cymbals. Danny looks out, his eyes instantly drawn to the flash of blue at the back, and he sees that it's Yin, in a blue flapper dress and matching blue wig. The guests stomp their feet on the sparkly resin floor. Danny feels the vibrations come right up through the stage and he digs his fingernails deeper into the leather, his head darting as he follows the spotlight bouncing off so many famous faces.

After one more playful swoop, the spotlight fixes on Danny, casting an impressive chiaroscuro around his prominent Adam's apple. The high lustre of the gold paint really makes it pop.

'Hit it!' Kelly hollers from over on the bar, and the slow creep of Gershwin's *Summertime* begins.

Swaying to the music, Kelly closes her eyes, coupe glass still in hand, not spilling a drop. And as the movement of the rhythm takes hold, her guests follow suit, coolly swaying along. And then, it's all eyes on Danny, like lasers boring into him.

It's a song he knows, albeit a different version, but he's familiar with the beat and the melody – he's glad of that. But with it comes pressure; he knows he ought to act, to do something. So, as the clarinet comes in, he starts to glide across the stage, taking long, languid sweeps with his feet, Nigel's words echoing in his mind: *'It's all about flow. Just gooo with the flooow.'*

After the "fish have jumped" and the "cotton has grown high," Danny stops, faces his audience, and brings all four of his hands in close to his stomach, balling them up together as one. With the music in his veins, the people stop swaying – Kelly too – and Danny becomes a gilded lotus flower blooming. Glistening under the lights, he gently opens his hands and lengthens each of his golden stems.

A profusion of tiny lights from above bathes him in sunshine. A few sharp intakes of breath can be heard from those with the best view, and his confidence grows, enough for him to arch his hips forward and dreamily sashay over to the giant Perspex wine glass.

When he reaches his destination, he is met with a classy ripple of applause, like that which follows a standard long shot at the *Crucible*.

Taking a slow lunge, Danny picks up the snakes with his little hands and holds them up high until the strain on his thighs forces him back up. It's an ungraceful manoeuvre, but once he's upright, he fills the wine glass with blue water. As the audience lets out a cheer, he tosses the snakes up with a swift motion, and the old fellas catch them. People rise to applaud, and he removes his thumbs from the buttons then casually blows imaginary smoke off his snakehead barrels – first left, then right. More people stand, earning Danny his biggest cheer of the night.

'Better make it a large, eh Kelly!' heckles someone at the back. Danny continues to fill the enormous glass while the spotlight finds Kelly, still perched on the bar, throwing her head back and laughing. The crowd laughs with her, seemingly finding amusement in her crime. Danny doesn't. He thinks it's in appalling taste. Yet, here he is, clowning around like some jester for her and her royal court.

Keeping a steady eye on her and struggling to mask the contempt on his golden face, he glides back to the armchair and prepares for launch.

It's a jerky ascent, but with his heady vantage over the crowd, he grips on tightly and spots Kelly, singing along.

'*Hush, little baby, do-o-n't you cry,*' she sings, holding out her empty coupe glass for someone to fill.

And it's Yin who swoops in to fill it. She even lights her cigarette, and as Kelly exhales, Danny watches Yin scowl, wafting the back drift of Kelly's smoke away with a cocktail menu.

Danny descends to glorious applause, and Kelly, assuming it's for her, bends forward and takes an elegant bow. But luckily for Kelly, nobody notices her *faux pas*, and she quickly realises that the applause isn't for her. She *styles it out* by rubbing an imaginary smudge off her black patent *sex shoe*. But Danny notices her cringeworthy display, as does Yin, who deftly stifles a laugh.

Moved by the crowd, Danny gives them a little wave with all four hands, and by the time he's touched down, he already knows his next move.

Slinking over to one of the many ceramic bowls filled with marbles and gems near the front of the stage, he plunges all four hands in, taking a moment to enjoy the texture of the gems rasping between his fingers. It's the flat ones he like best, so he picks out four.

Enticingly, he displays them between fingers and thumbs, not knowing what to do with them – he hadn't planned that far. But, rescued by the earthy sustain of the double bass, Danny quickly stuffs them into his pockets, freeing his fingers to click along to the beat, meandering through the various stage junk.

The contagion spreads, and soon the whole audience clicks along with him until he replaces his clicking with a light, rhythmic thrust of the hips. Danny's always had excellent rhythm; being a four-armed drummer would be something – talk about a gimmick.

Inspired by the thought, he plays air drums to the beat and bangs the sides of the Greek MDF column, which resonates deeply. Cheers and shouts fill the air. Rock hand signals are raised high, with some people head banging and stomping in unison.

The front lights switch. Danny is back lit and cast in a half-silhouette, creating a dramatic shift in atmosphere which throws him off his rhythm. But Danny holds steady, as though touched by King Midas, and freezes like a statue. Even with someone jeering him on the second row, his head doesn't turn, his eyes don't flicker. Rock steady, he remains as whispers of "circus monkey" and "Kelly's circus fodder" float around him, until the spotlight swoops back on him, silencing the scathing undertones.

But with the music now building to a wild crescendo of brass and flutes, there's no time for hurt feelings. Shining like a bedazzling jewel beneath the lights, the audience rises to a standing ovation, causing Danny to fall to his knees, all four arms yearning and stretching as he gives himself to the crowd – really *gives* himself to them. It's the closest thing to love he's ever felt.

A salty tear drives down his golden cheek, cutting through the paint and exposing his skin. Ad nauseam, the cymbals crash. A bouquet is thrown onto the stage, narrowly missing his head. Rose petals rain on the audience, and the curtain drops down to Danny's big toe, poking out over the edge of the stage and visible to anyone looking closely enough on the front row.

CHAPTER 4

Danny's alone, out on the roof terrace after having thrown up. It happened only seconds after the curtain dropped – nerves, adrenaline, possibly.

And while he was down on all fours, heaving like a cat with furballs, nobody seemed too bothered – except Monty, who gallantly handed him a towel, a breath mint, and a bottle of water. Nigel's only concern was that Danny's stomach enzymes might burn through the high-gloss laminate of the stage floor, after seeing the way they ate right through the gold paint around his mouth and chin. His *Superstars* are still nowhere to be seen. Monty said he'd have a look.

The roof terrace is a soulless place. There has been a heavy downpour, evident from the saturated floor and the air, thick and humid – the smell of the city's grime being washed away, if only temporarily.

Crunching the last of his breath mint, Danny waits ever hopeful for his shoes, without so much as a pat on the back or a "well done." No coupe glass of champagne for Danny. Kelly's done with him – she's had her fun and discarded him like a used tissue.

Wrapped in a royal blue, velvet cape, given to him by Monty, he waits. Its silk lining is already smeared with sweat and gold paint. No shoes, no rucksack, no phone. No way of knowing whether Jem or this Heather woman are even here. And no sign of his money. A brown envelope, Jem said. Maybe Danny should head down to the foyer and hail a cab, but with no shoes? Grinding the flat gemstones together in his pocket, he decides to hang around and wait for Monty.

They're singing "Happy Birthday" down in the party room. Someone's banging it out on the baby grand with gusto. The thought of Kelly sprawled across it, posturing suggestively with her coupe glass still glued to her hand, makes Danny shrink a little.

The heavens open. Lifting the blue cape over his head, he makes a dash for it across the terrace to take shelter under a bar awning soaking his socks on the way, only to find the awning offers precious little in the way of protection.

Leaping to a dry-ish patch of decking, he heads for the double doors that lead back inside.

A flash of blue in his peripheral vision comes from behind the bar.

'Yin?' he shouts, huddling the velvet cape around him. But the rain is hammering too hard on the awning for her to hear. The wind picks up. 'Yin! Yin! Over here!'

With tongue poking out in fierce concentration, Yin fills coupe glasses on a silver tray with champagne.

'Yin!' A strong gust of wind flips Danny's cape up over his face. 'Yin!' he calls again. But by the time he claws the heavy, wet velvet away, she's gone. A string of paper lanterns above the bar dance erratically in her wake.

'Yin?' he says, running over and leaning over the bar. He sees a closed hatch. Curious if she went down it, he gives up on his shoes and squelches around to the other side of the bar to see if it will open.

A gentle pull is all it takes for the hatch to spring open and snap back on its hinges. A ladder leads down.

'Yin? You down there?' His voice echoes down the hatch. 'It's me, Danny! I'm coming down!'

It's a tight squeeze. His cape flaps up and bunches around his neck as he threads himself through, scraping the sides of his arms.

Hunching his frame, stepping off the last rung, a fluorescent strip light swings precariously from the ceiling. Grabbing it to steady its momentum, he feels the rumble of a tube train underfoot.

'Curiouser and curiouser...'

Walking on, the floor begins to slope beneath his feet,

43

and the air grows hotter – hot and humid. He unclips the silver clasp of the velvet cape, still weighty from the rain, and he holds onto it.

The tunnel narrows, its walls seeming to close in with every few meters. Danny's little elbows scuff against the rough, uneven walls, and heading towards a red glow in the distance, he tucks in the little fellas, balls up the cape, and squeezes it tightly. Pocket-sized Yin wouldn't have any trouble navigating this wormhole, Danny thinks, his ears popping disconcertingly.

Another tube train thunders by, much louder than before, and he realises he's been gripping the cape-ball so tightly that his muscles are tense. A voice is telling him to turn back, but he presses on, convinced that the tunnel must lead to an exit eventually. Beads of sweat drop from the bridge of his prominent nose, pooling on his upper lip.

'Yin!'

Wiping his face with the cape, a mix of sweat and paint stings his eyes. Strange, wandering piano music grows louder and an EXIT sign gradually comes into view ahead. 'Oh, thank God.'

Its presence is undeniable, but the arrow points back the way he came. Defiantly, he trudges on, only to reach the end of the tunnel and find himself face-to-face with a brick wall.

'Fuck's sake,' he moans, throwing the cape-ball down and kicking the wall, forgetting he's not wearing shoes.

But he feels no pain. A light rebound, yes, but no pain. It's as if the wall absorbed the impact. Some of it even crumbled. Picking at it with his nail, he chips it away with ease, reminding him of those bio-foam bricks used for flower arranging. Pressing his ear against it, a circular section of the "wall" pops open, and the piano music grows louder, accompanied by the clinking of glasses and laughter.

The circular section is covered in exposed brick 3D effect wallpaper. It looked so real until he touched it, and behind it is another door, made of wood and fitted with a magnetic latch mechanism and a keyhole.

Kneeling uncomfortably, he looks through.

A room, a gentleman's club, dim and smoky. The back of a rusty, red leather armchair, like the one he sat in on stage, only in better condition. The smell of cigars. Deep, throaty voices, overly relaxed.

'You're very pretty girls, aren't you? Don't sit so far away – move closer,' says a man with an ominous cunning, reminding Danny of that poem about the spider and the fly. The armchair shunts back against the door. Danny ducks away as the man settles more comfortably into his chair. *That must be the spider*, thinks Danny, daring another look.

A bald head. Sausage-like fingers, with a black onyx ring almost cutting off the circulation to the spider's *digitus minimus*. The spider is smoking a cigar. Low tables and a red neon sign above a bar, the lettering blurred and obscured by smoke that makes Danny's eyes water.

Pulling back for a moment, he gives it a good rub before refocusing.

Two legs, clad in black fishnet tights. Three legs. No, four. All wearing fishnets. Danny spreads his knees wider, lowering himself for a better view.

A red stiletto, dangles from a swinging foot. It's far too big – too big for the foot, *way* too big. Thin legs, so thin that the tights bunch and sag at the knee. Two red crushed velvet dresses. Strappy things. The skin is young and fair. Two girls dressed like they've raided their mothers' wardrobes. Two very young girls – *the flies*.

An unmistakable flash of blue. Yin's face comes between the girls' heads, smiling and offering out a packet of strawberry laces. The girls turn to face her, their train-track braces glinting, thin legs swinging back and forth as they pull out long, gelatinous red strands. A red stiletto slips off and drops to the floor. Yin picks it up and slides it back onto the foot. The chair jolts again. Spooked, Danny stands, brushes the dirt from his knees, and heads back towards the hatch, forgetting his cape.

'*Shit.*'

Luckily, he doesn't get far before realising his mistake and turns back.

'*Fuck.*'

He grabs the cape and bolts, glancing over his shoulder until the strange door is out of sight.

CHAPTER 5

The intercom screeches. Danny wakes bolt upright. *Bloody kids. They'll get bored and give up soon.* Summer rain pelts against the skylight and as soon as his head hits the pillow, the intercom blasts again.

'For fuck's sake!'

It's almost two-in-the-morning. Once Danny made it back out of the hatch, he eventually found the foyer. Monty was there waiting with his shoes and brown envelope, and Nigel was at reception, on the phone looking at Danny like he was something on the bottom of his shoe. After Nigel finished on his call, he casually informed Danny that Kelly had moved on to a suite at the Ritz with '*ses amis*,' and that the afterparty was already in full swing.

'Afterparty?' said Danny, tying his laces. 'I could just go for a cold beer. Okay if I freshen up first quickly? Which way are the toilets? Down there? I won't be long—'

'Well, err... there's no point in you hanging around. I've just booked you a car to take you home. It's on its way.'

Another ear-splitting screech forces Danny – still smeared with sweat and gold and far too pissed off to be self-conscious about his recent metamorphosis – downstairs.

'Think this is funny, do you?' he says, unbolting the door, just able to make out the figure of a growth-stunted youth behind the frosted glass. 'Right. That's it—' He pulls the door open.

'Yin?' Her eyes are bare, unadorned. They look smaller, younger. Her dark nipples press against the damp fabric of her white ribbed tank top, wet from the rain. 'What are you doing here?'

'I know it's late. But your bag. You left it.'

'Oh,' he says, picking it up from between her feet and

spotting a large canvas shopping bag close behind. 'Cheers. Nice one.'

'Where did you go? I was looking for you. Lots of people were.' She folds her wet arms across her chest. 'I was sent on a *white-goose chase* trying to find you.' Another idiomatic slip that Danny lets slide. 'Kelly wanted to meet you and everything – but she got bored and moved on.'

'Yeah. I heard.'

Two urban foxes cry out, *ack-ack-ack-ack-ack*, into the night. The wettened tarmac amplifies the rumble of a passing night bus.

'Can I—'

'So, d'you wanna—'

Their voices collide in the night air.

'Come in?' finishes Yin. 'Yes. Yes, please.'

Danny takes her bag, and she follows him up, masking the paranoic state she's been in ever since discovering a flat, green gem left outside the secret entrance to *The Lounge*.

'Sorry about all the stairs. I'm all the way at the top, I'm afraid,' says Danny, praying the smell of sick has long gone by now. There's a bit of a stain. He cleaned it up the best he could.

But Yin has bigger fish to fry.

Initially, she thought the gem must have somehow stuck to her shoe and transferred itself as she went through the door. But if so, then why didn't she feel it on the thin sole of her ballet pump? And why was the door slightly open? She always makes sure to pull it closed afterwards.

'Just one more flight. Nearly there.'

But maybe she didn't. She's been pulled in so many directions lately, and after all, she was sure she'd locked the hatch – yet she knows she didn't. Someone ventured down; the green gem is evidence. But who? Danny? Did Danny find *The Lounge*, look through the keyhole? See her working there?

This is why she has come equipped with a ferociously expensive bottle of tequila she swiped from the Motoko Bar – she must find out.

'It's a bit of a pigsty, I'm afraid. Here—' He throws her a towel. 'Don't worry. It's clean.'

While Yin dries herself off, Danny looks away and thinks about earlier:

Braces, strawberry laces, baggy stockings, skinny knees – Yin smiling?

'Yin, I… you know earlier?' he says, picking the limescale off the kettle.

'Uh-huh,' she answers, rough-drying her hair.

'Well, I… I saw this… I saw…'

Her blood runs cold. 'Go on,' she says, trying her best to act nonchalant as she continues to dry her hair.

But noticing her toned midriff, Danny refrains. After all, what right did he have going down there? Following her like some stalker, some creep, with his weird little arms. He turns his head to view her pierced belly button, the dolphin tattoo peeking out above the low-slung waistband of her jeans as she shakes out her hair, then quickly resumes picking at the limescale.

'Cut to the fluff, Danny,' says Yin, his hesitancy a slow torture. 'Just tell me. Say it. What did you see?'

'It's… your hair, that's all. It was blue. Before, I mean. Wasn't it? Or was that a wig?'

Breathing a mutual sigh of relief, they smile.

'Well, yeah – *dummy*. You saw my real hair when I was painting you, remember?'

'*Duh* – men, eh.'

The gem must've got stuck. He's way too big to have squeezed through that hatch, she thinks, narrowing her eyes.

'And your eyelashes. They've gone. Makes you look… a bit…'

'Look what, Danny?' laughs Yin, her paranoia lifting.

'Different, that's all. *Really* different. Without your

makeup.'

'I don't wear *that* much, do I?'

'No, no. I didn't mean... It's just that you look... you look – better. Better without it. You don't need it, I mean.'

Blushing, Yin reaches for her bag, takes out a ceramic tequila bottle, ornately embossed with blue and gold.

'Come on. Let's celebrate.'

'What's that?'

'Tequila,' says Yin, drinking straight from the bottle. 'You're going to be famous, Danny. A big star.' She passes it to him.

'Yeah? You really think so?'

Although he can't stand Tequila, he drinks, and they discuss Kelly's *faux pas*.

'She stinks like an ashtray,' says Yin, and it's not long before Danny feels comfortable enough around Yin to gesticulate naturally and expressively with his arms, as if they've always been there.

'The little fellas?'

'Yeah, that's what I call 'em. The little fellas.'

Tequila flowing, they laugh and tumble onto the bed. Yin grabs his hands reassuringly and tells him that he's set for stardom, made for it. Danny's never spoken to anyone this tactile.

'Your mother never hugged you? Not even when you were small?'

'*Nah*. Never even touched me, unless she was giving me a whack.'

With more than half the bottle gone, the mood has shifted, and he starts to dominate the conversation with morose talk about his childhood, really spills his heart out. With a quavering lip, he tells her how he only got one G.C.S.E., and everything that happened with Gramps. As they near the end of the bottle, he's a wreck.

'You know, the bitch didn't even let me go to the funeral?'

'I know. You said.'

Wrecked and troubled, but sensitive and honest. If he'd gone down that hatch, seen anything at all, Yin's sure he would have said by now. Someone as maudlin as Danny couldn't help himself.

'Oh my God,' says Yin. 'Look at the time. It's gone four.'

Squinting at the blurred display of his radio clock, an acid reflux rises in his chest. 'Sorry I got a bit – *you know* – weepy just now. Dunno what came over me.'

Yin found the details about his granddad particularly harrowing. 'Just popping to the loo,' she says, gathering up her bag. 'The birds will be tweeting soon.'

And while Yin is in the toilet, Danny remembers her through that keyhole, offering sweets to inappropriately dressed minors. It was only a matter of hours ago, yet here in his room, she has seemed like an angel to him. She certainly looks like one, but has the booze clouded his judgement? Or is he reading too much into it? Women *are* thin these days. It's the fashion. And plenty of women have fixed braces and eat strawberry laces.

Watching for the door, he brings the tequila bottle to his lips and kisses it – French kisses it – like he used to with his FHM magazines when he was fifteen.

The toilet flushes and not being one for washing her hands after only a No.1, Yin comes back in sooner than expected, buttoning her jeans.

'What are you doing with that? There's none left.'

'Nothing,' he says with rising inflection. 'I wasn't doing anything.' Holding it at an angle, he gently exhales, his breath spilling over the rim, coaxing out a tuneful note. 'Makes a nice sound, that's all.' He puts it down by the sink. 'Or a nice vase. It would make a nice vase, I guess. Maybe put a rose in it or something.'

'*Aw*, that's sweet. Keep it. Maybe it will bring you luck,' she says, with a smile that warms his soul – his loins.

The most awkward silence ensues while the rain taps

steadily against the skylight.

'Yin, it's pissing down. Why don't you—'

'Look, I really better get going—'

'No, yeah. Of course.'

'I've got to work in the morning.'

Work. '*Shit.*'

'What's wrong?'

'No, nothing. I'm meant to be in soon myself, that's all.' He glances at the radio clock. 'In less than two hours.'

'I thought you were going to quit, go to Tenerife,' she says, picking up her bag. 'Unless you've got the taste of limes.'

'Eh?'

'*Limes*, the taste of *limes*. You know, the limelight. Fame. Stardom. That's what they say, isn't it?'

'No, yeah. Yeah.'

Yin heads for the door.

'Wait. Hang on a second—' Danny quickly pulls the gems from his pocket. 'Look, lucky charms.' But he only counts three. 'I thought I had four. One for each arm. Or four, like a four-leafed clover. Must've dropped one somewhere. Oh well—'

As he plops them into the bottle, Yin's face turns ashen.

'You okay, Yin? You're not gonna chunder, are you?' he asks, reaching for the sink bowl.

'No, no, I'm fine. I was just trying to remember that expression. Oh, what is it you British say? "Two's company, three's a – charm"?

'Yeah, something like that. Hey, listen. How are you getting back?'

'I'll get a cab out on the street.'

'Here, wait—'

Diving under his bed, Danny takes out two fifties from the brown envelope he safely stashed inside a shoebox as soon as he got home. 'Here. Take it,' he says, thrusting them into her hands. 'Come on. I'll see you out.'

Re-entering his room after another mighty stair climb, he notices an empty packet of strawberry laces on the floor.

~

Danny's phone rings from inside his rucksack. Squinting at the radio clock, his head pounding, he sees that it's gone ten.

'Fuck. Shit. Gerry.'

Scrambling to answer it, he relaxes when he sees that it's an unknown number.

'Hello?'

'Danny. Heather Harridan. At last, we speak. How *are* you?'

It takes a few seconds for Danny's brain to engage.

'Ah, of course! Heather, from the business card.'

'From *Complete Celebs*. Danny – you were hot last night, a total *riot*. Kelly's still going strong. She moved on to *Harpo's* this morning for Bloody Marys and Peruvian pancakes. That finger-clicking thing you did – in*geni*ous. Right up Kelly's street. Well done.'

'Yeah?'

'Yes. The phone's been glued to my ear ever since. I've had calls from Milan, Paris, New York – all wanting pictures of last night's show. *Grazia. Vogue. Cosmo.* And there's interviews, articles: 'The Ultimate Capsule Wardrobe for the Modern Four-Armed Man About Town.' There's *London Fashion week*. Catwalk…'

'Catwalk?'

'Runway, Danny. *THIN – IS – IN*, and "heroin chic" is back. They're saying you could be the face of its return. And it's not just fashion – there's newspapers, panel shows, reality TV, a documentary.'

'A documentary?' Danny sits up against the headboard. 'About what?'

'About *you*, of course. There's a meeting about it today,

at *RipCurl* HQ. They want you there for two o'clock.'

'*RipCurl Entertainment?* The television channel?'

Danny grew up with their programmes as a child: Saturday morning giveaways, custard pies, phone-ins, celebrities getting gunged, reruns of *Grange Hill.* But it's not all television light. *RipCurl's* late-night subsidiary channel: Pre-Loader TV, covers the more hard-hitting topics: drug gangs, torture, religious cults, sex-doll brothels. Just the other week, they ran a gripping feature on Tramadol addiction. Another followed a man who has spent the last ten years turning himself into a lizard with surgery and tattoos. Danny's watched them all. Resisting the urge for a morning piss, he listens on.

'I've emailed you an information pack. I got your email from Jem. He'll be at the meeting. I won't, I'm afraid.' Jem is *RipCurl's* Head of Creative Diversity. 'Familiarise yourself with the pack as much as possible. Everything's in there. Did you get your fee?'

'Err... yeah. Yeah, I did,' he says, feeling for the shoebox under his bed. It's all there, minus the two fifties he gave Yin. 'Yeah, thanks very much.'

'Good. Well, there's plenty more to come. And I promise we'll have a little sit-down, go through your work schedule for the next six months and all that jazz, get the contracts out of the way, that sort of thing. I've sent a car to collect you at one o'clock to take you over to head office. And Danny?'

'Yeah?'

'Don't worry if you don't see much of me. I work behind the scenes. I wear many hats. Jem is quite aware of my working rhythms. I'm very much a night owl. But I can assure you, under our management and care, between us, nothing will be missed. Oh – and Danny?'

'Yeah?'

'Welcome to the world of celebrity, darling. *Ciao!*'

If what Heather says is true, Gerry will soon see Danny's ugly mug splashed all over the papers and have his P45 in the post by tomorrow lunchtime. There's no point calling him now, or ever again, probably.

'*To create a truly entertained nation by delivering the wacky, the weird, and the wonderful through the unexpected and alternative.*' That's *RipCurl's* mission statement on the front of the info pack.

The rest of it is heavier going: all slides and graphs on *RipCurl's* generated revenue and global advertising spend – stuff way over his head. And besides, he's far too preoccupied about the prospect of a documentary to focus on anything else. Braces. Strawberry laces. Spiders and flies. Yin's smiling face between those two girls – a fragile bloom in a poisoned garden. A glitch in the atmosphere. That all seems distant, irrelevant now.

~

'Jeremy Quimby', reads the nameplate on Jem's office door. Not *Jem*, or *Gem*, like he'd assumed. 'Quim,' he whispers, softly. Something about the name just tickles the part of his brain that never quite grew up.

The bohemian-looking receptionist glides Danny over to Jem's office. 'This way,' she says, pushing the door open with a casual grace and floating away, as if she were part of the air herself.

'Danny – *the star*. Welcome. Please, sit down.'

Jem carries a notably different energy – keen-eyed and much fresher-looking than the last time Danny saw him. Clean-shaven, with his curls tight and shiny with gel. Holding onto the straps of his rucksack, his little fellas tucked neatly behind, he walks forward.

'You're looking good, Danny. How's everything feeling?'

Choosing the seat directly opposite Jem, Danny removes his rucksack. The hippy-dippy receptionist drifts back in with some water, and before she's even placed it

55

down on the desk, Danny erupts in a paroxysm of praise for the genius of the channel – a sycophantic gushing that Jem allows to go on for nearly a minute.

'Danny, as you know, *RipCurl* has a reputation for making gritty, hard-hitting content – introspective, award-winning documentaries, which is *why* – oh, if I could just get you to cast your eyes over this—'

Jem spins the contract towards him, and Danny, choosing a black biro from Jem's desk tidy in reckless haste, signs it, spins it back, then leans back on the mesh fabric chair.

'Which is *why*…' says Jem, popping the lid off a dry-wipe marker and heading over to the whiteboard.

The door opens. A dozen or so people file in.

'Quickly guys. Come on. Make a line.'

As they line up against the back wall, Jem starts to draw a stick figure. 'Which is *why*, Danny…' he says, adding four arms. 'Which is why *RipCurl* needs you to be… *cool.*' Jem writes the word on the board in blue and underlines it.

Loosening his tie, Jem takes another marker, a red one. 'Tell me about Danny, people. Come on. Talk to me,' he says, removing his tie completely.

'The ponytail,' contributes someone from the Upstyling Department.

'What about it?' says Danny, looking behind and pulling his hair to one side.

'Well, it's got to go,' adds Jem. 'Too much cultural baggage: poor hygiene, poor sense of style. Split ends. Social awkwardness – overall bad vibes. It's best we move away from the whole tortured poet slash nineteen-nineties university lecturer thing.'

'I agree,' says someone from Manipulative Editing.

'Yeah, it's inappropriate,' says another.

'Inappropriate?'

'I say, shave it off. All agreed? A quick show of hands, please.'

It's unanimous.

'Good.' Jem crosses the word "ponytail" off the board. 'Really nice energy guys. Okay, let's keep it going.'

'*Ear-piercings.*'

'*Tattoos.*'

'But I don't have any.'

'Don't worry. You will, you will,' says Jem, offering a reassuring pat on the shoulder. 'Next—'

'But what about my arms? Don't you want to know about *them*? That's what the documentary's going to be about, isn't it? My arms. Me and my arms? Man, did I feel alone. And it was agony when they first birthed, I can tell you. And gory. That's cool, isn't it? Pain and gore? Here, we could do one of them drama reconstructions – an hour-by-hour account of what happened to me, make it look super realistic. I almost lost my mind at one point.'

'*Irrelevant.*'

'*Boring.*'

'I beg your pardon?'

'They're right, Danny. It's depressing. We're aiming for hard-hitting content here, not an episode of *Casualty.*' People snicker. 'We want our viewers glued to the screen, not reaching for a razor blade.'

'But the documentary *is* about me – isn't it?'

'Well, yes, in a way, kind of. Come on, guys. Keep it going.'

Attributes continue to be ascribed to "Danny" – whoever that is. All Danny knows is that it's not him.

'*Leather biker jacket.*'

'*Sleeveless,*' adds someone from wardrobe.

'*A gold tooth. A grill.*'

'*Cigarettes.*'

'Cigarettes *are* cool,' says Jem, adding one to *Stickman Dan's* mouth complete with curly puff of smoke. 'Yes. I like that.'

'But I don't smoke!' protests Danny. 'Never have.'

'Oh, don't worry about that. You'll soon pick up the

habit. There's nothing to it,' says Jem, glancing at his watch. 'Okay. Great energy, guys. Keep it going, keep it going.'

'*He's a Casanova.*'

'*A bit of a charmer.*'

'*A complete slag.*'

'Wait a second. Slow down. Let me get this up on the board: **CHAR**... **MER** – **CAS**... **AN**... **OV**... **A** – **SL**... **AG**—'

'But I've never even had a girlfriend,' Danny pleads, all four hands raised in innocence towards the jury.

'I don't think a man who rides a *Lambretta* G350 with a liquid-cool engine has much trouble getting girlfriends, now, do you, Danny?'

'But I can't even ride a bicycle.'

'Stop *worrying*. The ABS braking system provides a smooth feel and a confident ride. A monkey could handle one.' More snickering. 'And besides, it's a total icon of Italian style. It's going on the board. Next!'

Stickman Dan expands and fills the board. His image now belongs to *RipCurl* – he's owned, he's their plaything.

'That *thing* on there,' says Danny, rising from his seat. 'Whatever it is, it ain't me. That ain't me. I like fishing. Ferrets. Koi carp.'

'Well, this is *RipCurl Entertainment*, not *Dementia TV*.' More snickers. 'Settle down, settle down.'

'I can't believe this.'

'Why? We're letting you keep your name.'

'Oh – thank you. How thoughtful. Thank you. Thank you so much.'

'Danny's a cool name, I think we're all agreed on that.' Rapid, enthusiastic nods from the back wall. 'Yeah, really cool, actually. Let's see, there's Danny Zuko. Danny Dyer. Danny Ocean – George *Clooney* plays him...'

'Why not change it to George then? God, this is impossible,' says Danny, flopping back into his chair.

'*Danny DeVito...*'

'*Danny Baker...*'

'Alright, that's enough. Let's move on to the script.'

'Script? You're joking, of course.'

'No, straight up. It's all there in your contract. The meticulously drawn up contract you just signed without bothering to read. It's all there in black and white.'

'But I... what do you mean, script? Are you saying I've got to learn lines for my own bloody documentary?'

'And here's the first draft,' says Jem, reaching behind and pulling down a stack of papers. 'Everyone, take a copy. Becky-Jo, want to lead? From the top? Danny's opening line?'

Danny's words will be scripted. Every detail will be mapped out by a team of people he has never even met. He will be shaped, plucked, and preened.

These are the stipulations of the contract, and they will be henceforth.

'But not the ponytail,' says Danny. 'You leave that alone. That's staying.'

CHAPTER 6.

Guy is an oversexed, incessant gum chewer, with wooden beads around his neck, and he's been Danny's personal trainer for the past month.

Danny's waiting for him in *RipCurl* HQ's in-house gymnasium, in ill-fitting shorts and a brand-new pair of size twelve trainers, courtesy of the wardrobe department. He fiddles with his bright white laces, gazing down at his big banana feet.

Guy's lewd. He's relentless with it. It makes Danny feel uncomfortable, but he laughs along to hide his embarrassment. When Guy's not in the gym, he's having sex; and when he *is* in the gym, he's talking about sex.

Guy has a lot of sex.

Here he comes, with his sports holder casually slung over one broad shoulder.

'The things I would do mate,' he says, approaching Danny, enviously eyeing his arms and popping a fresh piece of gum in his mouth. Danny knew it would only be a matter of seconds before the bawdiness began.

'Gum?'

'No thanks.'

'I mean it. I'd be having orgies everyday if I had what you had. A load of us, oiled up, all slipping and sliding about on one of them giant plastic mats. Know what I mean?'

'Yeah.' Danny has no idea what he means but protrudes his lips and squints his eyes as if he does, trying his best at looking coarse. '*Phwoar.*'

'Blindfolded we'd be. Blondes. Brunettes. Redheads. Oh, *man.* All those hands groping about. The things I would do – *you lucky bastard.* You must be having the time of your life with those things.'

'Yeah, well, I've not had 'em long, have I?' says Danny, struggling with his locker door. The pound coin falls out again and drops to the floor. 'Not had much of a chance to – *you know* – do anything like that. Not yet anyway.'

'Well, you wouldn't get me hanging about. I'd be straight in,' says Guy, gathering up his tackle with one hand, and edging forward. 'I'd be *beating my meat* every chance I could. Oh, *man*,' he says, his minty breath blowing across Danny's face as he tries to get his locker to stay closed. 'Getting hard just thinking about it – *jammy bastard*.'

And although Danny wishes Guy would stop, his cheeks flushing hot with embarrassment, he must give the man credit where it's due. Guy's already got Danny's little fellas curling three kilograms – a feat Danny never thought possible. During their first session, he could barely lift them off the floor. His posture has become more streamlined too, and Danny stands a bit taller than he did four weeks ago. It's all part of Danny's *cool* new image.

And steadily, the gigs have been coming in, just as Heather said they would. Tonight, Danny is appearing at an alternative nightclub, *The Pink Toothbrush*. With its sticky floors and plastic cups, it's a far cry from *Isabella's*. The fee is much lower – only a few hundred, but Danny's not complaining.

'Here. Try one of these,' says Guy, handing Danny a meat jerky as they head over to the bench press. 'High-protein beef jerky, from South Africa. Got a box of them out in the car.'

Danny gives it a sniff.

'They were a total gamechanger for me, mate. Try it.'

Danny tries to bite off a piece and nearly pulls his head off in the process.

'Right. Dead lifts,' says Guy. 'Ready?'

With all the script learning and intense gym workouts often lasting late into the evening, Danny prefers to take the Tube home instead of all these cars they've been laying on for him. After a gruelling day, the last thing he wants is to make small talk with a stranger behind the wheel.

The glamour of his first gig has already faded, and there's workplace politics just like with any other job. The same gossip and grumbling about being overworked and underpaid. The same cliques and power trippers, the fake smiles. Nothing new. Danny can't help but hear things: how he's a slow reader, how there are plenty of people with two arms and far more talent who would *kill* for a shot at fame. Classic water cooler moments. He knows he's little more than a box-ticking exercise to help *RipCurl* meet its diversity and inclusion quota.

The sliding doors close just as Danny reaches the platform. The Tube pulls away. He catches his dispirited reflection in the glass, tugging at the stubborn strip of beef jerky, and he is reminded of the doleful expression on those girls' faces, biting down on their strawberry laces. What were they doing there? In baggy, bunched up fishnets? The image leaves him with an unpleasant taste in his mouth. Stepping back from the platform edge, he gobs the jerky, now impossible to swallow into his hand and discards it under a sleek metal bench before the next Tube pulls in.

Gripping a vertical pole once inside the carriage, he wonders what kind of world he's gotten himself into.

'Ready?'

Danny gives the man behind the mixing desk two double thumbs-ups, then places the cans over his ears. 'I'm ready,' he says, bringing the condenser microphone to his mouth and psyching himself up to deliver his line for the thirteenth time:

'*Be fair to yourself. Always gamble responsibly. Quit while you're ahead* – how was that? Better?' says Danny, lowering the cans around his neck.

'Again, less emphasis on *gamble* and more on *always*. Take fourteen – *one – two – three…*'

Massaging his stomach, Danny misses his cue.

'What's wrong now?' the sound engineer asks

dispassionately.

'It's just these protein shakes Guy's been giving me. Playing havoc with my guts. I've constantly got the urge to—'

'How's he doing? Got it in the bag yet?' says Jem, bouncing into the recording studio over an hour late. He takes a seat behind the mixing desk with no apology.

'Not quite,' the sound engineer responds. 'Still a bit too lively. Needs another take.'

'I see – Danny?' Jem speaks through the talkback mic. 'The duller and more lifeless the better, remember? Let's make this the one, yeah?'

Aware that Danny has about as much charisma as a dishcloth, Jem is banking on the paradox of Danny being so bad that he's good – so unfunny, he becomes funny.

'Dead as a dodo, yeah? Flat as a pancake. Nice and slow. *And a one...*'

'*Register today with SpeedyBet and get the first five bets free. Two-hundred-and-fifty free spins and one hundred bet credits with SpeedyBonus codes.*'

'We'll be here all *bloody* day at this rate,' says Jem, glaring at the engineer. He leans across to speak again into the mic. 'What's with the urgency, the rush? Let me give you your motivation, imagine this: you're an accountant who's just been made redundant. You're an accountant who's just lost their job, you're at a funeral, and you've been taking a high-dose antidepressant for years. *That's* the energy we're after. Okay?'

'Got it. Hang on a sec...'

'For God's sake, what *now*?'

'Oh no. Oh, *God*—'

Unable to hold it in any longer, Danny breaks wind loudly inside the booth. The audio level meters picking it up, flash up and down

'Right, cut!'

Fifteen minutes later, Danny returns from the toilet.

Again, they count him in:

'*No need to be greedy, when you bet with Speedy.*'

'That's a wrap! Oh, thank God,' rejoices Jem. 'Lunch!'

Feeling a wave of relief, Jem decides to take the sound engineer out for a late lunch at an award-winning gastropub down the road. All wood-panelling and Burford Brown scotch eggs. Lobster croissant. Confit of duck and potted Cornish crab.

'Great,' says Danny, putting on his rucksack. 'I've never tried lobster.'

Jem and the sound engineer exchange a glance.

'Well, best you make your way up to the staff canteen, eh, Danny? Carry on with your lines. It'll be closing in twenty minutes,' says Jem. 'If you're quick, you might get a jacket potato or something.'

And without hesitation, they leave without him.

A woman in a hairnet fits the lid back on an industrial-sized tub of margarine. Danny steps up to the counter and stares down at a hard-boiled egg and a corned beef roll wrapped in cellophane.

'Is that all that's left?'

'Yeah, that'll be £2.90, please, love.'

The shutters roll down behind him, and Danny takes his tray over to a table by the window.

Biting into the egg, he sees that the yolk is pale yellow and grey. He sets it back on the tray.

Three hours later, Danny is taken down to the studio for part two of today's *SpeedyBet* scratch card advertising campaign. It's your everyday domestic setting: dining table, chairs, cheese plant in the corner. Danny sits at the table, filmed from above, scratching away at four *SpeedyBet* scratch cards glued down to keep them from moving.

The clapperboard goes down. Danny looks at the camera and mouths the words that will be dubbed over later:

'*Have you had a scratch? I'm 'avin a scratch right now. Go on – 'ave a good old scratch.*'

The camera cuts away to a Jack Russell, expertly trained by its owner to scratch its ear with its back leg on command.

'*See*,' mimes Danny. '*He's 'aving a scratch. Thousands of winners – everyday!*'

A clothing rack speeds through a set of swing doors as Danny is rushed through to wardrobe where he is told to wait on a stumpy, grey stool between two more racks of clothing. A wardrobe girl, with a measuring tape around her neck and carrying a bundle of leather jackets, comes over and hands Danny a pair of leather shears. They get to work hacking off the sleeves. Danny, accustomed to repetitive, menial work, doesn't mind and soon finds his rhythm.

The swing doors burst open, followed by a familiar laugh. Without having to turn his head to look, Danny knows it's Guy.

'Can you take your vest off?' asks the wardrobe girl, holding out a newly sleeveless, white leather and gold-studded jacket.

'What? Why?'

'Because the Upstyling Department wants you topless for the documentary. We need to see how it'll look.'

'Topless? But I... oh, what's the point.'

Standing with his arms limp, Danny lets her dress him while eavesdropping on Guy's conversation near the doors.

'Funny bloke. I've got him on the jerky.'

'Jerky?'

Another man's voice. By the fretful tone, Danny immediately knows it's Jem.

'Yeah. Fifty percent more protein. It was a game changer for me. If I cut his carbs and up his protein levels...'

'*Jerky?*'

The swing doors open again. Guy and Jem swerve to

65

let an equipment trolley rattle through. In the commotion, Danny loses track of their voices.

'What, the dried meat stuff? It's going to take a lot more than *that* to get the kind of muscle "Them Upstairs" are demanding. They want muscle and they want it fast. Muscle opens a lot of doors in television. A *lot*. Reality TV. Fitness videos. Naked dating shows. We can only go so far with this circus freak thing. *Jesus*—' says Jem, suddenly spying a topless Danny, arms outstretched between the racks. 'Just look at the state of it. More meat on a butcher's pencil. *Christ*.'

'Well, he's bigger than he was four weeks ago,' observes Guy, craning his neck just enough to see Danny.

'Shoulders like bloody razor blades.'

'Keep your voice down,' says Guy, quickly leading Jem out of earshot. 'Anyway, I thought you said he was made for catwalk. Male model stuff. He's certainly got the bones for it.'

'In the short-term, yes. But this is television. "Them upstairs" have a very specific brief for what they want long-term, and that's muscle.'

'Well, with a more intense workout regime, combined with a switch-up of diet plan, I reckon I can—'

'Diet plan? Workout regime? Look at him over there!' says Jem, glaringly, running both hands through his curls.

'You've got to believe, man. Think positive.'

'Believe? Think positive?'

'Listen. I know how to get results, Jem. You think I've always looked like this? I was a slinky malinki once as well, you know. It just takes time, that's all. A bit of time.'

Having lost its flavour, Guy exchanges his gum for a new piece.

'Time. And you think that's what I've got, do you? Time? You know those *bastards* up there have brought the fucking thing forward? By a whole *month*.'

'What thing?'

'The docu*mentary*, you idiot. Something to do with

advertising constraints, contracts – things way over my paygrade.' Jem moves in a little closer to Guy. 'Look,' he says, 'all I'm after is a bit of... a bit of *gym candy*, that's all. Can you get any?'

Lifting his wooden beaded necklace up over his chin, Guy pretends he didn't hear.

'Well? Can you?'

'Look,' says Guy, in a low tone, retreating further back. 'No one's doing anabolics anymore.'

'No? Yeah, yeah, I know they're not.'

'Not if it's results you're after,' says Guy, checking around.

'Go on.'

'But results don't come without a few – side effects.'

'Oh, what's a few headaches, the odd sleepless night?' A rack of faux fur coats zooms through the doors. They step aside to let it pass. 'I haven't slept in *weeks* thinking how the hell I'm going to deliver this – that *thing* over there. They want me to turn it into a sex-symbol. *A sex symbol?* Just look at it.'

They look over at Danny, still standing between the clothes racks, trying on another jacket. It swamps his jagged, gangling frame.

'It's an Adam's apple on a stick, that is,' says Jem, leaning back against the wall. 'Please, Guy. You've got to help me.'

'No, no. That's not fair. He's come a long way over these past few weeks. Those little arms can curl three kilos now. I know they don't look it, but they're bloody strong. Wiry little buggers. His BMI's shot right up, too. Almost in the healthy range. His cardiovascular capabilities have improved—'

'You know Colleen's kicked me out?'

'No, I didn't? *Fuck.* Sorry, mate.'

'Slept in my car last night. *My fucking car.* She wants a divorce. That's it. It's over. We're done. The bitch is going to take me to the fucking cleaners, while "Them upstairs" are threatening to demote me if I don't deliver on this.'

'They can't do that?'

'I won't even be able to afford a fucking one-bed flat in Croydon. How am I supposed to have the kids at weekends? All of us in one bed, an inflatable mattress on the floor or something. So don't talk to me about headaches and a few side effects. My whole life is nothing but one long side-effect.'

Smelling the desperation radiating from Jem, Guy steps back, folds his arms across his chest.

'So,' says Jem with a thirsty grin. 'Can you help?'

'There's a bit more to it than that,' says Guy, looking up at the ceiling. 'It's not something you have a dabble in and then move on. There's risk.'

'Oh, come on. What's a few pills? You pop 'em and go, then take a couple of paracetamols for the headaches. You could crush them up, put them in his protein shakes, he'll never even know,' chuckles Jem, lending some gallows humour to the uncharted dilemma.

'You do know, as a personal trainer, I have an ethical code to abide by. You need his consent first,' he says, still looking up.

'And what if he says no? What then? Shove a bicycle pump up his arse and inflate to the desired size? He'd go straight to the papers. No, no. It's better he's in the dark.'

Guy can hear Jem grinding his teeth.

'Look, Jem, I don't want to get involved.'

'Listen,' says Jem, gripping Guy's thick forearm and flashing a smile at odds with the hunger in his eyes. 'I'll make it worth your while.'

'Do you know what kind of damage this stuff can do? You wouldn't be so blasé about it if you understood.' Jem's grip tightens. 'I'd let go of my arm if I were you, mate.'

Jem lets go. 'Guy – please. You're my only hope.'

'No Jem. Don't do this. No way. You're talking crazy,'

he says, rubbing his arm. 'The risk isn't worth it.'

'Well then, what *is* it worth? Go on. Name your price.'

Silence.

'How much? Seriously, Guy. Five? Six?'

'Ten.'

'*Ten*? I haven't got that sort of dosh. You think I'm made of money?'

'Alright, bye then.'

Guy pushes himself off the wall and starts walking.

'No. No, wait.' Jem grabs Guy's forearm again.

'Now, I'm warning you,' says Guy, shaking him off like dust.

'Okay, ten. Ten it is.'

'Well,' says Guy, leaning back against the wall. 'There is this doctor I know…'

CHAPTER 7

Danny's little fellas can curl five kilograms now, his old guys even more. And for the first time in his life, he feels good about himself, and even likes looking at himself in the mirror.

Guy insists it's all the peanut butter Danny's been adding to his protein shakes, along with hard work on Danny's part. His jaw seems broader, his voice deeper. Some evenings, after training, he's so energised that he jogs home – all the way from Mayfair to South Ealing – and still finds the energy to crank out a set of push-ups on the lino before finally hitting the hay.

But he does get these dreadful headaches in the morning, and he's had an unsightly outbreak of acne along his jawline, something he's never experienced before. And his libido. It's gone through the roof, which can be distracting at times. Oh, and it sometimes burns when he pees. And he's been forgetting things, important things, like his pin-number or where he's left his keys, his phone. But every day, he is transforming before his very eyes. In his wildest dreams, he never thought he'd be able to build muscle so quickly, and it's left him with this strange feeling – confidence? Self-esteem? Whatever it is, it sure makes up for all the niggling annoyances.

But the enduring, nocturnal, raging hyper-boners are becoming a real nuisance. He's losing sleep.

Guy's told Danny that all the "niggly" things – like the acne and short-term memory loss – are down to something known in the trade as T.A.P., a completely bogus acronym that Guy made up to assuage Danny's fears, and maybe not getting enough fluids.

'That'll be the Temporary Adjustment Phase,' Guy explained to him. 'Everyone goes through it when they start gaining serious muscle.'

Thus, Danny has been wearing his headaches and his

acne as a badge of honour, and is truly starting to like who he is, even *love* who he is. Yes, Danny's starting to feel comfortable in his own skin.

But Danny hasn't mentioned the thundering erections to Guy. He thought it best to leave that out, avoiding any probing questions about the nature of his nightly fantasies. Last night, for the first time, Yin popped into his head, with her toned midriff and her dolphin tattoo, her softly parted lips, and the pearly shine to her perfect teeth. The little fellas began to roam, and the old guys, too, got rather hot under the collar, running their fingers through Danny's hair, caressing his face and neck. It felt almost as good as the real thing, only it lasted much longer.

But it left Danny feeling sick with shame afterward. Who is she, after all? *What* is she? In that den of vice, grinning away without a care in the world with those girls, done up like little madams in strappy dresses and high heels. He doesn't know her. Not really. Yin's no more real than a glossy *FHM* centrefold – all pout, no pulse.

Firmly placing his mug down by the sink, he wrestles with the creeping doubt this whole Yin situation is giving him. Can she really be such a devil-woman? With her silky voice and her silky hair? Can he trust her? *With her tattoo and her golden skin. Those eyes, those dimples...*

Splashing his face with water, Danny tries to snap out of it – Guy must be rubbing off on him more than he realises.

But it's not all sex romps and profanity at the lockers with Guy. Guy has proven himself to be the consummate professional, taking his career as a personal trainer very seriously. If it hadn't been for Guy's quick action and concern, Danny would have no idea about his vitamin B and D deficiencies. As soon as Guy spotted the signs a few weeks ago, he took Danny to see a private "doctor to the stars", who administered a series of vitamin shots straight away.

'Intravenous vitamin therapy. All the stars do it,' Guy told Danny. 'Trust me. It's magic.'

'Whatever next?' laughed Danny. 'Botox? Teeth-whitening?'

If only these magic shots could help Danny remember his lines. The script just isn't sticking. Danny's never been much of a reader, it always makes him tired, and any mental energy he does have left of an evening is being utterly consumed by his new sex drive.

Closing his eyes, trying to remember his opening line, his phone rings. Where from, he doesn't know – it went missing last night. Following the sound with his ear, he opens the fridge.

'For fuck's *sake*.'

And there it is, next to a high-protein egg and avocado pot.

It's Jem. 'Oh, what does *he* want now?' After an eye-watering yawn, he answers.

'Danny. Where the hell are you?' blasts Jem, before Danny's even placed the chilled phone to his ear. 'Tell me you've left already.'

'What? Why?'

'For the script run, that's why. The script-run that started ten minutes ago?'

'I thought that was tomorrow – Thursday.'

'No, it's today. Tomorrow is Friday.'

'Is it?'

'*Yes*. Look, just get here, will you?'

Another torturous and humiliating script run, set to be more undignified than ever because Danny hasn't even showered. He's kicking up quite a pong, but he's finally on the Tube. Luckily, the carriage is empty.

A flash of last night's fantasy about Yin briefly stirs his loins, only to leave him cringing in disgust. A gust of wind blows in from the carriage window as the train accelerates. An empty crisp wrapper dances across the floor, quickly diverting his thoughts to the empty packet of strawberry laces in his bedroom for the continuation of his journey.

'Where the hell have you been? Reception said you were here fifteen minutes ago,' says Jem.

'I got lost,' answers Danny, stifling a yawn. 'Took the wrong corridor. They all look the same. Couldn't find the room.'

'Lost? What on earth... It's always this room. For *weeks* now it's been this room.' Jem's fists clench beneath the boardroom table.

'I know. It's these corridors. They all look...'

'Don't tell me – the same? Well, you're here now. Just sit down, will you?' Sandwiched between the length of the oval board table and the wall, Danny squeezes along to find a seat. 'Don't you think you've wasted enough time?'

'Time?' Danny glances at the clock. 'Just gone half past three.'

Danny's behaviour is becoming as worrying as it is infuriating. The production team can't help but gawp at his jawline as he passes. Jem looks aghast as he watches Danny sit down at the far end of the table.

'Good. Right then. Top of page twelve, Danny. Line three, where Danny has just finished his cigarette and swung over the metal railings by the bandstand, he faces the camera and he says...'

Smoothing out the crumpled script from his back pocket, Danny traces his finger along the page, trying to find his place.

'Earth to Danny?'

'Huh?' says Danny, looking up and around.

'Danny,' says Jem, clicking his fingers. 'It's your line.'

'Yeah, I know. Calm down.'

'Calm down?'

'Just gimme a second, alright?'

The production team imperceptibly slumps. The Beta Blocker Jem took this morning is wearing off and his heart's back to racing. People talk quietly amongst themselves about Danny's shocking complexion, until finally, he looks up with lips parted, and—

'Yes,' says Jem, eyebrows raised, a silent wish hanging in the air.

'What page is it again?'

~

Eyes watch from Heather's black convertible as Danny stretches out in front of the mirrored wall opposite the running machines, visible through the gymnasium's full-height glazed wall. For the past six Fridays, Yin has been watching, waiting for Heather's greasy, Chinese takeaways to be prepared in the height of summer.

Lifting herself up over the gear stick, she slides into the passenger seat. Tilting her baseball cap down over her face, she takes Heather's 'Jackie Ohh' sunglasses from the glove compartment and puts them on, almost covering her face completely. She's got fifteen minutes. Fifteen minutes to slide a little lower in Heather's air-conditioned convertible, with the top down, to watch Danny. She's not sure why she comes. It's not that she's fixated on Danny – nothing like that, nor does she think he's particularly handsome, or has much of a personality, come to think of it. It's just that he's the only person she's spoken to lately that's not Heather, a paedophile, or a child. And she's lonely. It was only after spending time with Danny that she realised how much.

She knows he went down that hatch and saw something, very possibly her. The ceramic tequila bottle holds the evidence. If Heather knew... it doesn't bear thinking about.

Standing with his feet shoulder-width apart, Danny reties his ponytail, then lifts four blue dumbbells high over his head. He combines this with a low lunge and repeats for eight minutes.

And that's it. Yin's time is up. She takes one last glance

before Manoeuvring herself back into the driver's seat, preparing to collect Heather's takeaway and spit in her egg fried rice.

Heather's away this weekend on a sailing course. After demolishing her takeaway, leaving not one prawn cracker spared, she grabbed her suitcase and headed for the coast. *The Lounge* will be closed for the entire weekend, marking a rare occasion for Yin.

Slipping on her Marigolds, Yin clears away what's left of Heather's takeaway, counting exactly seven grains of rice in the foil container. Shaking it out into the recycling bin of Heather's well-appointed Mayfair penthouse, she gazes out at the panoramic city view. Designer sofas. Designer sound system. Vaulted ceiling. Cool gadgets to distract Heather from the moral decay of her life, as well as making it easier. A marble-topped kitchen island stained with two red wine rings. Royal Egyptian bath towels left sodden on the bedroom carpet. Mulberry silk bedding, unmade and hanging over her four-poster bed. A Japanese toilet which Heather regularly leaves pebble-dashed, despite the twenty-four-karat gold-plated toilet brush propped up next to it.

'Do you have no shame woman?' grumbles Yin, flushing the toilet and giving the seat one final wipe. Removing her gloves, she goes to strip the bed.

There's a heavy thud as she pulls back the sheets. Something has fallen to the floor – something requiring two AA batteries, which have landed by her feet.

'*Ugh.*'

Gloves back on, she quickly pops the batteries back into the pink rubbery device and shoves it under a pillow.

Helping herself to Heather's unfinished bottle of red wine, Yin makes a start on the kitchen. Taking a sip, she looks back across the open-plan space that leads to Heather's bedroom – and her now perfectly made bed. A devilish idea comes to her. She toasts to her fiendishness, downs the rest of her glass, and dashes across the square.

Mission accomplished. She managed to grab a couple of dead batteries from the battery recycling box behind the franking machine of *Isabella's* reception before the evening staff changeover. No one saw. She kicks off her ballet pumps and darts back to the kitchen to glove back up, and, laughing like a demon, she rushes back to the bedroom and makes the switch. 'And now for my next trick,' she says, wriggling her toes contentedly into the high pile of Heather's cream carpet. But all out of ideas, she settles on helping herself to Heather's expensive moisturising cream instead.

Rubbing the cream into her shins with *MTV* blaring out from Heather's *Bang & Olufsen* TV, she lies back on the sofa with her legs in the air. A whole weekend away from *The Lounge*. No having to make up the girls, often younger than her sisters; no having to dress them or bribe them with sweets. Soothe them. Hush them. Sense their fear.

She takes the green gem out of the pocket of her cut-off jeans and stands up tipsily on the sofa. Hoisting her low-slung waistband up, careful not to lose her balance, she holds the gem under the light of a swivel spotlight and admires its lustre.

Creative juices beginning to flow, she removes the antique silver chain from around her neck. Playing with the frayed denim strands of her shorts, she wonders how she can attach the gem like a pendant.

Thread, that's what she needs.

Rooting around in Heather's underwear drawer, she pulls out something lacy and luxuriant – a pair of gold knickers.

'Gold – perfect.'

Teasing out the lace, she decides to wrap the gem onto the chain. And with her handiwork complete, she rushes over to the hallway mirror to admire her creation.

'An emerald, if ever I saw one,' she says, lengthening

her stubby neck, wishing it were longer.

A key turns in the door. She gasps, then wipes the red wine from her lips with the bottom of her coral cami.

'Oh. You're still here. I'm surprised to see you here so late,' says Heather, struggling with her suitcase. 'Well, don't just stand there watching. Help me, for God's sake.'

Jolting herself into action, Yin grabs the case and drags it through to the bedroom. Heather kicks the door closed.

'What a waste of *fucking* time that was,' says Heather, collapsing on the sofa and taking off her shoes. 'Portsmouth, all the way to *fucking* Portsmouth and back. *Sweetie?*'

Yin rushes over and stands to attention. 'Yes.'

"Sweetie" is not a term of endearment. By no means does Heather consider Yin *sweet*. When she says it, her bottom teeth show. Yin said it back to her once, when she first started working for her and was still navigating the minefield that is British culture. She thought it was just how women addressed one another to be polite, but when it earned her a black eye, she never said it again.

'I need wine, sweetie, wine. I left half a bottle out there somewhere in the kitchen.'

'Wine? What wine?' Yin polished off the rest of that bottle, stood empty on the marble island.

'Yes, wine. Bring it through will you. And a glass. Jesus, my *feet*.'

While Heather's rubbing her bunions, Yin swiftly places the bottle in the recycling, praying there's another red in the wine rack.

'Your bed is made if you'd like to take a nap,' says Yin, searching the rack. 'You must be exhausted from all that driving.'

Foot in hand, Heather looks over at Yin speculatively. 'What are you doing? What are you still doing here?' she says, turning on the television, which comes on at full blast. 'Oh my *Christ*. Why is it so loud?' Yin got a bit carried away when a *Legendary Girl Groups* special came on. 'Why can't I turn this damn thing down?'

Spotting a bottle of red right at the back, she uncorks it unnoticed while the TV blares, then pours half the bottle down the sink.

'Here, let me,' says Yin, swapping the remote control for a glass and successfully managing to turn the volume down.

'Bloody tech these days,' says Heather, shoving her foot in Yin's face. 'Why does it always have to be so complicated? All these buttons. It's like something from the *Borg*, I swear.'

Taking the ball of Heather's foot in her hands and massaging it with her thumbs, Yin wonders what the "Borg" is – a fashion house, or a tennis reference, perhaps?

After a substantial gulp of wine, Heather says, 'Now, tell me—how are the alterations coming along?'

'Alterations?' Yin changes feet.

'Yes, on the dresses.'

'The dresses?'

If it hadn't been for Heather's impromptu return, Yin would have had all weekend to finish them.

'Well, you must have made good progress with them, because it doesn't look like you've been too busy here. This place is a mess. Just look at the *floor*.' Stray snippets of gold surround Yin, kneeling on the carpet.

'I finished the dresses *first*, and *then* I came here to clean.'

'Finished?'

Nodding, Yin pictures the dresses by her sewing machine, still covered in pins and fabric pencil.

'And a good job too because *The Lounge* opens in two hours,' says Heather, savouring her wine.

'*The Lounge*? Tonight?'

'Yes, tonight. Do you think I would have abandoned my once-a-year sailing trip for anything else?' She knocks back her glass. 'I could do without it, believe me, but we've a "major new client in town" – *apparently*. So, good call on those dresses. The apartment can wait. I'll send the girls down to you in an hour or so. All the bloody way to Portsmouth – for *nothing*. A designer suitcase lovingly packed with nautical chic – for *nothing*.' Heather holds out her empty glass. 'Wine, sweetie. Wine.'

Filling her glass, Yin's skin crawls. 'Well, I guess I'd better be going then,' she says, placing the bottle down.

'Well, you can do a few things here first, surely? Like giving the sides a quick wipe, at least. Oh, and run me a bath. Have you cleaned the toilet?'

Hastening to the bathroom, Yin runs the waterfall spout tap on full. 'Come *on*. Come *on*.'

'And Yin?'

'Yes!' The tub's so big, it's like filling a swimming pool with a teaspoon.

'Make a note in the diary to take my car in next week, would you? The roof seemed rather slow opening and closing, a bit delayed. A bit, sluggish. And there's this whirring sound, have you noticed?'

'*Come on.*'

'Yin? Have you noticed?'

Shutting off the water, Yin races through to the hallway and puts on her ballet pumps.

'What's the rush? What's all the hurry? You've got over an hour yet.'

Narrowing her eyes, she turns herself around on the sofa and sees Yin, flushed by the door. 'It's the dresses, isn't it? You haven't done them, have you?'

Yin looks down, picks at her thumb.

'I *knew* it,' smirks Heather. 'Don't worry. It's no big deal.'

The muscles in Yin's shoulders relax a little. 'Really?'

'In fact, it works out better this way.'

'Yeah?' A ray of hope, a chink of light.

'*Yeaaah*, much better, considering the new client and all. Send the girls up naked.'

'Naked? No, Heather—' Yin runs in, drops to Heather's feet, hugs her ankle. 'Heather, please. They're just children. Punish me, not them. If I go now, I can finish the dresses. I know I can—'

'Off,' says Heather, shaking her leg. 'Naked works much better, actually.'

Holding her wine glass out chalice-like, she walks across the room.

'*Yes*, a special night. A new client ought to have a show. I'm almost glad I'm back now. I'm beginning to have fun.'

Looking up, Yin's green pendant glints beneath the spotlights.

'What's that?' says Heather, putting her glass down on the coffee table and lifting the pendant off Yin's décolletage.

'You like?'

'You know you're not to go to the antiques market without my permission.'

'I didn't. I made it. I made it for you.'

'Well, it's obviously not a *real* emerald,' says Heather, pulling at the necklace to inspect, causing Yin to shuffle forward on her knees. 'Where did you get it? Been snooping around the props department again? It looks just like the ones that four-armed *buffoon* was prancing about with on stage. Cheap tat. *Ghastly*.'

'No, no – I found it.'

'You found it?'

'Yeah, on the floor.'

'On the *floor*? And you made if for *me*?' says Heather, twisting the chain tighter like cheese wire, her knuckles digging into Yin's throat. 'Trying to be funny, you little, *bitch?*'

Her eyes bulging, Yin digs her nails into Heather's wrists as Heather yanks the chain up with both hands, so forcefully that Yin's knees lift off the ground. She gasps for breath

'Stubborn this chain, isn't it. Not as flimsy... as... it... *looks.*' Jerking it back and forth, her knuckles punch into Yin's windpipe. '*It... just... won't... break.*'

Snap. Yin drops to the floor, clutching her burning neck.

'What's that?' says Heather, noticing something jutting out from beneath the coffee table. 'Is that my French face cream? What's it doing in here?'

'Yes,' rasps Yin, only too pleased that attention has shifted away from the gem's provenance. 'Yes, it is. Look how smooth my legs are.'

Watching Heather slowly pick up the cream, Yin instinctively covers her head, bracing for the heavy glass pot to be hurled at her – likely followed by a prolonged verbal battering. Her left shin takes the full force of it, and she tucks her legs in, moaning as she watches Heather brush down her striped linen culottes and slide back into her *Valentino Espadrilles* from under the coffee table.

CHAPTER 8

'Oi, look. It's that bloke from the advert – you know: *Don't be greedy – bet with speedy,*' says the man leaving his girlfriend by the precinct fountain and heading straight for Danny, who's doing quad stretches after his run.

'It *is* you, isn't it – you, off the tele?'

Pulling his foot towards his right glute, Danny sees the man coming over.

'Don't, Olly. Leave him alone,' the man's girlfriend pleads, but Olly ignores her and keeps walking towards Danny.

'Go on, do it. Do the line: *Don't be greedy…*'

'*…bet with Speedy,*' says Danny, dropping his foot down and rolling his eyes.

'You look a lot different in the flesh. A lot bigger.'

'Yeah?' says Danny, watching the man's eyes dance all over him.

'And all them tattoos. You don't have them in the advert.'

'Come on Olly. Let's *go.*'

'What's that one say – BUM?' Danny wishes it did.

'Err, no. It says MUM.'

Lowering his arm, Danny shows him a beating heart entwined with a thorny rose and the word "MUM" in bold lettering, now etched on his skin forever. Danny had no say in it. It's all part of his image. He can tolerate the anchor on his right old guy's bicep, and the sugar skull on his left. And even the Celtic cross on his right little fella – as cliché as it is. They're still a bit sore; he only peeled off the protective film this morning.

'Nice. And that earring—'

'*Olly.*'

'You never had that in the advert, did you?' says the man, noticing the silver stud in Danny's left earlobe. 'And your skin. What's happened to it? Looks nasty that.

Angry—'

'*Olly!*'

'It wasn't like *that* in the advert.'

Fame's not turning out like Danny thought it would. He's never liked attention, but he didn't think getting recognised would feel like this.

Covering his face with his towel, he jogs off past the fountain and out through the automatic doors.

'Wait! Can I get your autograph?'

'*Olly!*'

Heather's got him a gig with *The Shopping Channel*, modelling watches for a price-drop bonanza tomorrow. A car will pick him up at five a.m., and he needs all the beauty sleep he can get. His acne has flared up something rotten along his jawline.

'Your eyes look sore, really red,' says the makeup lady. 'Let's see if we can't brighten up those peepers with a couple more eye drops. Now, head right back—'

Yet another dreadful night's sleep. Danny's raging libido had him up half the night. He slept away most of the car journey here. But he's here – even if he is half-asleep – being styled in a black, fringed, sleeveless leather jacket with nothing underneath; a bootlace tie, black ripped jeans, and a red bandana to hide the newly formed zits on his forehead, which sprouted overnight.

But beneath the heavy foundation and concealer caked on his face, no one would ever guess what's lurking. The makeup artist has performed nothing short of a miracle.

'Just a little more kohl on those lower lids, and you're done. Let's make those peepers *pop*.'

Sue and Sandra, the show's presenters, head over. Danny sees them in the makeup mirror as he downs his second double-espresso.

'Doesn't he look fantastic, Sandra?' gushes Sue, giving Danny a shoulder squeeze. Danny looks ahead at their reflection.

'Like a young Mark Knopfler crossed with Adam Ant, only with more muscle.' Another firm squeeze. 'Doesn't he, Sue?'

After an eternity of shameless flirting and endless fiddling with Sue's earpiece, the autocue finally begins to roll:

'Now, ladies and gentlemen, we've got some *lovely* watches for you today, modelled by the equally lovely, Danny. Let's give him a hand everybody – although I don't think you'll be needing another one of those in a hurry, will you? Come on over, Danny!'

Putting on a sprightly façade, Danny bounces onto set to the upbeat rhythm of the signature production music and squeezes himself in between Sue and Sandra. Their perfume – rich with notes of cinnamon, clove, heat, and passion – is overwhelming, giving off a predatory allure. Not ideal on an empty stomach and a belly full of coffee sloshing around. Danny tries not to breathe too deeply.

'That's it, don't be shy. We don't bite – do we Sue?'

'Oh, I dunno Sandra—'

Giving Danny a playful pinch on the bottom, Sue smiles suggestively, while Danny squints and pouts as if he's enjoying it. Having Guy as a personal trainer has certainly helped him hone this particular craft.

'And if we could just get a close-up of what Danny's modelling for us today on his left wrists, Grahame?' asks Sue.

Grahame, the cameraman zooms in.

'His left wrists Grahame, that's it. And yes, viewers, you heard that right – that was plural. Danny has, of course, *two* left wrists. And just look at those *arms*.' Sue gives his bicep a squeeze. 'Tense it for me, Danny. Oh, I say.'

And on and on it goes. It's a far cry from *Isabella's*, that's for sure. When Danny came alive under that spotlight, he was free to do what he wanted, how he wanted. Yet look at him now, beneath the harsh lighting of a specialised broadcasting studio somewhere in Surrey, with Sandra and Sue dropping their urgency sales tactics and time-limited offers, brazenly trying to shift a job lot of costume watches to an audience of middle-class housewives, widows, and drunks. Danny's seen better quality pulled up by the jewellery claw down the arcades.

'Now, let's get serious for a second, bargain seekers, because these watches are *really* special, aren't they, Sue?'

'Yes, they are. But to all our friends at home, I do have to point out that this is not the sort of watch you would give to your everyday man. This is a watch for the man who is after something extraordinary – so if you're a man, or lucky enough to have a man who is after that unique, standout style, then this is the watch for you.'

'That's right, Sue. And they come with a choice of four fabulous, 100% *genuine* buffalo leather-coloured straps, so you can switch 'em up, change 'em around...' Sandra takes one of Danny's wrists and sniffs at the leather. '...And let me tell you, you can smell the quality coming off that leather. Just have a whiff of that, Sue, go on.'

Sue takes another wrist and sticks her nose in close. 'Wow, that is *incredible*. When you get a smell like that, you know that you're dealing with 100% quality.'

'Yes, and that's what we are offering you here today: 100% genuine buffalo leather and that stand out quality that you only get here on...'

The klaxon sounds. Danny's first instinct is to duck and cover his ears as the studio goes wild with flashing lights and the ringing of cash register sound effects. It can only mean one thing:

'That's right. You guessed it. It's... *PRICE DROP*. Danny, drumroll, please.'

Coming back up from crouching position, his head pounding, Danny drums and slaps all four hands on the display desk.

'Wait for it... hold it... here we go...' It's like a fair

85

ground, and way too early for Danny. 'Let's get that *PRICE DROP* going… and what's the price? It's dropping… it's dropping…'

'No! *No*, Sandra. I can't believe that. Forty-nine ninety-nine?'

'Well, you better had, Sue. And what did I say, shoppers? I told you today's *PRICE DROP* was going to be crazy, but this is unbelievable. Now, I know we do some crazy things here on *PRICE DROP*, but this has got to be the craziest. Just remind our viewers of that price again, will you, Danny. That's it, Danny, over there where Grahame's giving you a little wave.'

Dazed and confused, Danny's eyes find Grahame. 'Forty-nine ninety-nine,' he repeats to the camera, his lips spasming with nerves.

'And it's affordable luxury, isn't it, Sue.'

'It certainly is, Sandra. Oh, wait a minute — what was that?' Someone comes through on Sue's earpiece. She places her finger on it and looks away to the side. 'No. Are you sure? What, *already*?' Removing her finger, she looks back at Grahame. 'Now, I'm afraid you're not going to believe this, but I'm being told that the black has almost gone. The black has almost gone, everyone. Danny, show Grahame that lovely right wrist again.'

The klaxon sounds again. Red flashing lights. *Cha-ching, cha-ching, cha-ching.*

'It's another — tell 'em Danny,' says Sue, holding Danny's wrist up in the air. Bemused and unwilling, he searches for Grahame. 'Price drop,' he says, rubbing an eye and enduring three more excruciatingly loud and energy-draining *PRICE DROPS*.

The brown sells out. The purple, the green. The watches end up going for just £2.99 in the end.

'Hasn't our Danny been *fabulous* helping us out here today? Everyone, let's give him a big hand—'

Tired and beat, Danny waves himself off the set and makes his way to the green room.

'And you can look out for Danny on the *fabulous* Pre-Loader TV, brought to you by *RipCurl Entertainment*, as he's got a documentary coming out: "Danny: The Man with Four Arms" and filming starts in a couple of weeks and it's going to be *fab*. And remember – you heard it here first on... *PRICE DROP.*'

After pressing the vending machine button, Danny waits for his coffee and looks up at the little screen bracketed to the wall, where Sue and Sandra's unyielding momentum continues.

Taking his coffee from the drip tray, he walks over to a wall emblazoned with *Shopping Channel Best Sellers*: a carnival of cheap tricks aimed at the gullible. *The Banyan Heavy Duty Garden Bag. The Zane Spelman Egg Separator. Dr. Wuu's Facial-Flex. The Custerdome Freshwater Potato Pearl Christmas Collection.* Gimmicky, overpriced impulse buys and unnecessary gadgets no one asked for.

Jem said he'd be here, but seeing no sign of him, Danny waits on an aqua-marine, green room chair next to a lush and leafy boston fern, his neck aching as he tries to drown out the inexhaustible Sue and Sandra on the screen above. They're flogging midi skirts now, being modelled by "our Chloe."

'Give us a twirl, our Chloe. Look at that movement, that swish. These really are stunning. Now, I know what you're thinking – midi skirts? At this time of year? But if you look at that beautiful swoosh our Chloe's giving...'

Rubbing his eyes, Danny watches the billowing fabric.

'And these are not that heavy kind of velvet we are all used to; this is crushed *British* velvet, and as you can see from that lovely motion, they have that light, summer feel, perfect over a bare leg. The underside is viscose...'

A man in rhubarb trousers with a moustache, sidles up to Chloe.

'All of my fabric is sourced from the only remaining velvet weaver in the UK right now, but if you're thinking,

"Can I really get something like this into my everyday wear?" I'm here to tell you that you absolutely can.'

'These skirts are so versatile,' adds Sandra. 'You can dress them down with a funky trainer, like our Chloe has done here, or up with a bit of a heel...'

A strange sensation starts to creep over Danny, like a low buzz building in his head. A wave of nausea hits him, and quite overcome, he slumps forward in the chair, his chin on the edge of the table taking the weight of his head.

'And just *feel* that quality. I can't stop stroking this. If you could feel what I'm feeling here, shoppers...'

Over to Sue...

'So, Chloe is wearing the crimson, the ultimate colour for crushed velvet wear. It's perfect for that Christmas party or that special occasion where you want to be truly unforgettable...'

Leaning back, he opens his eyes. Seeing that there's still no sign of Jem, he slumps forward again, all four arms hanging limp by his sides and chin back in place. *All that coffee on an empty stomach was not a good idea*, he thinks, nestling his head in the crook of his left elbows.

'And with the lace bodice underneath, don't be afraid to team it up with silk or satin...'

Like a drunk at a wedding, Danny tries to snap out of it, forcing his head up towards the screen, where he sees Chloe swishing her skirt.

'So, ladies, if you're looking for your *Mr. Darcy* this Christmas, then this is the skirt for you. It also comes in a stunning marigold yellow...'

'And just look at that gorgeous, crushed velvet trim. It screams Regency – I'm talking that period drama fashion that's just so *in* right now. The way it catches the light, the way it moves – just *look* at that.'

Hypnotised by the crimson velvet, Danny's eyes are transfixed. Sue, Sandra, and Chloe blur into a half-dream, and then – he's gone.

'Danny? Danny, are you okay?'

A hazy figure rests its hand on Danny's shoulder. A heavenly host? An angel?

'Danny? Danny, can you hear me? Look, sorry I missed it. Had the usual nightmare out there on the roads. London bloody traffic. I could have walked faster. Danny? What happened, pal?'

Scouting the green room for assistance, Jem spies a po-faced studio runner popping a mini quiche into his mouth. 'Well, don't just stand there – get him some water!'

'I tried waking him,' says the runner, bringing over a bottle of mineral water. 'But he was out like a light before the lunch buffet came. We all just thought he was tired, didn't we?' A handful of entry-level crew, busy minesweeping the cold meats and cheeses, look up from their phones. With mouths full, they nod. 'He's been here since the crack of dawn. Maybe his blood sugar's low?'

'What? He's diabetic?' asks Jem, snatching the bottle from his hand. 'Who told you that? Anyone here know basic first aid?'

The minesweepers shake their heads in unison and look back at their phones, some fixing their gaze on the screen where Sue and Sandra are demonstrating a dual-basket air fryer.

'Danny?' Jem gives him a few light slaps. 'Where's your insulin, mate?' Jem searches Danny's pockets. 'Danny? Danny, can you hear me? Oh *God*—'

'We need a first aider. Look, I'll go find somebody—'

'No,' says Jem, seizing the runner's arm. 'I mean, no need for that. *Er...* it'll be the lights. It's just the lights, that's all – the studio lights. It's very hot in here, isn't it?'

Pulling a half-eaten packet of strawberry laces from his inside pocket, Jem wafts them under Danny's nose. Acting like smelling salts, Danny comes to.

'I'm not diabetic,' he mumbles, looking up at Jem's face, a big mushy blob of confusion. 'Jem? Is that you?'

'See, he's coming round already. No need to panic. *Oh,*

thank God. Danny? Try and eat. The sugar will help.'

The crumpled outline of a pink strawberry with pigtails ' and a smiley face slowly comes into view. 'Strawberry laces?'

'Yes. Sugar, you need sugar.'

'You? You as well?' Danny tries to focus.

'Danny, just eat one,' says Jem, laying a red lace across his face. 'Breathe, Danny. You're confused.'

'You're telling *me.*'

'Your blood sugar's low.'

Squirming, Danny flicks the lace off his face, and grabs the water, taking a swig.

'Them girls,' he says, wiping his mouth with the back of his hairy hand. 'They were wearing velvet dresses, just like – and them sweets.' He grabs the laces from Jem's hand. 'You as well? You're in on it too?'

'What's he saying?' asks the runner. The minesweepers, filming on their phones, begin to gather.

'Nothing. It's just the hypoglycaemia talking—can you stop filming, please?'

'You know, don't you? Were you down there? Monday night? Strawberry laces. That's where you got them things from, isn't it?'

Energy surges through Danny's body, and he shoots up from the floor, grabs Jem by the lapels, and slams him against the *Product Wall of Shame:* a collection of items that didn't quite make it.

'You're part of it, aren't you?' A framed picture of the *Instant Salad in a Can* crashes to the floor. 'Course you are!'

'Part of what? Danny, please – you're hurting me.'

'Part of it! Them girls. They were eating these!' Squeezing the sticky packet, Danny throws it at the wall. Then, using the force of all his arms, slides Jem across, pressing him up hard between the *Glow-in-the-Dark Yoga Mat* and the *7-Blade Banana Slicer.*

Someone carrying a first aid kit appears. 'Well, he seems fine to me.'

~

'You know, Danny, you had me rather worried back there in that green room. Thank God, I could get us this car. There's no way I would have been able to drive us back, not in this state. Just look at my lapel – it's all sticky. That'll have to be dry cleaned now. Smashing. Just smashing—'

Jem and Danny got off the M25 about twenty minutes ago. Having been slumped forward most of the way, Danny is only just managing to sit in a more upright position.

'I thought you were going to hit me. They almost called security over, you know. I've never seen you like that. I never thought – I didn't think...'

A black cab juts out and cuts the driver off, but he doesn't flinch – just taps the brake and adjusts his cuff, smooth as silk, guiding the car like a moving room. Danny sips his bottled water and, for the first time on the journey, speaks.

'Who gave you them sweets?'

'What? Sorry, Mum. Will I ruin my appetite? Who gave you them sweets? Are you for real?'

'Why would a grown man – a professional man like you – have a pack of sweets like that? Yin had a pack of 'em too.'

'Who?'

With bloodshot eyes smudged with black kohl eyeliner, Danny turns his head. 'Look, I know what I saw, Jem. They were eating strawberry laces. The exact same ones, same brand. I saw it crystal clear, and it's still crystal clear in my mind.'

'Saw what? Danny, you're sounding crazy. Nuts.'

'Oh, come on, Jem. *You* know.'

'I can assure you, I don't.'

'It all makes sense now. I get it. *I* get it.'

91

'Get what?'

'You think I don't know what's going on down there, in that place, behind that secret door? Some kind of – some kind of secret nightspot for – for men. *Old* men. Old enough to be their bloody granddads. It's fucked up, man.'

'Who? Whose bloody granddads?'

'The girls. There were girls in there. Up that late on a Monday night before school? Surrounded by booze and cigar smoke?'

The car accelerates as the driver navigates a roundabout. A wave of nausea rises from Danny's stomach, settling uncomfortably.

'They were eating strawberry laces,' says Danny, trying to focus on the city's stabilising architecture through the window. 'Clear as crystal.'

'Now listen, I have no *fucking* idea what you're talking about. You sound *fucking* nuts – mental. I should have known someone like you wouldn't be the... the full ticket.'

'Someone like me? You wanna be careful. The Head of Creative Diversity shouldn't be saying things like that, now.'

Approaching the next set of traffic lights, Jem pulls the armrest down between them. The emo-acoustic rhythm of the car's indicator ticks softly. The light turns green. Danny looks up through the sunroof as they pull away.

'It's an underage knocking shop,' he says, reaching both right arms up to the sunroof and sliding it open, filling the car with engine fumes. 'You know it, I know it,' he says, over the roar of traffic.

'Danny? Are you high, by any chance? What are you on? Ecstasy? Coke? Ket? The agency has a strict policy against drug use among its talent, you know. We simply can't condone this type of—'

Lunging over the armrest, Danny thrusts out his tongue and waggles it wildly, combined with a cartoonish growl.

'Right, that's it. You're a bloody madman. I'm calling

Guy,' says Jem, taking out his phone.

'Go on, then. Do it. But it won't change what I saw, saw with my own eyes. I went down there.'

'Down where?'

With the diesel fumes worsening his nausea, Danny closes the sunroof, leans back, and breathes.

'Down this hatch on the roof terrace,' he says, looking at the floor between his spread knees. 'Got any aspirin, mate?' he asks the driver, giving the partition window a couple of quick raps.

'A hatch? What hatch? I've never seen one up there.'

'Behind that bar. That bar with all them… all them lights, them lantern things.'

'Lantern things?'

The driver passes back a couple of aspirin. Danny knocks them back with what's left of his water.

'The Lantern Bar, yeah, that's it. There's this hatch, see – a hatch that leads right down under *Isabella's*, down into its underbelly.'

'Underbelly?'

'Yeah, and there's this door. This weird, round door. Only it's not a door. It's not real.'

'Not real?'

'No. It was made of…' Rubbing all his forefingers and thumbs together, Danny tries to summon the right word, reminding Jem of a spider silently extruding silk from its spinnerets. 'Something crumbly. Like a hard polystyrene, or a super soft breeze block.'

'Polystyrene doors? Secret tunnels? This is *W. H. Bonkers* – and, seeing as we passed Broadmoor twenty miles back, I'm calling Heather.'

'I could hear Green Park Tube it was that far down.'

'And how many leagues under the sea was it? You sure they were aspirins you just took?' laughs Jem.

'There's nothing funny about this. These are kids I'm talking about here. Children.'

Jem gestures to the driver, who slides the partition window closed.

'Keep it down, Danny, yeah? You think the driver wants to hear all this? You're saying all sorts of things. I mean, *kids*? This is sick. Just stop, okay?'

'But they're pimping them out down there! I swear.'

'Pimping them out? Where are you getting this stuff? You partied last night, didn't you? Whatever you "imbibed" must still be in your system.'

'Driver?' says Danny, unclicking his seatbelt and reaching for the door release. 'Stop the car. I wanna get out.'

'You're not gonna be sick back there, are you?' Danny reaches for the door release. '*Oi* – you better not be—'

'Just stop the car—'

'You do know any valeting fees have to come out of my wages?' the driver grumbles, searching for a sensible spot to pull over in the congestion.

'You can stick your documentary!' blasts Danny, swinging the door open while in motion and scraping it against the curb.

'Whoa, *whoa*! What are you *doing*?' The driver slams on the brakes. The partition window opens. 'Is he being sick?'

'No, no he hasn't. Everything's fine. Isn't it Danny?'

Seeing what he's done to the bottom of the door, he sits back down and shuts it.

'Thank you,' says the driver, quickly getting them back onto the main drag.

'Now, Danny. Danny listen to me,' says Jem, closing the partition window. 'Let me explain. There's been a – misunderstanding. Those girls you saw. They were actors. *Child* actors. Dancers from a local theatre troupe, that is *all*. Precocious little madams if you ask me, but extremely hardworking ones, I'll give 'em that. They've been using that space to rehearse, sometimes right into the early hours.'

They hit traffic; the car starts to slow.

'Rehearse? Rehearse what?'

'Bloody awful stuff. *Bugsy Malone*. Can't stand it, personally. All that musical theatre *crap*. Colleen couldn't get enough of it.' A wistfulness comes over Jem as he realises this is the first time he's referred to his wife in the past tense. 'Show tunes, she loved all that, bollocks.'

'Bugsy what? Never heard of it. Child actors? You must think I was born yesterday.'

'Or on another planet, possibly.'

'Okay. So maybe I don't know *exactly* what those girls were doing down there, but it wasn't bloody tap, modern, and ballet.'

'*Bugsy Malone*, Danny. Good clean fun. All perfectly innocent. All above board.'

The traffic starts to move again.

'*Bugsy Malone*?'

'You know, I took her to see *Blood Brothers* once. It was our first date. Some rubbish by Willy Russell, peddling the dream that anyone can better themselves if they really want to – *please*. And who's that other one? Oh, what's his name? Does everything. Everywhere you look down the West End, it's always him.'

'What, Lloyd Webber?'

'Yes, him – Andrew *bloody* Lloyd Webber. I've had my fair share of *him* over the years, let me tell you. That's one thing I *shan't* miss about Colleen: bloody Lloyd Webber. I remember when *Joseph* came out, it was as if the whole city was being strangled with neon signs. Every colour of the *bloody* rainbow. Everywhere you turned—'

'Wait a minute,' says Danny, clicking the fingers of his right hands. 'Neon. There was this neon sign down there, behind that door. Red. A red neon sign, shaped like a pair of lips, it was. Yeah, that was it... and it said... oh, what did it say...? *Got it*!' he says, bringing both pairs together in a sharp clap. '*The Velvet Lounge*. That was it. Where they were eating them sweets, them laces.'

'Sorry to pop your bubble on this, but I'm afraid that sign was nothing more than a stage prop.'

'No stage, no set. This place was real. A proper gentleman's club. Whisky and cigars. *The Velvet Lounge.*'

'And plenty of child performers eat strawberry laces, Danny. They need to keep their energy up, so enough. Stop it with these baseless assumptions, these wild allegations, just stop. You're making yourself look stupid – crazy, even. You could get us into a lot of trouble, you know, so drop it. That's the end of it. God knows why you keep pushing with this... this nonsense.'

'But dancers look happy, don't they,' says Danny, his gaze drifting over the concrete sprawl below as they speed along the Brent Cross Flyover. 'Energetic. Happy. Always jumping, bouncing around. Like Tigger.' The aspirin having kicked in, enables Danny to accompany these words with a couple of boings in his seat. 'Sparkly eyes. They're always smiling, dancers. Can't stop smiling. These girls weren't smiling. They looked like lambs to the slaughter. And their eyes were dead. It was as though all the life had been sucked out of them – zapped. Like zombies.'

'Zombies? Neon lips? Listen to yourself.'

'Jem, I know what I saw. Dancers don't look like that, they just don't. Something's going on down there, something serious. I can feel it.'

'You can, can you? Danny, look, I didn't want to say anything, but – you don't look... you don't well. Acne's a sign of stress, you know.'

Catching sight of his bumpy-jawed reflection in the window, the makeup wearing off, Danny shrinks a little in his seat.

'You've been pushing yourself too hard lately. *We've* been pushing you too hard. *I've* been pushing you too hard. Heather said I was overloading you, and now I see she that was right. I should have listened.'

Inching along Chelsea High Street, alive with its

shimmering storefronts and polished façades, Danny looks out the window at the parade of beautiful people, the *bon chic*.

'You're burnt out, Danny. Overthinking. Reading too much into things. Stress and paranoia – they're closely linked, you know. Seeing things that aren't there. Forgetting where meeting rooms are. Fame, Danny. We've thrown you in at the deep end. Too much too soon. But don't worry – *Complete Celebs* takes mental health very seriously. In fact, I'm calling Heather.'

'Heather? But...'

Pulling his attention away from the window, Danny sees that Jem has already got her on the line.

'Heather? Yeah, yeah, I'm good. Listen, I'm putting you on speakerphone for a three-way with Danny, okay?' He places the phone on the arm rest.

'Danny? Can you hear me? I just caught this morning's re-run – you were amazing! The camera *loved* you. You looked fantastic. How'd it feel up there?'

Before Danny can answer, Jem cuts in.

'Heather, I'm afraid it's not all good news. Danny's had a bit of a – how do I put this? – meltdown. I think that's a fair assessment, wouldn't you say, Danny?'

Saying nothing, Danny turns back to the window.

'A meltdown? What kind of a meltdown?'

'I told him about the kiddies' troupe – you know, the *Bugsy Malone* rehearsals which have been going on these past few weeks – but he doesn't believe me. Maybe he'll believe you.'

They exit Cadogan Gardens. A man in olive-green Jodhpurs, carrying a small, white dog, passes them at the crossing. 'Wait, was that guy wearing jodhpurs? *Jodhpurs?* Ascot's back that way, mate! Where's the pony? Parked round the corner?'

'What was that, Danny?' asks Heather.

'*See?* He's completely out to lunch. Gone "*lo-co* down in

Ac-a-pul-co." HAVEN'T YOU DANNY.'

'Heather, I'm fine.'

'He's playing it down. At one point I thought he was going to hit me.'

'Is this true, Danny? *Complete Celebs* does not and *will* not tolerate violence of any kind.'

'Well, he had me up against a wall, and he's been rambling on about – what was it again? Some secret brothel, hidden **deep beneath the *bowels* of *Isabella's*** – ever since.'

'I'm sorry, you've lost me.'

'Well, I've had a whole bloody car journey of it. Tell her, Danny. Go on, tell her what you told me. You're going to love this, Heather—'

'Oh, shut up Jem and let him speak. Go on, Danny.'

'That night, after my gig at *Isabella's*, I saw something. This place. *The Velvet Lounge.* And there were these girls – well, a couple of them, so young, they had bloody braces on their teeth, for God's sake. In fishnets. Kids? Fishnets? They were dressed up like, you know, like little women.'

'"*Going lo-co down in Ac-a-pul-co – if you stay too long...*"'

'Jem!'

'They looked terrified. Really scared—'

'"*Yes, you'll be going lo-co down in Ac-a-pul-co. The magic down there is...*"'

'Shut up, Jem. This sounds serious to me. Danny, I believe you.'

'You do?' Jem and Danny echo.

'I believe you *believe* you saw something, but really Danny, you're putting two and two together and coming up with four million. Danny, sweetheart, those girls are part of an acting group. They *are* using that space for rehearsals. You've got the wrong end of the stick with this one. Have you ever seen *Bugsy Malone*?'

'I don't care much for musical theatre.'

'He's never even heard of it, Heather. How can you have never even heard of it? *I'm* your age! You must have heard people at school talking about it, surely…'

'Jem, that's enough. Danny didn't know. It's an easy mistake – anyone could have made it. Let me explain, Danny. The girls in *Bugsy* are supposed to look like – well, like little madams, as you put it. But it's a spoof. A musical comedy. Child actors playing serious adult roles.'

'Oh. Right.'

'Yes. It's a scream, set in New York City and Chicago, during the prohibition era. That's why they weren't smiling, Danny. It was a miserable time. It's a great film and an even better show. I recommend you see it. The cast are kids playing adults, so they're in full makeup and flapper dresses, but it's clean. It's for kids. Guns squirting cream instead of bullets. *Fat Sam* at the speakeasy. Great tunes. It even got a Best Musical Oscar nomination.'

Dipping his head, a rueful smile tugs at his lips. 'I think I owe you both an apology.'

'No, you don't,' says Heather.

'Danny – *I* accept your apology.'

'Oh, *shut up*, Jem. Just maybe leave the detective work to Columbo from now on, yeah, Danny?' laughs Heather, taking the edge off Danny's embarrassment.

'I truly thought something terrible was happening down there. Oh *God*. I'm such an idiot, such a dick.'

'Believe me, Danny, if anything like that was going on, I'd be the first to know. The very first.'

'She would, Danny.'

'I would. I know that place like the back of my hand.'

'I'm such a *dick*.' Danny covers his face with all four hands.

'No, you're not, Danny. It means you're a caring guy, someone who looks out for people, someone with a heart, a conscience. But you must remember to put yourself first sometimes. You've got to look out for yourself, not just other people, remember that. This is your time now. You've got a bright future ahead. You were brilliant this morning, a real star. Everyone's talking about it. The phones haven't stopped ringing.'

'Yeah?'

'Yes, Danny. Maybe start believing it? You're a natural. Think about what you're going to do with all that money once it comes in from the *SpeedyBet* campaign. You could invest or even buy your own a place. You can't rent a room forever, not now you're a – celebrity.'

'I'm a dick.'

'No, you are not. *Isabella's* is a total Tardis of a building. There are rooms I've never even been in, floors I've never set foot on. It's a thriving hub of activity. There's always something going on.'

'I'm so sorry. I'm sorry for…'

'Look, I'm signing you off for a week – nervous exhaustion – then you can come back replenished, refreshed, and raring to go, okay?'

'A whole week? Wow. Okay. Maybe I'll watch *Bugsy Malone.*'

'That's the spirit. Well done. *Ciao, ciao.*'

Heather hangs up, pulls her bottle of vodka out from under her desk. 'Bollocks.' She takes a swig. 'Shit, shit, shit, *bollocks.*'

CHAPTER 9

Rummaging through his pencil case for a felt tip pen that hasn't dried up, Danny tries out the blue on the back of his page. The tip's a bit frayed, but it'll do for the plumage, at least.

Feverishly sketching away in his room all morning, he's been thinking about what Heather said on speakerphone the other day. She's right. He's making money he's only ever dreamed of. Soon, he'll have more than enough to revive his dream of running a beach bar in Tenerife, and his celebrity status could be one hell of a draw.

But earlier, when he was mooching about on the landing, he started peeling away a flap of wallpaper by the old sash window. It was hard and brittle, and he got to thinking: *Why go all the way to Tenerife when I could do the show right here?* The idea came to him in a flash. Run a pub. Be a landlord. Renovate the place. Murphy might take some convincing, but having something down on paper – something solid – would certainly help him convey his vision.

'The Finch's Arms,' he says, holding the A4 sketch out in front of him.

Something's not quite right. It's the perspective. It's all wrong, and the overall style looks too – cutesy. It's more *Tweety Pie* than the proud finch he was going for, with its conical beaked head set in profile, complete with ponytail, and four wings folded boldly across its breast. Art was never Danny's subject, but nothing ever really was. He outlines the beak with a black biro and holds the page out again.

'It's a start at least,' he says. 'It'll do for a preliminary pub sign sketch, anyway.' And he's pleased with how the feathers have turned out. The fluffed up, worn marker tip has created a lovely painterly effect. But knowing he can do better, he gets to work on another design.

A loud coughing coming from downstairs makes Danny jump, and his 2B pencil streaks across the page. 'Jesus, Murphy,' he says, throwing his pencil down.

Danny was hoping to speak to him about his renovation plans once his signage designs are ready, maybe make him an offer, but the man doesn't sound well. It sounds like a load of geese are playing with a blender full of gravel down there. Trying his best to drown it out, Danny puts pen to paper and presses on.

Pub sign design number two: Danny as Vitruvian Birdman, with four arms outstretched inside a circle – he used a compass for that bit – and with Danny's signature ponytail.

He holds out the page.

It's the feet. Something's wrong with the angle of the feet. *I'm not sure Old Leo had them set at ten-to-two like that*, he wonders, filling in the conical beak with an orange highlighter. *Do finches have orange beaks?*

A loud bang sends Danny's orange highlighter skittering across the page. He hurls it at the wall. *Murphy*, of course. Again.

'Everything alright in there?' Danny asks, banging on Murphy's door.

'Who's there?' Murphy croaks, only to be cut off by another full body coughing fit. The heavy thud of footsteps reverberates through the room, and then the door creaks open, letting out an unmistakable stench of whisky.

'Everything alright in there? I heard a bang?'

Nicotine-stained fingers creep around the doorframe

'How many of yers are there?' Murphy asks, seeing two heads, two bodies, and too many arms to count. 'What do you want? From the council, are *ye*?' It's the first time Murphy has seen Danny since his "metamorphosis."

'It's me, Mr. Murphy. Danny, from upstairs. Can I come in?'

'Danny? Aye – aye. Who's the other fella?' Murphy's

steaming.

'Nobody. It's just me. Just Danny. I've changed a bit since the last time you saw me. I look a bit different now...'

'Right so. Ah, *Jaysus* – I'm seeing double. I thought there were two of yers. Come in, come in.'

Murphy cackles and coughs. Danny steps into the room.

'Having a bit of a party, are we, Murphy?' The air is thick with cigarette smoke. Blue carrier bags litter the floor. Empties are lined up along the old bar of what used to be *The Tavern*. The original brass foot rail still runs along the bottom. 'On a lovely summer's evening like this, and you're cooped up in here?' he says, drawing open the curtains.

Perching precariously on the sofa arm, Murphy clutches a bottle of whisky.

'*A gypsy curse – until my last kiss...*'

'You're gonna fall off there if you're not careful. Why don't you sit down properly?' says Danny, spotting the likely source of the loud bang.

'*...no pot of gold – no pot of gold – just an old gypsy curse...*'

Murphy takes a swig from the bottle.

'Don't you think you've had enough of that?'

Another coughing fit takes hold of Murphy. A deep, guttural hack laced with a sharp, high-pitched wheeze.

'You seen a doctor about that?'

Thick, phlegmy – whisky sprays from his mouth.

'Mr. Murphy?'

His stained, mustard T-shirt rides up over his bloated belly. It must have been four, maybe five months since Danny's seen him, and his gut was nothing like that then. Danny imagines jabbing it with a pin and nothing but *Jameson's* bursting out.

'How about a coffee, Mr. Murphy? Nice and strong—'

'*A gypsy curse – until my last kiss...*'

'I'll brew some up, shall I?'

Going through to the kitchen, Danny smooths his hands over the bar counter. Although neglected, it has managed to retain some of its shine.

Watching Murphy belching and sucking on his bottle, Danny abandons the coffee and goes behind the bar. Leaning his elbows on the counter, he looks through the bay window opposite, trying to get a feel for the place – that magic feeling people talk about on property shows. That gut feeling telling you it's the right decision. Then, imagining himself calling last orders, pulling pints, two at a time, he asks, 'Hand-carved this bar, isn't it, Murphy?'

'*That gypsy woman, gypsy rose – a curse until my last kiss. No pot of gold waiting for me…*'

'That's original up there as well, isn't it?' he says, stepping out from behind the bar and pointing up at the Lincrusta wallpaper on the ceiling. 'Flapping up a bit, mind, but easy enough to fix. You see, Mr. Murphy. I've—*err*—come into a bit of money. I ain't got much. I ain't won the lottery, nothing like that – but it's enough.' Danny picks at the Lincrusta. 'Enough to sort this place out. And there's more on its way.'

Murphy lets out a loud fart and rolls down onto the sofa. Danny instinctively covers his nose.

'Found my old pencil case this morning,' he says, stepping out from the bar, the foul stench no longer lingering in the air. 'Been doodling. Sketching.' He sits down and swivels on a creaky bar stool. Complimentary drawing gestures with both right hands accompany his words. 'Pub sign designs. All morning I've been at it.'

Bringing the bottle to his lips, Murphy knocks his teeth.

'*The Finch's Arms*,' says Danny, hopping off the stool and dramatically spreading his hands. 'That's what we could call the place. *The Finch's Arms*. Get it?'

Danny could have ten arms and still, Murphy wouldn't notice. He hops back onto the wobbly stool.

'Put this place back on the map, eh, Murph? You and

me. Together. Restore it back to its former glory, like when you used to run it – imagine that!'

Slumped over on the sofa, Murphy sings into its armrest, slurred and painfully off-key.

'It'll need a bit of modernising though. Gastropubs – that's what today's punters are after. An honest pint isn't enough these days, not for this London lot. They want decent grub now, an 'all. Giant scotch eggs. Four-cheese tarts. *Hummus*. Decent service, which won't be hard with my – advantage. It'd be like three of us working behind there. And think how we'd save on staff costs.'

Staggering towards the bar, Murphy's bottle dry, he's thirsty for another. 'No Murphy. No more, eh?' says Danny, blocking his path. But there's madness in Murphy's eyes as he brushes Danny aside, reaching over his shoulder for the hand bell. 'No, Murphy, please.' Danny covers his ears, bracing for the clang.

'Last orders! Last orders!' he gargles, coughing and spluttering whisky-fuelled catarrh into Danny's face as he struggles to prise the bell from Murphy's surprisingly strong grip.

Six hands grapple at once until Danny finally frees it from his grasp, the reek of stale smoke infused in Murphy's skin, hair, and clothes hitting Danny's nose as he steers him towards the sofa.

'Now sit down, for God's sake,' says Danny, pushing him down onto the sofa. Murphy slumps forward and burps. 'Jesus.' Danny can smell sick. 'You let one go again? Knocked all the wind out your sails that did, didn't it. *Bloody piss head*. Now sleep, will you, for God's sake?'

Pulling Murphy's T-shirt down over his belly, another coughing fit takes hold. Danny pats him on the back until the coughing subsides.

'You had me scared there for a minute. Jesus, Murphy. You have let one go, haven't you? That fucking stinks! So, you *do* have *some* wind left in you then!' says Danny, trying to defuse the grisly situation with humour.

Leaning Murphy's head back on the sofa, Danny shakes his head in disbelief and moves over to the far wall.

'It'll take me no time at all stripping these walls, you know, Murphy, not with these bad boys,' says Danny, flexing his biceps. 'A nice colour scheme: brick red and slate grey? Heritage green and maroon? No... how about mahogany? What d'you reckon?' says Danny, looking back to see Murphy cupping his hands under his mouth. Danny had only turned his head away for a moment, but now there's blood spatter all over Murphy's T-shirt, his mouth.

A liquid gurgle followed by more blood.

'Murphy?' Danny rushes over. 'Jesus. I'm calling an ambulance—'

'No,' gargles Murphy. 'Don't, boy. I'm fine...'

'Fuck it,' panics Danny, realising his phone is all the way upstairs. 'Wait. Wait there. I'll be right back. Stay there, okay? Don't move—'

Flying up the stairs, the dreadful noise coming from Murphy growing quieter as he nears the top, Danny grabs his phone, races back down, and finds Murph slumped to his right, his head hanging over the sofa arm.

'Come on!' he says, trying to lift him, but Murphy's a dead weight. 'Fucking, come *on.*' Danny shakes him firmly by the shoulders, but there's no life. Nothing. He feels for a pulse.

'Mr. Murphy? Can you hear me?'

Nothing. 'Mr. Murphy? *Please,* Mr. Murphy!'

Against his better judgement, Danny leans in closer, slaps him lightly across the face. Then harder.

'Mr. Murphy!'

Shakily trying to dial for an ambulance, Danny covers his mouth with his two little fellas.

They'll tell me to do CPR.

It's ringing.

I've never done CPR. I don't want to do CPR.

Murphy's bloody mouth foams.

The kiss of life? No way. No way, I can't.

He switches off his phone. *What if they call back? What if they can trace this address?* 'Fuck. Fuck. Fuck.'

A strange hissing sound coming from Murphy, cuts through Danny's shock. 'Murphy?' For a moment, he almost believes he's alive and tries to rally him with a song. '"*A gypsy's curse*" – come on, Murphy. Sing it. "*A gypsy's curse…*"'

As Murphy begins to emit gas from every orifice, Danny sinks to the floor.

He's never seen a dead body before – only on the telly. But he knows he must get him out before his sphincter relaxes and his bladder empties pure *Jameson's* all over the place. He saw it on an episode of *Autopsy: Life and Death*, and he knows that soon, he'll have to get hands on with the body.

Wiping his eyes with the bottom of his vest, Danny gives him a prod.

'Wake up! Wake up you, bastard!'

Some kids mucking about outside past the window makes Danny get a grip of himself. Staying low, he goes to the front door, slides both bolts across, and creeps back in the room unable to stop shaking.

Gnawing at his thumb nail, thirty regret filled minutes go by. Regret at not having called that ambulance. *It's too late now. They'll think I had something to do with it.*

It certainly looks suspicious. What if the ambulance is on its way after having traced the call? It's possible. Danny saw it on *Bodycam Squad UK*. And if he calls them now, they'll question why he waited so long before calling for an ambulance. Then it'll be straight down the station. Only murderers wait that long before calling an ambulance. Guilty people.

With his thumb cuticle stinging, he switches to another hand and spots Murphy's blood spatter on the back of it. Snatching it away from his mouth, he wipes it on his jeans.

'You idiot. You fucking idiot.' He punches himself in the head – left, right, left – his sharp knuckles digging into his temples. '*Stupid, stupid, stupid.* Dick, dick, *dick.*'

What if he'd never bothered coming downstairs and hadn't knocked on Murphy's door? He'd still be dead, wouldn't he? He still would have died. If he hadn't come down, his body might have lain here for days. Rotting for weeks, until the rancid stench of putrefaction drifted up the stairs.

At least this way he didn't die alone. He didn't die alone. He didn't die alone…

Sitting up at the bar, drinking Murphy's whisky, he notices it's almost twilight. He can't put it off forever – he knows that. If he waits any longer the chemical changes will set in. Things will get too messy then. Too rigid. Too stiff.

Too real.

But he's stopped shaking. He's beginning to think more rationally.

In all the time Danny's lived here, not one person has bothered to even visit Murphy. Looking around, he sees no loved ones in frames, no children. It was one of the first conversations they'd had. Murphy always called him "Danny Boy" when he was sober. Danny liked it. And although they passed like ships in the night most of the time, Murphy was still the closest thing he's ever had to a father. Gramps never called him "Danny Boy" – only Tommy.

Taking Murphy's ring of keys off the hook behind the bar, he goes through the kitchen.

Lichen and mildew have crept through the gaps around the garden door. A frustrating struggle with the lock ensues, but eventually it gives.

A canopy of brambles overhangs his head above the door – nature's barbed wire. It's a balmy night. It will be dusk soon. Danny flicks the garden light. It doesn't work. He goes back in puts the main light on, trying to ignore

Murphy's pot belly expanding with gas in the corner of his eye.

If he's quick, he should be able to make it over to the DIY store by the precinct before closing. Wearing a fleece-lined hoodie in this heat is the last thing he wants, but staying anonymous isn't optional.

Taking a couple of fifties from the shoebox, he runs downstairs, pulling up his hood before heading out into the breezeless night, Murphy's keys jangling in his pocket.

The air conditioning in the Garden & Landscaping aisle is heaven. A woman with spiked blonde hair has gone to fetch him another spade from out back, as there was only one on display. He waits for her return.

'We're closing in two minutes,' she says, returning and handing him the spade. 'You'll have to use self-checkout.'

'Fine. That's fine.'

It's more than fine. Danny's grateful not to have to engage in any further human interaction.

Leaving the store, each spade concealed in a carrier bag, he looks up at the night's full moon. A scene straight out of a horror movie – it's almost too perfect. 'What the hell am I doing?'

The pub garden is dotted with weathered pub benches, their wooden legs heavily rotted and almost lost in the overgrowth. The tabletops seem to float above the long grass. The dim light spilling from inside casts an eerie glow along his path. Danny walks to the far corner of the garden, spades in hand.

The impressive trill of a nightingale brings an unexpected comfort as he peels off his vest and places his right foot on the edge of the spade. It's the old guys who cut first into the soil, softened by the recent downpour, and it's not long before he finds his rhythm. A pile of earth gathers evenly along the back wall behind the grave.

A grave. I'm digging a grave. Murphy's grave. Sweat already pouring, he speeds up.

Having been digging for nearly an hour, Danny alternates spades – old guys, little fellas, old guys, little fellas – but for some reason, not feet. His right foot is starting to ache from the constant pressure of standing on the spades, and when he notices the sole of his Superstar tennis shoe has split, he decides to switch feet.

Two hours in, and there's still a way to go, but the little fellas threw in the towel ten minutes ago and now hang loose by his sides, near wasted. The old fellas are on their own. They pick up the pace, and at four feet deep, he lies down, disappearing into the tall grass before facing the final hurdle.

After wrapping the body with an old bedsheet, Danny threads both pairs of arms under Murphy's armpits, and cradles the body, dragging it out backwards through to the garden. 'Jesus, Murphy,' says Danny, lining up the body beside the grave. 'Too many gut-buster fry ups, eh, old man?'

But before he rolls him in, he retrieves the carrier bags that covered the spades, and double bags Murphy's head to give the man some dignity. The length of the grave is adequate, but looking at Murphy's bloated body, it could have been a bit wider.

'Oh well. Here it goes. *One – two – three…*'

Murphy lands with an undignified thud, face down. 'Sorry, Murphy.' It's a tight fit. His jeans have slipped down, revealing his arse crack.

'I guess this is it, then. Last orders—*wait.*'

The hand bell. Danny goes and gets it and rests it on Murphy's back. 'Last orders, Murphy. Last orders.'

Backfilling the grave, a tear rolls down his nose and drops in. When his strength returns tomorrow, he'll drag a bench over to cover it. Not now.

'Life will breathe again through these walls, Murphy. It will,' sniffs Danny. 'You just wait and see.'

CHAPTER 10

Since the burial, Danny's been in a daze. Losing things. Forgetting the names of familiar kitchen appliances like the kettle and the fridge. Thunderclap headaches. And all the while, his angry acne has been bubbling away along his jawline. And to top it all, his recently pierced earlobe is red and swollen, with this solid, pea-sized lump inside of it that feels tender to the touch. He hasn't stuck to the routine with the surgical spirit and the cotton balls. It's hard to believe this was meant to be his recuperation week.

There's a dead body buried in the garden.

Moving back from the kitchen window, he goes through to the front room rehearsing what's he going to say if someone comes looking for Murphy – *when* someone comes looking. Funny how he never thought anyone would when Murphy was alive.

The front room windows are covered with black bin liners, and every day that passes, every minute, with the front door going un-knocked or the intercom going un-buzzed, feels like a victory.

Danny is currently the highest bidder on a 1955 Wurlitzer jukebox; an 1800 model; bright fluorescent tubing and with a walnut finish. He has the perfect spot for it, just as soon as the new carpet goes down. The renovation is the only thing keeping him sane.

In the end, he settled on Vitruvian Birdman. Once the décor's done, he'll have an oak sign made and hang it out front. He's already added a few touches, like string up some fairy lights around the bar with Sellotape, and he's placed Yin's tequila talisman on the mantlepiece above the fireplace. Angel or devil, it's hard to say. But Danny's not in a position to be picky. He'll take all the luck he can get.

'Three's a charm' he says, giving the bottle a shake, the gems gently tinkling inside.

His phone pings. The bright screen was hurting his

eyes, so he moved it away, but knowing it might be about the jukebox, he goes and gets it, takes a look.

It's an email from Heather, subject: *Housewives' Favourite!*

He opens it.

A major celebrity gossip magazine wants him to do a double-page spread off the back of his *Shopping Channel* gig. Heather did say that gig would act as the perfect springboard for him. She was right. Squinting and massaging his temples, he reads on.

The magazine wants Danny sprawled out on black satin sheets and surrounded by puppies. He's to have his teeth whitened, get a pedicure, and a spray tan. A schedule for his vitamin-shots is attached, which he's expected to continue with for another three months. And he's been offered a runway debut in Milan for *Fashion Week* - catwalk training schedule attached.

Oh, and documentary filming starts in three weeks.

'Three weeks?'

A sudden pressure in his head forces Danny out to Murphy's kitchen for a glass of water. As the tap runs, he gazes out at Murphy's grave, and buckles.

There's a dead body under there. In the garden. A dead body. Murphy's body. Only four feet deep.

It's like his brain is being stabbed repeatedly with an ice pick; his eyes flash, and for a second, it's like that scene in *Jaws*, with Chief Brody and the dolly zoom. Only, instead of that gut-wrenching moment, "Get Out of the Water! Get Out of the Water!" it's Murphy's grave.

After lying down for a bit, Danny decides it's time to clear his head. He slips on his trainers, planning a slow jog – South Ealing to Mayfair – and then he'll catch the tube back.

Passing Gino's, he stops for a panini and sits on the low wall behind *Isabella's*, watching the exclusive clientele come and go from expensive cars, green pesto and butter oozing out onto his knees. But keen not to be spotted, he decides not to hang around.

Scrunching the oily panini paper into a ball, he stands up and turns to go. Then something catches his eye by the fire exit. A small figure, coming down the steps with a rubbish bag. *Yin?*

Leaning into the shadow of the adjoining building, he sees it is her, standing on tiptoes beneath an exterior wall light, hurling the rubbish bag up and over the lip of an industrial metal bin.

Her eyes are puffy and strange. Lifeless like a doll's. Leaning back further, he sees her untying something from around her neck and recognises it as one of those chokers girls wore in the nineties. Yin had fashioned it from some cut-offs while altering the girls' dresses. Now, Danny sees her neck, black and bruised. Gently pressing it, she winces and traipses back up the steps.

'Yin!' Danny shouts, stepping out of the shadows. She doesn't hear him. 'Yin!' he shouts again, louder this time, but she's already up the steps. 'Yin!'

The heavy fire door seals behind her.

Gripping a blue pole in a near empty Piccadilly Line carriage, Danny stares vacantly at his hooded reflection as the sliding doors close.

Who did that to her?

The Tube roars, accelerating over worn metal rails. His head's pounding. The "slow jog" was a mistake. The seven-and-a-half-miles took him over three hours – he walked most of it. Usually, he runs it in an hour and twenty.

People get on at Hammersmith. Danny steps aside to let a mother and her little girl sit down.

'Sit *down*, Izzy,' the mother snaps, as the little girl in a rainbow dress, swings on a vertical pole banging into Danny's leg.

'I'm sorry,' the mother apologises.

'It's alright,' says Danny, his face partially covered with

113

a hand. The girl ignores her, has one last swing.

'Isa*bella* – don't make me tell you again. Now you sit down right now, young lady. Isa*bella*.'

Isabella's. Rooms she's never even been in? Floors she's never been on? Knows the place like the back of her hand? Shadows lurch across the carriage as the train hurtles forward, joints groaning and rattling with every twist in the track. The darkness outside presses against the windows, as if the train is burrowing deeper into something it shouldn't. Danny doesn't blink. He just stares, thoughts louder than the noise.

B- u -g -s -y - M - a -l -o -n –e Danny types into the search engine on his phone, seated at the bar. With a tumbler of *Jameson's* in hand, he zooms in on Tallulah, recognising her from *Silence of the Lambs*.

But she looks much older than the girls he saw.

He trawls the internet for youth theatre groups. Rehearsal spaces for hire. London dance troupes, but nothing relevant pops up. He pours another drink and types in "*The Velvet Lounge*" just for the hell of it.

To his surprise, a discussion forum comes up.

He registers and creates an account.

DannyDan-83 has entered the chat.

Most of it's crazy. Conspiracy-stuff, but someone going by the handle of: **BonzoDooDah-49** says he's heard of the place and invites Danny into a private chat.

'So, what's this Bonzo got to say for himself?' he says, waiting for Bonzo to finish typing. 'Come on, *Bozo*.' Another sip. 'Bono.'

An alert on his phone beeps. He opens his account in another browser while he waits.

'Yes. Yes! Get in.'

Danny's won the jukebox. The excitement almost knocks him off the bar stool, and he sees that the seat isn't properly attached. He makes a mental not to get some new ones. 'See, Murphy, what did I tell you?' He raises his glass over to the tequila bottle on the mantlepiece, and by the time he's processed his payment, Bonzo's responded.

After chatting for a while, Bonzo reveals he used to be one of *Isabella's* delivery drivers – or so he says. He claims to have seen all sorts of things over the years, including "this oriental bird" who used to let him in round the back. He says *The Velvet Lounge* is common knowledge among the delivery drivers.

'Turn a blind eye,' types Bonzo. 'More than my job's worth. That's what most of the delivery guys did and probably still do. Not me.'

'Turn a blind eye to what?' Danny types.

Bonzodoodah-49: typing…

Danny pours another whisky.

Bonzodoodah-49: typing…

'Kids. Little girls being dropped off in posh motors.'

DannyDan-83: typing…

'You heard of the *Bugsy Malone* theatre group?'

Bonzodoodah-49: typing…

'Bugsy Malone? What you smoking, bruv? LOLZ!'

DannyDan-83: typing…

'Do you know if the "oriental bird" is involved?'

Bonzodoodah-49: typing…

Danny looks over at the tequila bottle.

DannyDan-83: typing…

'You there?'

Bonzodoodah-49: typing…

Bonzodoodah-49: has exited the chatroom.

Watching *Bugsy Malone* on his phone, with a slice of takeaway pizza in his hand, he studies Tallulah – the chanteuse in her flapper dress, exuding the deadpan sincerity and droll charm of a young Mae West. Bold. Confident. Razar-sharp wit. Nothing like those girls he saw.

'It's fucking night and day!' he says, marching over to the mantelpiece, pizza still in hand. He grabs the tequila bottle and smashes it against the stone hearth, then takes a bite. The chorus number – *Fat Sam's Grand Slam* – plays from his phone on the sofa behind him.

Staring down at the ceramic fragments on the floor, he wants out, but he wants the money – to get *The Finch's Arms* off the ground. If he can just hang on, turn a blind eye, until the documentary airs. And maybe Milan. *Would that be so bad? Would that make me... complicitous?* He means *complicit.* Would it?

"At Fat Sam's grand slam – speak easy – always able to find you a table – there's room for just one more – at Fat Sam's grand slam – speakeasy..."

Danny shuts off the film.

A celebrity landlord. Clearing glasses. Small talk with the punters. Changing the barrels. Danny grabs his pad and pen off the bar.

'Cellar management course,' he writes down. 'New bar stools. A sheepskin rug to go by the hearth. Taxidermy. A stuffed badger. An antique fire grate. A hand-made, copper-bottomed frying pan...

A stuffed albatross...

A set of chrome and leather bar stools...

There's a dead body in the garden...

Tiffany lamps...

Tables...

A 52" LCD Flat Screen TV

Chairs

Yin's neck all bruised

Braces. Strawberry laces...

"The only thing necessary for the triumph of evil is for good men to do nothing."

An Edwardian umbrella stand...

A mahogany chaise-longue...

It's the last day of his recuperation week. It's four in

the morning, and unable to sleep, Danny is writing a letter to Yin, putting it all down.

How he saw her with those girls. Saw her neck the other night. Smashed tequila bottles, Bonzo – the lot. He tells her everything.

He tells her he feels stupid for spilling his heart out that night in his room – about his mum, his childhood. Tells her all that "shit" about the overdose was made up. "You think I'd tell someone like you something like that if it was true?" he writes. "I'd have to be mad to trust someone like you."

He tells her that after the documentary airs, he's going straight to the police. Says he'll give names, a witness account, a statement. "I'll even draw them a bloody map!"

After barely any sleep, he posts the letter on his way to *Ripcurl* HQ, pausing halfway up the stairs to platform two. 'Shit,' he mutters, reaching in his back pocket for his script. Rush hour commuters barge past. Propelled by the throng, he is swept to the top. 'Shit.'

He's forgotten it. The Tube pulls in.

'Danny? It's your line.' Jem's voice is pained.

Midway through a yawn, Danny looks up.

'Danny? The line? I must say, I was expecting you to be a tad more *with it* after your week off. Where's your script? He doesn't even have his script,' says Jem, to his team around the board table. 'Not that it would make the slightest bit of difference—'

'Now look here,' says Danny, pushing back his chair as he stands. 'I'm trying my best, alright? I told you I ain't much of a reader, let alone an actor.'

A script gets passed along to Danny.

'Thanks,' he says, as it reaches him. 'It wasn't my idea to memorise an entire script for my own bloody documentary. You can't expect me to reel it off like I'm... like I'm bloody...'

Too wiped to even summon the name of a single well-

117

known actor, Danny draws a blank.

'…like I'm bloody… bloody, thingy…'

'Are you quite done?' asks Jem.

Danny sits back down.

'What's that?' says Jem, sliding his glasses down from his head.

'What's what?'

'Your ear. It's all red. Your ear stud. Where is it?'

'Oh, that.' Danny touches his sore earlobe, uneasy. 'I took it out.'

'Took it out? Why? They said six weeks, Danny. You were supposed to keep it in, twisting it at regular intervals. It'll have closed up now. You'll have to be pierced all over again.'

'But I had to take it out. It was hurting me. Especially at night. Against my pillow. I couldn't sleep.' Danny glances at the soft-featured lady beside him. 'And there's this funny lump inside it. Inside my earlobe. Look. Can you see?'

Looks of repulsed concern sweep across the table.

'Right, that's it! Meeting adjourned. Danny, wait for Guy out in the corridor. We'll *reconvene* later.'

'But, what about my…'

'Danny, just go, will you?'

As people file out, Danny trails behind. Jem notices a bald patch, dead centre at the back of Danny's head. It wasn't there a week ago. He hangs back, closes the door. 'As if I haven't got enough on my plate,' he mutters, begrudgingly picking up the phone to inform the Upstyling Department of this morning's "developments".

Jem's been sleeping under his office desk in one of his kids' sleeping bags. Hotels are a privilege ill afforded to someone going through a messy and expensive divorce. He drank two bottles of Malbec last night, then watched porn on his phone until he passed out.

'Jem. Wake up,' says Heather, placing a large cappuccino and croissant on his desk, her eyes momentarily entertained by the empties in the wastepaper basket by the photocopier. 'You look like shit.'

'Thanks,' he says, his eyes levelling with Heather's high heels as they recede from under his desk.

'It reeks in here,' she says, cranking up the air-conditioning. 'Where have you been showering? You have been, haven't you?'

'The gym.'

Stretching and yawning, Jem radiates body odour and morning breath. Heather fans away the stink with a letter she pulls from her handbag. 'I bring news.'

'Good, I hope,' says Jem, reaching up for his cappuccino and pulling down the navy-blue paper bag from Gino's. Bleary eyed, he takes out the croissant. 'What – no pecan plaits?'

'No. Now listen. This is important. I intercepted Yin's post—'

'None at all?' he says, sulkily lifting the lid off his cappuccino and tasting it expectantly for hazelnut syrup. There is none.

'*No.*'

'It's bad news, isn't it. Don't tell me – "Them Upstairs" again, right? I am, aren't I? Go on, just put me out of my misery. *Oh, what a beautiful morn-ing...*' he sings, his voice hoarse and his lips stained with tannins.

'This is *serious,* Jem.' Heather stamps her foot and some of her caramel latté spills over.

'It's that Becky-Jo from Manipulative Editing, isn't it?' says Jem, straightening up and putting on his glasses before biting into his croissant. 'Absolutely useless. God knows how she got the job. Living proof that evolution really *can* go in reverse, that one. Gormless isn't the word.' Brushing pastry flakes off his sleeping bag, he takes another bite. 'Makes our four-armed friend look like bloody Einstein.'

'Well, it seems that our "four-armed friend" isn't

buying our story.'

'What, the *Bugsy Malone* shit? I came up with that. Thought it was pretty good myself.'

'Well, evidently not good enough. Here—'

Frisbeeing the letter over to him, she takes a sip of her latté and lets out an anguished sigh.

'Yin left the *sodding* hatch unlocked on the night of Kelly's party. And now we're in the shit. Deep shit. You and me.'

'Who?'

'Yin.'

'Yin?'

'Yes, *Yin*. A nobody. A menial. A Becky-Jo. Oh, it doesn't *matter*.'

Yin's as unfamiliar to Jem as Becky-Jo is to Heather.

'His handwriting's awful. I can barely read this.'

'I know. It took me quite some time to decipher as well. It's like a cryptic forest code.'

Parting the vertical blinds, Heather surveys the vibrant street scene below, while Jem battles through Danny's appalling handwriting.

'Finished?'

'Yeah. *Jesus*. That penmanship should be declared abstract art. Almost needed divine intervention to get to the end of that,' says Jem, gladly casting the letter aside. 'Nobody else knows, do they? Just this Bonzo. And this Yin. And what about the hatch? I mean, it'd better be locked now. It's not still open, is it?'

'Of *course* it isn't. It's been covered and refloored. I oversaw the work this weekend – a*ll* weekend. And what a way to spend it. Unseemly, to say the least. Absolutely *arse*-cracking.'

'Well, it beats being stuck in here, under this desk.'

'All weekend I've been up on that roof, having to *commune* with a bunch of cock-eyed concreters in ill-fitting jeans.' Heather darts a look at the wine bottles in the bin. 'Hardly the little *soirée* you seem to have had. If I never see a builder's bum again it'll be too soon.'

'But what if he blabs? *Before* the documentary is aired. What if he goes to the police, what then? We can't trust what he says in that letter.' Jem rubs his eyes under his round-framed glasses. 'What are we going to do?'

'Nip it in the bud,' says Heather, now pacing with hands on hips. '*That's* what we do.'

'Nip it in the bud?'

'Yes. Silence him.'

'What – kill him?'

'No, of *course* not – but he'll be wishing he was dead by the time we've finished with him.'

'So, what then? Threaten him? Blackmail?'

'Better than that. We press his buttons. Set him up. Make it so his word is mud.'

'Mud?'

'Yes, *mud*,' says Heather, aiming her empty latté cup at the wastepaper basket and successfully landing it between Jem's empty wine bottles. 'We launch a smear campaign. Make people *loathe* him.'

Straightening the cuff of her blouse, her eyes narrow. Jem watches as a self-approving smile creeps on her face.

'Make them believe he's gone nuts, lost his mind, that he's making it all up. Baseless, unsubstantiated claims. The mere ramblings of a madman.'

'Mad him off?'

'Precisely. A few well-coordinated shots in the papers. A couple of stories about how "hands-on" the four-armed *fuck* can be should do it.' Her eyes smoulder as she crosses the room.

Uncertain whether it's the copious amount of porn he's been watching lately, Heather's looking hot to Jem right now, smoking. He slips his hand inside his sleeping bag...

'After a couple of weeks' bad press, he'll be about as credible as a chubby child locked in a chocolate factory, with chocolate smeared all over its disgusting, grubby face, insisting it hasn't touched a thing.'

'So – what else you got *cooking*?'

'Well, to start, I thought a light sex pest scandal, with just a *pinch* of "tin-foil-hat" thrown in, just enough to make him look crazy. Let that simmer on a low heat for a while, and that way, we can always add herbs and spices as needed.'

'*Mmmm*,' purrs Jem, Heather's arse snug inside her fitted skirt. 'And more *meat*.'

'No,' says Heather, turning sharply from the window, somehow sensing his eyes on her. Smoothing down her pencil skirt, she strides back across the room. 'Nothing too heavy. Just enough to discredit him, make any crazy allegations he makes seem like nothing more than an act of revenge. Danny's bitter about being dropped, that's all.'

'Dropped?' says Jem, flinging his hand well out of the sleeping bag. 'But what about my documentary? If I don't deliver on this, I'm toast. You know that. I'm out – that's it. Filming starts in three weeks. Danny was supposed to be my protégé. The ratings are set to go through the roof. And what about the Diversity Awards?'

'Jem, my dear man, you are forgetting that your "protégé" is unhinged, unsafe. Impossible to work with. A sexual predator. A sexual predator prone to violent outbursts on set. A sexual predator with a substance abuse problem and "mummy issues." He says so himself in that letter.'

She comes over, palms flat on his desk, looks over, and whispers, 'Nip it in the bud.'

'Nip it in the bud?' Gazing up at her cleavage, Heather's desirability is fading fast. 'What, now?'

'Now, Jem, now. Nip it in the bud. Strangle it at birth.' Heather wrings out an imaginary flannel. 'Terminate it. *Get rid.* Pull the plug *before* he speaks, before he even gets the chance. Nip it in the *bud.*'

'So, no documentary? And what about *London Fashion Week*? Surely that's still going ahead.'

'Can you imagine the wrap party, with that ten-gallon mouth of his? Chewing the fat? After a few drinks, there'll be no stopping him. And *Fashion Week*? Are you serious? With all that champagne and those male models coked up to the eyeballs? Hind legs and donkey spring to mind, we may as well shout it from the rooftops ourselves. Forget it, Jem. Not going to happen. Can you get his phone.'

'Excuse me?'

'His phone. His PIN. I need his phone so I can tap it.'

'Tap it?'

'Yes, Jem. We need to track his movements online, his emails. He's al*ready* building a presence on social media with this *Gonzo* character. No, no, no. We can't take any risks.'

'I guess I could sneak a look over his shoulder, in the gym or something. Distract him in the locker room, I guess,' suggests Jem, devoid of enthusiasm.

'"*Deranged D-list celeb – still bitter after being dropped – seeks revenge by making wild allegations against agent.*" Yes, yes – I like that. We'll make the whole thing look like his own undoing. No one will have the foggiest that we're behind it. Not even "Them Upstairs." We'll let the *SpeedyBet* campaign run its course, milk Danny for all he's worth, and I'll go ahead and cancel his upcoming gigs. Tell people Danny is "struggling with his mental health," his "anxiety." Play the victim card. *Yes, yes.* Make people feel sorry for him, rather than angry. A pitying public, not a maddened one. *Then* we'll go in with the violent outbursts, the sex pest stuff.'

'He really would have been great, you know. I was *this close* to winning that Diversity award. It would have looked great up on my mantelpiece.'

'*Your* mantelpiece? I thought Colleen was getting the house?'

It's times like these when Jem wonders what it would feel like to punch Heather square in the jaw – and then

123

kick her in the tits.

'Oh, come on, Jem, don't be such a *sulky slug*,' she says, trying her best to pout her non-existent lips. It's like a cat's anus, or the tied end of a party balloon. Rising up, he heaves his slug-like body over to his desk, his nipples exposed and erect above his sleeping bag.

'I guess I could bring filming forward,' he says, switching on his PC. 'We can poke the bear during filming. Feed the fire a little.'

'Create the perfect catalyst to have him dropped. I like it.'

'Exactly. Really rattle his cage. Mind turning down the air-con a bit?'

'I knew you'd get on board – see sense in the end,' says Heather, going over to the A/C unit.

'See sense? This feels anything but sensible,' says Jem, as his PC begins to boot up.

'It feels like madness. Like I'm hanging myself.'

CHAPTER 11

In the garden of a West London pub, Danny, dressed in the same Adam Ant/Mark Knopfler get-up he wore for his *Shopping Channel* gig, fiddles with the magnetic ear stud the Upstyling Department has made him wear.

Seated at a pub bench, he enjoys the invisible pull of the magnets. They snap into place with a satisfying click either side of his sore, closed-up earlobe, and he likes the way it hurts. But as Jem heads across the lawn, he savours the pinch one last time before relaxing his hands on the table.

'Shouldn't be too much longer now,' Jem assures Danny – for the second time. 'The crew's almost ready.'

Remaining doubtful, Danny swishes the last of his lager around his pint glass.

'Fancy another? Another drink?' offers Jem. It's barely noon.

'Alright. But make it a shandy this time.' Danny knocks back the last of his drink and hands his sun-warmed glass to Jem.

'And Danny?' Jem eyes the pack of unsmoked cigarettes on the table. 'Your smoking style – it still looks a little affected. A little...odd, like you're not enjoying it.'

'Well, that's because I'm not. I don't smoke.'

'Well, no better time to start. It's the way you're holding it. Look—' Jem lights up a cigarette to demonstrate. 'Hold your fingers *over* the filter, like this, not between. You're Danny Finch, remember, not Dot Cotton.' He coughs, passing it to Danny. 'Prefer a jazz cigarette myself. You know – a giggle stick.'

Mimicking the grip, Danny takes a drag. The smoke stings his eyes.

'That's it. Much better. Smoke up, yeah?'

The garden gate unbolts from the other side. Jem turns. 'Heather! You're here. How's this for weather, eh?

Perfect or what?'

Padding over to her in his Birkenstocks and silver toe ring, Jem leaves Danny in a smoky haze.

A runner comes over with a tray of drinks, hands Danny his shandy. 'Thanks,' he says, quickly stubbing out his cigarette. His eyes catch on a red, sparkly drink in the centre of the tray. It reminds him of a Cherry Bakewell.

As the smoke clears, Danny watches the crew set up their equipment, strangely detached from the scene. The lager must've gone to his head. Heather waves at him, lifting the red drink from the tray with a smile so forced it pulls her ungenerous mouth taut. She purses her lips around the skinny red straw, cheeks hollowing vampirically, like she's sucking up blood. Then, just as quickly, her expression shifts, and she holds out the drink as if it were raw sewage.

'You, boy. Come back. Come back here.'

The runner hurries over, all fawning and half-bows.

'I said cranberry soda, cranberry soda. *Wakey, wakey!*' She claps her hands sharply. 'Cranberry *soda* – come *on*. It's not rocket science, is it? It's sodding soda water. Cranberry soda.'

Lifting his pint to obscure the scene, Danny accepts that she's unbearable.

'Da da da – *dah* da - da da da – *dah* da - da da da – *dah* da,' he finds himself gently drumming on the table's edge. There's something about the way she spat out those words –something familiar, like a song he can't place. Enough to give him a creeping sense of déjà vu.

'Cranberry soda. *Da da da - dah-da – da da da - dah-da.* Cranberry soda.'

A conversation between two of the camera crew behind him thankfully distracts him from the itch in his mind. Casually, Danny tilts his head, angling his ear towards their chatter.

'Check the gate, and don't neglect those smooth eyelines. And don't be afraid to throw in a few unexpected close-ups, yeah?' one says to the other, effortlessly smoking a cigarette that clings to his bottom lip as he speaks. His skinny jeans hang low, coolly skimming his hip bone. 'Experiment, yeah? Have fun.'

'Okay, how about starting with a Dutch angle? What do you reckon?' says the other.

'Yeah, cool. That would work. Chuck in a couple of low angles maybe?'

The pair slink across the lawn in their hipster jeans, cigarettes dangling from their mouths. Less reluctantly than before, Danny lights up.

Through the smoke, a woman in a floral dress – far too frumpy for her voluptuous frame – sits down opposite Danny.

'Sorry,' he says, extinguishing his cigarette and wafting the smoke away, surprised that she's chosen to sit here when there are plenty of other tables.

'Oh, I don't mind,' she says, laying her notebook down, her freckled cleavage glistening in the sun. 'Used to smoke myself. Twenty a day. I'm Maggie.' She extends her freckled hand. 'Short for Mairead.'

Danny doesn't shake, just stares at the gold cross nestled between her bosom, flashing in the sun.

'Are you – alright?' she asks.

'Everyone called my mother Maggie. She was a Mairead. Wore a necklace just like that too. Here, you're not from Donegal an' all, are you?' says Danny, half in jest.

'Oh, my. Is my accent really that strong? Born and bred, I'm afraid – for my sins. Was *she* from there?'

'Who?'

'Your mother. She obviously means a lot to you,' says Maggie, clocking the "MUM" tattoo on his left little fella.

'No,' says Danny, dropping his elbows off the table. 'Not really.'

A camera boom lowers between their heads, and a camera is pointed at Danny's face. Make-up artists swoop in to trowel more concealer on his jawline, and he wonders if it's thick enough to cover his tattoo.

'We rolling?' Jem asks. The crew nods.

'What? We're rolling now?' asks Danny. 'But – what about her?' He points. 'Sorry, love, but you're gonna 'ave to 'oppit. Nice chatting to you.'

'It's okay. I'm the interviewer.' Maggie picks up her notebook with a smile.

'Interviewer?'

'Yes, I'll be the one asking all the questions.'

'Questions? Nobody said anything about questions.'

'Jesus, Danny.' Jem grabs the clapperboard. 'And here was I thinking you'd jump at the chance to go off-script. Let's go, everyone – it's showtime. Remember, we want this raw and organic, true *RipCurl* style. No edits. And Maggie – keep it quickfire, yeah?'

'Ready?' says Jem, walking backwards away from the table. 'And – *action.*'

The clapperboard snaps shut, marking the start of the scene, and Maggie dives straight in with the first question. The camera crew rotate around Danny in a low Earth orbit.

'How old were you when you had your first pint?'

Maggie's deadpan delivery is spot on – she's clearly understood the brief. Danny, on the other hand is totally stumped by the inconsequential question, and Jem's giving him a hurry-up hand-roll. 'Oh, too young,' blurts Danny, 'far too young.'

Camera One zooms in on Danny taking a sip of his shandy, leaning back, his old hands gripping the edge of the table, knuckles white, while his little fellas fiddle with his flip-lighter.

'Do your arms have names?'

His grip loosens. 'Yeah, they do, as it goes. I call this pair the old guys' – Danny gestures accordingly – 'and this pair, the little fellas, because they're littler. Smaller. But they used to be a *lot* smaller. Scrawnier.'

Another pint is placed in front of him. His fast-accumulating empties remain on the table.

Question three:

'Tell me about the first time you threw up from drinking.'

'What, you mean really chundered? Fifteen, I guess. Yeah, I was fifteen.'

Question four:

'What were you drinking?'

'Rum. White rum. A whole bottle. Can't touch the stuff now. The smell alone makes me wanna vom.'

A series of unrelated questions follow, ranging from vulgar to totally surreal. But, freed from the constraints of a script and nicely lubricated by alcohol, his eyes glazed, Danny is beginning to enjoy himself.

'Come on.' Twice, Danny snaps his fingers with all four hands. 'Next question.'

Question nine:

'Would you say you were on – a false ego trip?'

'Huh?' Danny leans forward. 'I don't know. I don't *think* so. I'm not exactly sure what you – a false ego trip?'

Danny looks up at Jem for guidance, an earnest smile on his face, but gets nothing.

'Okay, I get it. You're putting me under the microscope, aren't you.' Camera One closes in to study Danny's Adam's apple after taking a substantial gulp of lager. 'I'm right, though, yeah?' he says, expertly managing to suppress a burp.

Silence. Camera Two zooms in, filling the frame with a shot of Danny's right leg jiggling restlessly, while Camera One takes random shots of the back of Danny's elbows, his fingernails, his tattoos – and the bald patch he still doesn't know he has at the back of his head.

'What's a false ego trip? What's it mean? What d'you want me to say?'

Again, he looks up at Jem for supervision, his fourth

129

pint in hand. 'This shandy, yeah?' It's a struggle to maintain focus on Jem's bobbing head nodding affirmatively. 'Come on, man,' whispers Danny, Camera Two flying down on his ventriloquist-like mouth. 'Tell me what you want me to say.'

'But Danny, I thought you didn't *want* a script,' says Jem. People laugh, and Danny reddens. Something's off.

'Come on. Next question then,' says Danny, trying to mask his humiliation with attitude. But Maggie just repeats it with robot precision.

'No. I *ain't* on a false ego trip. There,' he says, and after a confident slug of his pint, he puts it down with force. 'Next question.' Another slug, his face screws. 'This the end of the barrel? Tastes a bit – funny.'

Silence. Danny fills it with a powerful burp and blows it in Maggie's face, making her jerk back.

'You don't like being put on the spot, do you,' she says, pinching her nose and staring at his arm.

'Does anyone? Next *question*.'

'Cockiness doesn't suit you, Danny.' Camera One follows her gaze and zooms in on Danny's "MUM" tattoo. 'You're still a little boy, really. I can tell. A little boy who still wants his "MUM".'

'Now look, what is this?'

A close-up of Danny's furled upper lip.

'A wee little boy who drinks shandy.' Some of the crew jeer at the baiting.

But Danny doesn't bite.

'This gonna be edited?' he says, lighting a cigarette. The cameras revolve around him, taking abstract shots of the guarded expression on his face. 'It better be. It's a load of crap, this, otherwise.' A close-up as he exhales. 'A load of bloody nonsense.'

Danny blows smoke at the lens of Camera One, hovering close.

'So, Danny. Tell me about the overdose.'

A roll of the eyes. A rapid shake of the head. Danny

flicks his cigarette at one of the cameras, and it bounces off, landing over on the lawn. The cameraman tracks it, continuing to film it smouldering in the grass.

'You want to tell your research department to get their facts right. Overdose? What overdose? *Jesus Christ.*'

'Daniel... you nearly died.'

'Died?'

Emboldened by the vodka-laced shandy-lagers he's been unknowingly consuming, he stands up. 'I see, I get it. Wanna play? Okay, let's play.'

'It was like this,' he says, stepping out from the bench, dismissing the question with another mighty burp. 'I remember sitting on the floor, up against the wall. It was my mate Roly who found me, strung out on the toilet floor. I only tried it once, during the school holidays. No one knew I was gonna try it, not even Roly. I just kept staring up like a zombie, unresponsive, with the foil in my hand, next to this mop and bucket. I bought the drugs with some money I borrowed off Roly, down the arcades. They thought I was dead. Everyone did. But I wasn't. I was alive. But I'd overdosed, see. I should have said no. But I didn't, did I? I said yes. Stupid, really.'

And, looking directly into Camera One with an authoritative point of his finger, he sings, "*No – just say no, just say no. No – just say no.*"

These efforts warrant a slow clap and a smirk from Jem.

'Very good – *Zammo*. I see what you did there. Very clever. Quite the performance.' Jem too was an avid *Grange Hill* watcher. 'Worthy of an Oscar, that was.'

A bag of cheese and onion crisps is thrown down onto the table. Danny sits back down and bursts them open. He drinks them back, his mercury fillings on display. Both cameras seize the moment. 'Didn't need a script, did I?' Crisps shoot from his mouth. 'Why are you doing this? Why don't you ask something – I dunno – about *me,* maybe? About my arms.'

'She was Irish, wasn't she?' says Maggie.

Another burp and blow. '*Gertcha.*'

'Thank you,' she says, wafting the boozy cheese and onion fumes away with her notebook before they get a chance to singe her nostrils. 'I take it that was for me?'

Drinking back the dregs of his packet, Danny laughs.

'Dumb insolence. *That* doesn't suit you either. Now, your mother. From Donegal, didn't you say?'

'Why do you keep banging on about my *bloody* mother?'

'Daniel, what was her name?'

'Look, I told you,' Danny picks crisps from his back teeth. 'Why do you keep calling me that?'

'What?'

'Daniel.'

'Because it's your *name*, Daniel. It's what your mother called you. Daniel.'

'Next – *question.*'

'What was your relationship with her like? She couldn't have been easy to live with.'

'Why? What would you know?'

Like a giant insect, Danny climbs back out from the bench, taking his drink with him. 'I've had about enough of this.' He knocks it back.

'Enough of what?'

'This! All these questions. I thought this was meant to be a documentary, not *Long Lost Family.*'

'Please, Daniel. Sit down. She liked a drink, didn't she, your mother?'

'For the hundredth time, it's Danny. Danny, *alright?*'

'A good old drink she liked, didn't she – your *mammy.*'

Camera One gets a shot of Danny's fingers, interwoven on the back of his head while Camera Two gets a close-up of his face.

'Not having a mother figure must have been difficult.' Weaving and ducking, he escapes the camera sandwich. Maggie and the cameras follow him across the grass.

'Come on, Daniel. Why did she leave?'

Like trying to outrun an alligator, he pivots, changes direction.

'You said you wanted to talk about *you*. Well, now's your chance. She could never put you before the drink, was that it? Was *that* the problem?'

Cornering him like a rat, the cameras trap him against the clematis wall trellis.

'It must have been tough for you, being a child, feeling so unloved... so—'

'Look, what is this, *Jeremy Kyle*? Why are you doing this?' he says, freeing himself from under their equipment.

'How old were you when you went into care, Daniel?'

They trail him back to the table.

'I already told you.' He gives it a kick. 'It's Danny.' Another kick. 'Danny. Look, who are you?' Now walking backwards. 'You lot MI5? MI6?' They move closer. 'Look, back *off*, alright?'

The boom grazes his cheek.

'Look, I'm warning you.' Maggie steps on his foot. He commandeers a tripod. 'I said, back off!'

The tripod goes airborne. Danny snatches the boom, swinging it like a machete. 'Come on then, you want some?!' he roars. 'You want some? Come on then!'

Two security men materialize seemingly out of nowhere, restraining him.

'Get off me! Get off!' he screams. 'They've set me up. Get off of me!'

But Danny's strength can't sustain, and he's forced face down, both pairs of hands cuffed before he's dragged through the pub, kicking and screaming, windmilling his arms, spitting, trying to bite. He's hurled into the back of a van.

'Doc?'

A familiar face. The van doors lock shut.

'Doc. Thank God. Thank God it's you. Doc, you gotta

help me. They're trying to' – Danny pauses to catch his breath – 'they're trying – *I don't know what* – they're trying to—'

The good doctor produces a syringe needle, then removes the air bubbles at the top with a practiced flick.

'A vitamin shot? What, *now*? Doc. You gotta listen to me, Doc. They're trying – they're trying to—'

But before Danny can utter another word, the doctor mercilessly sticks him with the needle. 'Drive on!' he orders, plunging the syringe down. 'And put your foot down!'

The crew mournfully recover their equipment left scattered across the lawn, and despite the damage, one of the cameras is still rolling.

'Think we got it all?' Heather asks Jem as they materialise from under a pub table.

CHAPTER 12

'We'll start over here and then get going on the stairs – depending on how much we get done today, that is.'

The carpet fitter pulls back the carpet around the hearth. It comes away with ease. '*Jesus.* Get a load of that.'

Carpet Fitter Two looks on in stunned silence.

'What, the floorboards?' Danny says, peering closer beneath the shadow of a huge roll of retro-arcade carpet, leaning against the hearth. 'They're original, those.'

'Yeah? Well, see all them holes there?' says One. 'Rot, that is. Woodworm. Gonna need a gel treatment, that. Both sides. The whole floor's riddled.'

'Riddled?'

'Look, I'll tell you what we'll do,' says One, scoping out the floor. 'We'll treat the wood tomorrow and rip up the carpet today.'

'How long will it take? You know, to lay the new stuff. A couple of days?'

'You're joking,' says Two, throwing down a section of underlay thick with mould. Dust and fibres fly up. 'We've got in here, then all the stairs, all your landings. How many floors you got again? Five?'

'Yeah, five. Including the basement – well cellar. So only four, really.'

'Only four he says.' The carpet fitters glare at each other.

'And you want that throughout?' says One, nodding towards the carpet: black with neon geometric shapes and lines. 'Up all your stairs, all your landings?'

Danny fixes on a spot of blood spatter by the foot of the sofa while the men telepathically size up the job.

'Four landings – that's five days.' One.

'At least.' Two.

Danny looks away from the blood. 'At least?'

'And it'll take even longer if we don't get cracking

soon,' says One, reaching for his toolbox while Danny awkwardly hovers above him. 'You mind?'

'Tea? Coffee?'

'Cheers. Milk and three, ta.'

'Milk and three for me too, please.'

Five days — at least.

The kettle boils. Danny stares out the window at Murphy's grave.

Five days of tea-making. Six times five is thirty. That's thirty sugars, even if they have only one cup a day. Which they won't. Danny picks a dead fly out of Murphy's sugar bowl.

'Oops,' says Danny, wiping the spilled tea off their toolbox after precariously placing the cups on the mantelpiece. There's not much room since his stuffed albatross arrived, which now has pride of place.

'Here, what's this?' he asks, pulling out a metal tool with a rubber-stamped end. 'It's heavy, ain't it?' he says, passing it to his second pair of hands then swapping back and forth

'Yeah,' says One, taking the carpet kicker from Danny, wishing he wasn't standing so close. 'Look mate — we really must crack on.'

'No, no. I understand. By all means, crack on, crack on.'

Taking a seat on one of his shiny new chrome-and-leather barstools — which arrived yesterday — Danny swivels, trying to keep out the way. 'Nothing worse than being distracted, is there?' says Danny, rotating on the squeaky, brand-new stool like it's some kind of musical instrument. 'Imagine I'm not here.'

The fitters turn up the volume on their heavy-duty jobsite radio. Lou Bega's, *Mambo No. 5 (A Little Bit Of...)* pumps out.

'So, you seen it then? *"Don't be greedy — bet with Speedy."* That was me. They dropped me, you know. Dropped. Just like that. Like a cold bag of sick. Brought this Maggie bird in — during filming. Started asking me all these *weird* questions. Mind control shit. Started pressing my buttons. Personal stuff – things she couldn't have known unless she was psychic, because *I* never told her.'

'But then I got thinking. I wrote this letter, you see. It was all in there. It was like she'd found it and started reading it out loud. All my feelings and stuff – like in that song, *Killing Me Softly*, you know it? Anyway, they must have gotten hold of it. How else could they have known all my weak spots? Yin must have given it to Jem, or maybe Heather got a hold of it – I dunno...'

'Maybe Yin didn't even read it. Wish I'd never sent the bloody thing now. Or maybe Yin just told 'em straight what I said to her – which was in the strictest of confidence, I might add...'

The sun, having moved across, casts a long shadow of Danny's gesticulating hands on the wall, his fingers like poles.

'You know, you can't trust anyone in this life. Only yourself. You can only rely on yourself,' he says, picking at the flaking varnish along the bar counter. 'We come into this world alone, and we go out alone. You can't trust anyone. But *dropped?* Nah, I wasn't expecting that. Wasn't expecting that at all.'

One stands up, brushes off his knees.

'Where you going?' asks Two.

'Just out to the van.'

'What for?'

'Just the gripper.'

'Well, don't be long.'

'Charged me with assault, they did. Can you believe that? Woke up in bloody police custody. I'd been asleep in the cell for hours, they said. Must have passed out or something. Probably stress. I've not been feeling right lately. My head's gone all – foggy, know what I mean? Here – look at this...'

Danny heads over, crouches next to Two.

'Look at that,' he says, jutting his chin and spreading the skin along his rainbow- coloured jawline. The lone carpet fitter withdraws on his kneeling pad.

'Yeah, looks nasty that.'

'I woke up with my pillowcase fused to my face this morning. There was an explosion in the night. The fabric had dried to my face. When I finally prised the bloody thing off this morning, my eyes were watering, I can tell you.'

As Danny heads back over to the bar, One re-enters with the gripper.

'You took your time,' says Two.

'"*A troubled soul with a tendency for unpredictable, violent outbursts while on set.*" That's what they say about me, here.' Danny reads from the newspaper. 'Mad? Violent? Unhinged? *Me*? Just look at that picture. Makes me look like a bloody animal.'

And what a doozy: the airborne tripod snapped mid-air, Danny's ponytail stuck to his hate-filled face with saliva and sweat.

'They set me up,' he says, digging at the picture with his right index fingers. 'That *thing* there, that ain't me.'

Tossing the paper behind the bar, Danny goes over to the albatross, two stone-cold teas under each wing. 'What we gonna do, eh?' he whispers to it, gently preening its feathers. 'We'll be alright. Me and you.'

Looking over their shoulders, the carpet fitters see Danny talking to the huge stuffed bird.

'Lovely, ain't she,' he grins. 'Real showpiece. Not as bright in the eyes as the badger, mind.'

They follow Danny's gaze to the badger, frozen mid-snarl and perched high on a shelf behind the bar. 'But ain't she 'andsome, my beauty, 'andsome. Feathers soft as silk.'

'Mind you,' says Danny, lighting a cigarette – he's gone through four packs this week alone. It's the first smoke in the morning he enjoys best. 'A couple of the claws are missing. Vicious things, badgers.'

'Sorry, but do you mind smoking that outside?' says Two. 'I've got asthma.'

Obligingly, Danny goes out into the garden, and Two turns the radio down. 'Carry on ripping that lot up,' he says, 'and I'll make a dash for it upstairs.'

'Wait,' says One, 'you hear that? Who's he talking to out there?'

Two sneaks a look through the kitchen window, then comes back. 'Himself. There's no one out there.'

'He's fucking crackers.'

'You're telling me. Now, if he asks where I am, tell him I've gone to measure up.'

A new gloom hangs pendent in the stale air, fibrous with must from the repeated ripping of a carpet so tattered it has turned to dust. The undrunk teas are still up on the mantelpiece, and Danny remains swivelling and smoking, glaring at the walls of this tragic ruin – this dreary wreck – with contempt.

How they mock him.

To think that this was once a house of merry-making, filled with happy barroom cheer, seems unbelievable when all within is dark as night. Windows boarded with bin liners against the light. Slates slipping. Damp rising. A garden marooned in a sea of weeds and brambles. Ivy climbs as a corpse decomposes. Danny stares down at the rotten, exposed floorboards that mirror his soul.

'Oh, *God*,' he wails, head in hands, foot tapping intently against the chrome footrest of his stool. He should have started with the bar refit first – not the carpet, or all the frivolous online bidding he's been doing. As soon as the carpet fitters finished for the day, he went and bid on another pool table.

'Idiot. Stupid. *Stupid*.' What he's got in the bank won't last forever. The pumps, the optics – all that costs money, not to mention the damp proofing. The jukebox wasn't cheap either: the beating heart of the place. Or at least, that was the idea. It's all such a muddle, a mess – ordering things now, thinking later.

The bar – should've started with the bar first, that's the beating heart of any pub, you fool. Idiot. Stupid, stupid, stupid.

He steps out into the garden to consult a rotting corpse for direction.

'Once the carpet's down, I'll get on with the paintwork, yeah, Murph? Decide on a colour scheme. A dark, gloss ceiling... I was thinking black,' says Danny, his subconscious dictating the mood of the interior. 'What d'you reckon?'

Not getting the direction he hoped for, Danny's now reduced to streaming endless repeats of the DIY cult classic, *Room Revolutions* on his new LCD flat-screen television. As episode two bleeds into episode three, all he's learned is how to distress an old mirror using poster paint and half a sink sponge. He's toying with the idea of covering the mould and damp with MDF panels. A quick lick of paint. Put it up with a staple gun.

A welcome beep from his mobile, cuts through the haze of half-baked ideas. He snatches it up, hoping it's a notification telling him he's been outbid on the pool table – but it's not. It's a direct message from Bonzo, urging him to do a live stream.

Within seconds, Danny is sucked back into the forum, perched up at the bar, cigarette wedged between his teeth.

BonzoDooDah-49: typing...

'It will be a chance for you to set the record straight. Put your side of the story across. *Live.* An interview. With me. On *my* channel: *Black Pilled TV*.'

And with well over five thousand subscribers, Bonzo proudly sends Danny the link.

DannyDan-83: typing...

'But wouldn't that make me a target? Speaking out might put me in danger.'

BonzoDooDah-49: typing...
BonzoDooDah-49: typing...

BonzoDooDah-49: typing…
DannyDan-83: typing…

'Hello?' types Danny, with repeated hourglass emojis. 'You taking a dump? LOL!'

BonzoDooDah-49: typing…
BonzoDooDah-49: has left the chatroom.
DannyDan-83: typing…

'!!!!!!!!!!!!!!!!!?'

DannyDan-83: has been ejected from the forum.

After three more cigarettes and five failed login attempts, Danny calls it a night. The carpet fitters are back tomorrow for the wood treatment anyway, and he needs to be fresh in the morning.

'Fuck's *sake*.' Voicemail again. He's already left two messages for the carpet fitters – he's not leaving a third. It's nearly ten now. 'Where the fuck are they?'

Washing his hair earlier, Danny noticed that the water wasn't draining properly. Sludge was circling around the shower drain, so he slid it aside with his big toe and fished out a slimy clump of hair. *His* hair.

After flushing it straight down the toilet, he angled the triple doors of the mirrored cabinet just so, revealing a perfectly smooth circle of skin. All pink and naked.

As mortifying as it was, he was ready to do what he always said he would if this day finally came: shave it all off.

But he held off getting his clippers out – just in case the carpet fitters turned up right at that moment.

That was over two hours ago now. He could have shaved his head three times by now.

Without another moment's hesitation, he pulls the clippers from the top of the cabinet, presses the button, and makes one clean, decisive swoop, centre-front, doing his best to ignore the heap of hair building at his feet.

The intercom screeches from Danny's room.

'Sod's *fucking* law,' he mutters, staring at the inverted mohawk running through the middle of his head in the mirror, the clippers still buzzing. 'Just a minute,' he calls down the stairs, wrapping a towel into a turban around his head. But when he opens the door, there's no one there – just a strange pile of gunk on the doorstep: tinned spaghetti, rice pudding, Jelly, cracked eggs, sliced wholemeal bread, frozen prawns. Hardly surprising. The footprint of a bored youth in the school holidays. The empties lined up on top of the recycling bins only confirm it: white wine bottles and cans of bitter – the hallmark of parental burnout, no doubt stolen from mum and dad, too fried to have even noticed.

'Little bleeders,' says Danny, stepping over the mixture.

His hands full with cans and bottles, the turban slips and drops to the floor. Before he can decide whether to bother picking it up, a series of rapid flashes blinds him, causing him to stumble back against the bins.

'*Danny! Danny, over here!*'

'*This way, Danny. Over here!*'

Hooded figures with spring-loaded telephoto lenses emerge from behind the bins, snapping him from every angle.

'*Danny! This way! Over here!*'

'Stop,' he says, shielding his eyes and his bizarrely shaved head with the bottles and cans. 'Leave me alone.' They close in, forcing him to stagger back towards the door, landing a bare foot in the doorstep gunk. Prawns and penne pasta squelch between his toes. 'Piss off,' he says, shaking the gunk from his foot and fumbling for the door. 'Leave me alone.' He throws an empty bitter can their way, makes it inside, and, clutching the wine bottles in shock, the little fellas slide both bolts across.

Leaning back against the door, he breathes. The letter box flaps open. 'Come talk to us, Danny!' a crazed paparazzo yells through. Without a second thought, he runs up to his room, leaving the sharks to circle below.

It's a four-armed feeding frenzy. Another set up, clear as day. Danny looks down from his kitchenette window, brushing the shaved strip running from his forehead to the nape of his neck with his fingers. Quite the front page this will make.

It's almost noon when the sharks finally retreat. He tries the carpet fitters again, but there's no answer. Is it any wonder? Maybe they were out there, trying to park up but the paps scared them off. Or maybe they really believe he's the monster in the papers.

This new bald look makes his eyes seem larger, like it did with Sinead O'Connor. It also makes his lips look fuller too, he thinks, pouting in the mirror. Not like Heather's. Heather's vanished into nothing when they were sucking on that skinny red straw.

'*Poof*, and they're gone,' he says, clapping his hands, Mick Jagger fashion, then following up with, 'Cranberry *soda*, cranberry *soda*,' playfully channelling Heather's energy, her cadence.

The déjà vu feeling creeps back, placing him in Yin's dressing room.

'Shiva – of course. *Cranberry soda, cranberry soda, cranberry soda.* Fucking Shiva.' As soon as Yin got off the phone, she started bitching about having to fix someone a drink. 'Shiva. Shiva skinny lips. Fuck me, it's her. Knows the place like the back of her hand? Rooms she's never even been in? Bugsy Malone? Bugsy *fucking* Malone?'

All out of cigarettes, Danny craves a smoke. The shop's only meters away, but he's not risking it. Not risking being seen, being papped. They could still be out there, lurking behind the bins. And all that weird *crap* on the doorstep? Leave it to the foxes. They'll clean it up better than Danny ever could.

Paps behind bins. Dead bodies in gardens. The suffocating cloud of unemployment looming. A supermarket wouldn't even hire him now – not with his reputation. It's a shame really. He would have made an excellent shelf-stacker, and any sorting office would have been lucky to have him.

And then there's the knock. The knock he's been waiting for. Any minute now, someone will come looking for Murphy. He can feel it in his gut.

The walls close in.

Resting on a roll of unlaid carpet, his phone lights up in the dark. Prostrate on Murphy's sofa, he reaches for it and his eyes flick over the screen. 'No. Please, no.'

He's won the bid on the pool table.

Kicking the roll of carpet out of his path, he goes behind the bar, grabs a bottle of Murphy's whisky, then kicks the carpet again. Lying back, he swigs from the bottle with the telly on low.

The morning craving for nicotine hits, and, forgetting he's out of cigarettes, he searches for where he might have left them, the bitter taste of whiskey still lingering in his mouth.

'Yes,' he says, spying a deck sheltering beneath his albatross. But the victory is short-lived: the pack is empty. He tosses it across the room.

Out in the garden, urinating before sunrise, he scrolls through the morning's headlines. And there he is, clutching the wine bottles, his back pressed against the recycling bins streaked with pigeon droppings.

"Has-bin celebrity looks worse for wear"
"Face of SpeedyBet hides the empties"

Apparently, Danny's back on crystal meth; he's "hit the bottle" since being dropped and desperately needs rehab. He's on suicide watch and, judging from the pictures, he almost believes it himself.

His skin has this sickly, greenish hue. His stomach looks bloated. *It has to be doctored*, he thinks, running a worried hand over his taut, toned abs. Zooming in, he spots track marks on his arms.

"Recently dropped celeb loses mind" runs one

tabloid.

"Ex-minor celeb back on the scrapheap" runs another.

David from Dunmow, United Kingdom says:

"Danny Finch marks a decline in the age of celebrity. Today's youth are a product of fame hungry, talentless, toxic-males like him, who do nothing but lift weights and get high, three-sixty-five."

Meg88, Canberra, Australia: "Promoting gambling? What a scumbag. It's a mug's game."

Noisy Oyster, London, United Kingdom: "Toxic masculinity at its worst. If he had a brain cell it would die of loneliness. Pathetic!"

Why2020, Basildon, Essex: "Is he doing a 'Britney' by shaving his head like that? Please don't – *hit me baby one more time – you drive me craaay-zee!*"

Mahadeva, Culver City, United States says:

"Meth face! Run away to the circus you four-armed f**k! Ever heard of Clearasil?"

A silent tear rolls off Danny's chin. He wipes it with the back of his right little fella and looks down at his little hands, resentment brewing. Without warning, he punches his left little fella hard in the bicep. Then, like a rabid cat, he starts scratching at his little forearms enough to draw blood.

Bathed in the dim glow of fairy lights taped to the bar and the screen of his, Danny can't stop scrolling. He's been at it for hours, unable to tear himself away. The headlines are coming thick and fast, and the negative press is now running on its own juice, with little involvement from Heather needed at all.

"Four-armed Finch talks to aliens after UFO beam ship lands on roof"

It's absurd. One picture shows a superimposed UFO on Danny's crumbling chimney, complete with little green man waving back through a porthole window. Now

they've got him tied to the English Defence League now –
a far-right drug-addled lunatic who believes in little green
men.

Could it get any worse?

Yes.

Desperate for a smoke, he's sifting through a flowerpot
he's been using as an ashtray, searching for any butt-end
with life in it. It's slim pickings, but there's still a couple of
decent drags left on some of them.

Numbing himself with Murphy's whisky up in his
room, he listens half-heartedly to the radio before
collapsing back onto his bed.

'*Tina, how did you find out that your husband was having an
affair? What were the warning signs?*' The late-night host, a
smarmy, posh-Scottish man, asks.

'*Genital warts,*' says Tina. '*He caught them in the nursing
home. But he's out now, living with his sister. At his age?*'

Normally, a call-in like this would have Danny
guffawing, but he barely reacts.

'*How long as he had dementia, Tina?*'

'*Dementia? Please, he only checked himself in for the skirt.
Everyone in the village knows now as well. He had to have them
burned off. Cried like a baby, he did.*'

'*That must have brought you some comfort, his pain, I mean.
Did it?*'

'*Yes, it did. It was a huge comfort to me. But the whole bloody
village knowing about it wasn't. And God only knows how many
more people know, now I've come on here. But I wanted to put my
side of the story across. I had to. There's an STI epidemic going on in
care homes right, and nobody's talking about it. At it like rabbits,
they are. People don't have a clue what's really going on. People need
to know.*'

With open ears, Danny sits up, listening intently.

'*Well, you've heard Tina's side of the story. She wants people to
know. Oh, Tina. I do hope things get better for you. Divorces are
such painful things, believe me – I've had two. But recovery starts at
the lowest points. The lovely Tina from Barnet there. Such a tragic*

story, but loving ourselves, owning our story is the bravest thing we can do, and remember, if you've got something, anything that you want to get off your chest, give us a call. Free speech is what we do best on this show, and if it's advice you're after – give us a call. If it's cheering up you need, give us a call. Or even if it's just a good old cry – GIVE – US – A – CALL. You know the number by now…0345…'

Fumbling for his phone, Danny takes a gulp of Dutch courage and does something he never imagined he'd do – he calls in.

It's the producer who answers, screening the calls, and slurring slightly, Danny tells her he wants to talk about whether chivalry is dead – and if so, should we care?

After juking the screener, Danny kills his nerves with more whisky and is kept on hold so long, that he's now seeing double, but eventually, he gets through.

'Next up, we have Danny,' says the host, with no warning beep or chime. *'First-time caller, long-time listener – from South Ealing.'*

'Hi.'

'Holding doors, paying for dinner, standing when someone enters a room… gestures once seen as noble – now sometimes called outdated or even patronising. What do you think? Is there still a place for chivalry in the modern world? Danny – you're live on air.'

'The *Velvet Lounge*. Heard of it?' Danny cuts to the chase, flips the script.

'The Velvet Lounge? It rings a bell. It's a book, isn't it Danny? No wait – it's a play…'

'Wrong. All wrong. Have you heard of a place called *Isabella's?'*

'The place in Mayfair? Of course I have. I was in there years ago. Mick Jagger was seated right in front of me. Lionel Blair…'

'Good, so you must know all about it and what a disgusting place it is then?'

'Well, I've heard the lobster thermidor isn't what it used to be, but Danny – we seem to be veering off-topic here. Now, back to

chivalry—'

'Lives are at stake. Children's lives.'

'*I must say, this all sounds terribly dramatic, Danny. You're not trying to scare us, are you?*' A ghostly-wind sound effect plays from the studio desk. '*It's not Halloween already, is it?*' A hammer-horror movie scream.

The spy app on Heather's phone beeps. She quickly shuts off the jets of her jacuzzi bath, dries her hands on the sleeve of her ivory spa robe draped on the back of the door, and activates the listening device with practiced speed.

'*The Velvet Lounge* is a secret club, underneath *Isabella's,*' Danny says, a burp taking him by surprise, cutting across the airwaves. 'Excuse me.'

The audio is poor. Danny's DAB radio sits directly above the bugging device, muffling his voice.

'*Idiots,*' Heather mutters, shifting the phone around for a better signal. It improves only slightly. The carpet fitter stuck it under the kitchen sideboard, and there's considerable interference.

'*The Velvet Lounge? Go on Danny. We're listening.*'

'It's an underage brothel for kids, basically. Deep underground, and I went down this tunnel. Neverending it was…'

'Get him off the air!' Heather yells to nobody, splashing and slapping the water.'

'Anyway, I went down this hatch up on the roof terrace and then this tunnel…'

A bottle of soothing geranium and eucalyptus bath oil strikes the heated towel rack, resonating like a gong. 'Get him *off!* Get him off the air!'

One might think it would be in the Fair Isle host's interest to cut him off, considering he was in *The Lounge* only last month.

'*Okay, Danny. I'll give you the benefit of the doubt here, but why, why, why haven't you gone to the police? If what you say is true, a late-night radio call-in show is hardly the place to discuss something like this, is it?*

'So, you don't believe me? You think I'd make something like this up? I'm talking about kids here. Children.'

'So, who's running this nefarious operation then? The Angami Naga tribe of India, perhaps? Bigfoot? Old Nessy?

Laughter erupts in the studio, quickly drowned out by a burst of bagpipes from the sound effects desk.

'Oh, I hope it is Nessy. I like her. Or the Beast of Bodmin? ET?

The *X-Files* theme music plays.

'You think this is funny?' The host's ignorance has a sobering effect on Danny. The *X-Files* theme plays on as laughter builds in the studio. 'I'm astonished, really, I am. I could mention names. I've got plenty. Okay, let's start with…'

Stillness. Silence.

'Danny? Are you there? Not sure what happened there, but we seem to have lost Danny from South Ealing. Maybe his tin-foil-hat fell off.' Canned laughter plays. *'It's always nice to have a member of the raving looney party on at this time of night. The show wouldn't be the same without them, would it? But next we have the lovely Sue from Twickenham. Now Sue, you're not one of these conspiracy nuts are you, Sue? You're not going to tell us that the moon landings were faked or that the earth is flat, are you?'* A medley of yawn sound effects. *'You're not going to bore us to death, are you?'*

Towel-drying her hair with fine cotton bath linen, Heather goes through to the kitchen and pours herself a large glass of red wine. There's more fight in Danny than she'd anticipated, and she's conscious that a considerable number of listeners are bound to have recognised his voice from the *SpeedyBet* ads.

Jem's mobile rings from atop his desk. Clambering up to grab it, he answers. 'Colleen? Colleen. Let me explain—'

'Good. You're awake.'

'Ah – Heather. How lovely to hear from you at this

149

ungodly hour.' Her voice cuts like glass 'Have you seen the time?'

'Never mind that. Jem – things have reached critical point. We've got to act fast if we're going to make tomorrow's headlines.'

'Wait, I've got you on speaker.'

'Well, take me off – take me off, quickly.'

'Wait a minute,' says Jem, feeling around for his glasses. 'Ah, here we go.' He can't see the phone without them. 'Shit.'

'What?'

'Have you seen this?'

'Seen what?'

'This.'

'This what?'

'This link.'

'Link? Nobody sent me a link.'

'Fuck me. He's off his face.'

'Who is? What is it?'

'He's only doing a live stream!'

'Who?'

'Danny, of *course*. Fuck me, he's a mess. I can hardly make out what he's saying.'

'Well try. *Try.*'

'Fuck. It's *The Lounge*, he's talking about *The Lounge*. There's two thousand people watching this. You gotta see this. Wait, let me send it to you—'

'What, and increase his views to two thousand and one? No, you won't, you idiot!'

'Well, it's just shot up to two thousand and nine. *Jesus*, he can hardly see he's that cross-eyed. Fucking *hell*, he's got two cigarettes on the go at once.'

'Read out the comments. What are people saying?'

'Haha! He's just spilled his drink. Looks like he's at some dive bar. Jesus, what a dump.'

'Jem!'

'Okay, okay.' Jem scrolls down and scan reads.

'Well, it's rather supportive overall. The common thread seems to be something about a radio call-in.'

'I knew it. Carry on.'

'Call-in? What call-in?'

'Just *read*!'

'Oh, wait – there's one here calling him a "four-armed freak, with a head like a Tic Tac." A Tic Tac? Oh, I see – they mean since he's had it shaved. That's quite funny.'

'How many views has he got now?'

'Two thousand one hundred. No, wait, two thousand one hundred and one; one hundred and two... He's banging on about lips? Something about lizard lips? Wizened old lizard lips? Who's that? A mouth like a paper cut? Oh—'

'What?'

'He's just mentioned your name.'

A tense lull.

'We've got to shut him down *now*. Start trolling him. Join the live stream, Jem.'

'What?'

'Start slamming him, bashing him – bring him *down*!'

'Two thousand three hundred...'

'Join it, Jem, *please*.'

'Alright, alright — how?'

'What?'

'Well, I don't know. I'm not what you'd call *social media-savvy*.'

'Well try!'

'Okay. I'm trying, I'm trying.'

Heather waits, her patience stretching thinner than the Wi-Fi signal in a basement.

'Are you in?'

'Not quite. I keep fat-fingering the keys. I've always found navigating an

actual keyboard far easier than typing into one of these *poxy* things, have you? I'll fire up the PC.'

In just his boxers and silver toe ring, Jem reaches around the back of the monitor and sits down.

'Jesus, it's like Spaghetti Junction back here,' he says, feeling for the power switch. 'Ah, here we go. Christ, this thing is slow. The IT department in this place has a lot to answer for. Three times I've asked them to update this thing…'

The PC chugs into action. 'Ah – *ha*, here we go, here we go. It's doing something.' The motherboard fan connector rattles like a warplane propeller. 'It's gonna take off in a minute, I swear.'

'Is it even on yet?'

'Oh yeah. It's on. It's just trying to connect to the internet now. It did some weird Windows update thingy last night. You ever had that? Took fucking ages. Better not be doing it again now. No wait – *yes*! Yes, I'm in.'

And not a moment too soon, Jem performs nothing short of a miracle and manages to pull up the live stream platform.

'Right, so how do you join this bloody thing then?'

'For God's *sake*, Jem. How hard can it be? It's a fucking live stream, you're not being trained for NASA!'

'No, wait. There's an instructions tab here: *How to join the live stream: click the live stream that you want to enter after selecting it…*'

Three thousand views. Three thousand and one. Three thousand and two...

'*…click where it says, "Live Chat" and start typing anything that you want to publish in the live box.* Live box? What live box? There isn't a fucking live box. *Step three: select the board hosting the stream.* The board? Oh, wait a minute. No, no, that's not it. *How to set a reminder for your upcoming live stream?* No. *Invite guests to join your live stream?*

'Come on, Jem.'

Three thousand and thirty…

'Oh—'

'What? What's the matter?'

'It's the screen. The screen's gone black. No, it's okay, it's okay.'

'Has it come back? Jem, is it back on?'

'Yeah, it's just restarting, that's all. God, this thing is slow. That dim-witted IT department. Is it really too much to expect them to provide adequate support for the business they serve? Three times I've asked them to come and take a look at this sodding thing…'

'Jem!'

Three thousand and thirty-one. Three thousand and thirty-two. Three thousand and thirty-three…

CHAPTER 13

"I felt his hand on my thigh and froze as I watched it creep up. Before I knew it, his other hand was up my skirt. Then two more started trying to undo my bra. So many hands. His hands were everywhere."

The latest press invention: sexual assault. It has been alleged that an anonymous crew member came forward claiming that Danny groped them on set. *It's as though the entire national press is marching in lockstep*, thinks Danny, reading on.

The ear-splitting screech of the intercom pulses in the rhythm of the *Eastenders* theme tune – the safe code Danny and the pizza delivery boy agreed on after Danny's craving for nicotine became too much. Recognising the code, Danny heads to the door.

'You remembered the cigarettes?' says Danny, through the letterbox, feeding through a fifty.

'Yes, boss. Two decks.' The boy places them on top of the large pepperoni, leaving the spoils on the doorstep.

'Keep the change.'

With a twist of the throttle, the boy rides off, face alight, the hum of his 50cc engine dissipating into the night.

Reaching for another slice, lying bare-chested across Murphy's sofa with a pizza box at his side, Danny flicks through the channels with greasy fingers before settling on the ten o'clock news. As Big Ben chimes, the dour face of the news anchor fills the screen. Danny, staring through the broadcast, bites into his pizza. A disc of pepperoni falls on to his chest; he peels it off, tosses it into the air, and catches it in his mouth against a backdrop of rising inflation graphics.

'Misery, misery. More bloody misery everywhere you go,' he says, tossing another disc into the air. He misses, shrugs, and tries again as the news drones on about energy price spikes and reduced purchasing power.

No discs left. Small bites of pizza crust will have to do.

Increased cost of living. Wage-price spirals – and resorting to broken-up pizza crust when you're all out of pepperoni.

'*One of the Big Four talent agencies, Complete Celebs, and the prestigious Mayfair club, Isabella's, have received death threats from the public following false allegations made by recently dropped minor celebrity Danny Finch.*'

A chunk of crust lodges in his throat, forcing Danny to sit bolt upright. After a panicked cough, he hacks it out, sending it splatting against the centre of his flat screen, leaving a greasy splodge. Meanwhile, a sliver of green pepper slides off his left nipple and drops to the floor.

Danny lunges for the remote and stabs at the volume button.

'*The ex-celebrity, best known for his SpeedyBet scratch card adverts, called into a late-night radio call-in show, alleging that…*'

An unlit cigarette hangs from the edge of his open mouth. Eyes locked to the screen, he leaves it dangling and slides another from the pack.

'*The famous nightclub will remain closed while the police investigation continues. Our reporter, Jane Burn, has more on the story.*'

The camera pans, revealing Heather, her head tilted, practiced and pitying, sitting opposite the reporter.

'*How did you feel when you received the first death threat?*'

'Terrified. I received another just this morning. I understand he's bitter and hurting, but he has no idea of the damage he's caused. *Complete Celebs* has always felt like such a close-knit family to me – to us all. But already, people are talking about leaving, moving away to protect themselves and their families. They're scared. *I'm* scared. These are people's *lives*. People with families, with kids.'

'You fucking liar,' Danny spits, using the pizza box as an ashtray. He takes another drag.

'*Why do you think he's doing this?*'

'Revenge. Pure and simple. He's bitter about being dropped. We missed the signs with his mental health – things we should have caught. There are lessons to be learned here, for all of us. But in the end, all these false allegations do is prevent real victims of abuse from coming forward. Why should they, when they know they won't be believed? These lies discredit true victims, giving them all a bad name. Nobody wants their experience invalidated.'

'Ask her about *The Lounge*!' Danny roars at the screen. 'Go on. Talk about the *real* fucking issue here!'

'*And yet, there is absolutely no evidence for a single thing Danny Finch has claimed. Are you angry?*'

'Of course I'm angry. But I'm also human. I have compassion. Mental illness is something I take seriously – I've suffered myself, so I know what it's like. I just hope he gets the help he needs before something terrible happens.'

'*Do you think Danny is aware of the emotional cost of these allegations?*'

'You know, I don't think he does. Danny was signed off for a week. He was acting strange – delusional. But we should have acted sooner, gotten him the help he needed. Maybe if we had, none of this would have happened.'

The reporter hands Heather a box of tissues. '*Are you saying this is a celebrity aftercare issue?*'

'Maybe. Maybe it is.' Heather's voice breaks as she dabs her eye. 'Celebrity aftercare is something *Complete Celebs* has always prided itself on. I feel like we've failed him.'

The reporter leans forward. '*He's accused you of some of the most heinous crimes someone can commit, yet you still show compassion.*'

'As I said, I'm only human.'

'Human? About as human as a nuclear missile.'

'*You show compassion, even after today's story in The Daily Mail detailing not one, but two accounts of sexual assault. One crew member claims that Mr. Finch pressured her into spending the night*' *with him. Another alleges that, in a lift, Mr. Finch cornered her and demanded she remove her tights because he wanted to wear them…'*

Unable to stomach another second, Danny snuffs out his cigarette in the middle of the pizza box, snaps off the TV, and flings the remote onto the sofa.

The warm glow of headlights filters through a chink in his bin liner curtain. The sharp sound of two vehicle doors slamming shut, one after the other, sends Danny creeping low towards the bay window, stealing a paranoid glance.

A white transit van is parked close enough for Danny to read the words, "CLEANED BY STEVIE WONDER," along with the crude outline of a penis etched into the dirt on the rear doors.

Suddenly, the doors swing open, and Danny scuttles to the front door. He lifts the letterbox and catches sight of the pool table – dismantled, its legs gone – being birthed by two unhealthy looking men through the rear door canal, then carefully manoeuvred onto a ramp.

'Oi, careful, ya muppet!' one of the men barks, his voice strained as they heave the pool table.

It's a difficult birth. The baby's a lot bigger than Danny expected. 'Just leave it there!' he calls through the letterbox. 'Just lean it against the front… the front of the building. Here—' he says, pulling a fifty out from his back pocket and waving it through the letterbox. 'Here. Fellas. Here, take this.'

The two men turn round, see a fifty-pound note flapping away.

'But what about the legs?' says the man taking the lower end. 'They need attaching.'

Danny waves the fifty with greater gusto. 'No, it's fine. Really. Just leave it all there. Against the wall.'

'You do know it's about to piss down, mate?'

England has been caught in a cycle of hot, sticky days giving way to sudden heavy downpours. It never feels settled – just muggy, heavy and airless. The weight of it all

157

dragging down on Danny's already low mood.

'That's a walnut finish you got on there,' says the other, hugging the top pocket.

'It's fine, really. I can attach the legs myself. Please. Just take the money.'

After leaning the table and legs against the front of the building, one of the men takes the money. 'You sure?' he asks, feeding the delivery docket through.

'Yeah,' says Danny, looking down at the docket in the gloom of the unlit landing.

The van doors shut. The engine revs up. Danny steps into the light. 'Antique snooker/billiards table? Ten ft playing size? Wait! —'

The letterbox flaps up. 'Wait! I didn't order this. There's been some kind of mistake. It'll never fit in here! Wait! Come back!'

The rain's really coming down now, but instead of trying to bring the table inside – or at least throw a plastic covering over it – Danny is busy raising a dispute on the auction site it came from and drinking.

'You fucking bastards,' he mutters, pouring himself a whisky.

It seems that, although the item wasn't technically listed as a snooker table, it also wasn't labelled as a pool table – just a "games table." Had he bothered to read the rich, detailed product description, he would have discovered its carved spandrels and intriguing provenance. Neglecting to do so, however, always carries the risk of not being eligible for a refund. The substantial dimensions of the "games table" were clearly specified. He'll have to sell it on if he's to scrabble anything back.

'You wanker,' he spits at the antiquarian seller, who's been trying to make ends meet ever since losing his wife to stage four cancer, lovingly restoring antiques by hand. 'Make the description clearer next time – fucktard.'

Incensed and drowsy from alcohol, Danny finally concedes and covers the ten-foot monster – its value depreciating with every minute – with an old groundsheet he's kept on top of his wardrobe.

It's incredible, really, how quickly things have unravelled. And even more surprises lurk in his purchase history – like the sheepskin rug he has no recollection of ordering. According to tracking, it should have arrived ages ago, and the money has indeed been deducted from his ever-dwindling account.

All sorts of things are due to be arriving: mirrors, lamps, collectable commemorative plates. Things still awaiting payment. One seller has reported him over a set of crystal tumblers. Danny vaguely recollects the purchase but didn't realise they were for collection only. 'Pickering? Where the fuck's that?'

The seller wants immediate payment; otherwise, he'll go legal.

But there's already a set of crystal whisky tumblers behind the bar. He's drinking from one now. They arrived last week – a set of nine. Danny distinctly remembers taking them out and lining them up on the shelf. The box should be lying around somewhere.

By the light of the television, he finds it, checks the label. 'Nine cut-crystal whisky tumblers. Derby. Derby? Is Pickering in Derby?' He drops the box and returns to his screen. *A set of twelve this should be, not nine. Shouldn't it?*

'A set of twelve crystal highball tumblers. Highball? Pickering?' He can't get a handle on it. 'Pickering?'

Maybe it's true what the papers are saying. Maybe I am losing my mind. A balding, violent, acne-ridden, four-armed freak. A violent, sexual predator. A drugged-up alky with a dead body in the garden.

The rain pummels against the groundsheet outside the bay window. He surveys the chaos and disorder – bubble wrap, miscellaneous boxes, filth, and woodworm – and laughs at the delusion of it all. *The Finch's Arms? A celebrity landlord? Nobody in their right mind would want to get served by*

159

me?

The intercom blasts in short succession. Whisky spills down the thigh of his jeans and a strange apathy sets in. So what if it's another setup? it's not like things could get any worse. And even if it's a long-lost relative looking for Murphy, they'll run a mile as soon as he answers the door – once they see the monster in the flesh.

So he answers the door, only to find there's no one there. Just a package – a white box, about the size of a shoebox, resting neatly on the doorstep. He stares at it for a moment before it clicks: probably the flameless tea candles he saw listed in his recent purchase history. He ordered them on a whim, thinking they might soften the place a bit. Create some ambience. All the gastropubs are doing it. Rechargeable, too.

Scooping up the package, he gives it a shake and locks the door behind him. *Surely, this has got to be the last of them*, he thinks, slicing the box open with one of Murphy's keys.

But when he looks inside, his sanity is tested again.

It's a duck. One of those rubber ones you have in the bath – a yellow rubber ducky. 'What the fuck?' A stuffed one would make more sense – a loyal companion for his albatross maybe – but this? There's not even a record of it in his purchase history, and no receipt in the box. Just a yellow Post-it stuck to the bottom, matching the duck exactly.

'Quack, quack' he reads aloud from the note, eyes lingering on the duck as he lights himself a cigarette.

A symbol of childhood nostalgia and innocent fun?

Someone passing judgement on his personal hygiene, maybe?

Or something more sinister – an invitation, crudely encoded in Cockney rhyming slang? "Fancy a rubber duck?" Surely not.

But if so... from whom?

Danny sets his yellow friend up on the mantelpiece, propping it upright beneath the sweeping wing of his albatross.

He sits on the sofa, thinking and smoking, staring up at it for nearly an hour.

And then it comes to him.

It seems so obvious now, he thinks, rising slowly from the sofa, opening a fresh pack of cigarettes. *Sitting.*

'Quack, quack.'

CHAPTER 14

For two weeks, Danny has been locked in stalemate. The gutter press has begun to lose interest, replaced by broadsheets taking a broader, more intellectual approach. Think-pieces on society's toxic obsession with celebrity – celebrity as religion, as cult, as construct. Essays on the harms of social media and its impact upon mental health. Yada, yada, yada.

And over many a pensive smoke, Danny has taken heed of his yellow warning.

But now, it's his move.

Skimming a culture piece in *The Guardian Online: The dark side of celebrity,* he steps out into the garden. It doesn't go nearly dark enough.

'They have no idea,' he tells Murphy, lighting a cigarette.

Isabella's reopened just two days after Heather's appearance on the news. As if nothing had happened. No mention of Danny's live stream in the press – despite the hundreds of strangers who've reached out to him on social media. People who see through the media machine. People who know his cause is worthy. Telling him to stay strong. To keep fighting.

But to fight means he's at war – and he's a pacifist at heart, Danny doesn't want that. To stay quiet makes him complicit in these crimes, this cover-up. Danny doesn't want that either. Which means this two-week ceasefire must end.

Danny's going over the top. He can't hide away forever.

'Confuse your enemy,' he says, taking his coffee over to Murphy's bench. 'They're trying to shut me up, Murph. Shut me up and go quietly. They may *think* they've won – whoever *they* are – but they haven't. A sitting duck? Me? Not on your nelly. It's gonna take a lot more than that.' He lights a cigarette. 'A lot more.'

'A pattern break, that's what this situation needs. A disruptor. Something to take her by surprise, cause a scene. Then it'll be check*mate*, me old matey. Check. Fucking. Mate.'

He stubs his cigarette out in the flowerpot ashtray and gets to work.

It seems his vow of "no more orders" has been short-lived. After some extensive research, Danny's just placed an order for a *Bullhorn 360°* megaphone, even paying extra for next-day delivery. He's left detailed instructions for his preferred safe place: behind the "games table" beneath the green tarpaulin groundsheet.

'Right,' he says, clapping both pairs of hands. 'Let's do this.' He starts rummaging through some of his larger boxes. 'A nice big bit of cardboard – that's what I need.' One of the boxes the bar stools came in should do it. 'Nice and long,' he mutters. He tears off a side and holds it up. 'Yeah, nice. Perfect.' Another quick double hand clap. 'Now paints... paints. Where's me paints?' He digs around, pulling out a fancy set of acrylics in little silver tubes. Paints he's had for years but never used.

The placard doesn't look anything like it did in his head. The post-box red paint has muddied and dulled against the brown of the cardboard. Most of the paints were rock hard inside the tubes – only the black and some of the red were still usable. The yellow was dry as a bone. He'd wanted to paint a duck right in the middle, you see.

At least he's blissfully unaware of all the spelling mistakes:

IZZABELLA'S IS RUNNING
A BROTHELLE FOR KIDS
SAVE THE KIDS!

Not very catchy, but it's straight to the point. And the megaphone arrived first thing this morning, which is good.

He'll think of something once he's up there.

~

Tourists mill about, doing the typical things people do when they visit London: eating ice-creams, feeding pigeons French fries in the square. A queue for the matinée performance is building outside the theatre. Kids run laughing through the pulsing jets of the choreographed fountain, cooling off in the spray. Nearby, a group of bucket drummers bang out rhythms on dustbin lids, and children dance. It all reminds Danny why he's here – why he's about to do something crazy.

Surveying the square one more time, his rucksack on his back obscuring the little fellas in the now-customary style, he steps up onto the first level of the war memorial.

The bullhorn megaphone is heavier than he expected, and he now regrets not attaching the shoulder strap it came with. Clumsily gripping his placard between his knees, he climbs up another tier of the memorial and pauses there to watch *The Golden, Floating, and Levitating Man* performing for the crowd below.

The street entertainer has drawn quite a crowd. He's been here for as long as Danny can remember, always painted gold from head to toe, dazzling in the sun. As the resident performer wows the audience, a sudden vapour of feeling washes over Danny. A pang. A pining. With eye askance, he thinks back to when he, too, had the crowd eating out of his hands.

How did it all go so wrong, so quickly?

A group of Japanese teenagers glance up as he shrugs off his rucksack and removes the faded blue British Army baseball cap – his dad's, worn today for the first time. He'd rather these kids were not here, exposed to the ugly truths he's about to unleash. But the Bullhorn 360°, with its two-and-a-half-thousand-foot sound projection, could make a butterfly's fart sound like an earthquake.

He brings the megaphone to his lips. 'Can I have your attention, please?' His voice, thrillingly audible, echoes across the square. Shakily, he steps up another level, knocking his baseball cap off in the process. One of the Japanese kids throws it back up, grinning like a jester to his giggling friends. It falls back down. Another kid tries. It becomes a game. It's distracting. Danny does his best to block it out.

'I'm here today to talk about that place over there,' he says, pointing to the back of the Georgian townhouse. '*Isabella's*. It's not what you think, you know. There's a hidden world inside. I've seen it. Seen it with my own eyes, and I'm here to tell you – every rumour you've heard about that *rotten* place? It's all true.'

The baseball cap sits idle at the bottom. The Japanese kids focus on him, laughing and pointing at his arms.

'Now, what I'm about to say isn't nice. I don't want to scare you or give nightmares,' Danny says, angling the megaphone over the other side of the square. He takes a breath. 'But someone has to say something about these – about these *perverts*. These *politicians*. These *paedophiles*.'

The bucket drummers slow to a stop, and a hush spreads across the square. Wiping spittle from his mouth, Danny climbs another tier.

'And no, I'm not mad. This *is* real. It *is* happening. I *know* they are running some kind of secret brothel in there. It's called *The Velvet Lounge*. Look it up if you don't believe me. For young girls. Kids. Children. I'm talking about abuse, and it'll be going on tonight, tomorrow night, and every night unless we bring awareness to it and put an end to this cruelty.'

A few people clap, raise their Frappuccinos and soy-milk lattés, while a homeless woman raises her can of cider and stumbles to one side. But most people disperse.

'Don't you care? These people should be exposed.'

The bin drummers start up again, and stunned by their

apathy, Danny lays down his placard, along with the little self-respect he had left.

'Don't be greedy – bet with Speedy!' he bellows out from the speaker, his arms flailing, desperately trying to win the attention of the crowd.

'It's that druggie freak from the scratch card adverts – look!' shrieks a woman, putting her shopping bags between her sandaled feet. The little fellas wave more frantically.

'Yeah, it's me. The four-armed circus freak. The tin-foil hat. That conspiracy nut from the papers. That—'

'Pizza face!' shouts a woman in green dungarees.

'Is that the best you've got?' Danny taunts.

'Get down from there, you ruddy hooligan!' a man in brown corduroy trousers shouts up. 'Immediately. I've half a mind to call the police.'

'Go on then!' says Danny. 'Come on, police! Let's be having you!'

'Get down, you bald bugger!' says the woman with the shopping, slipping Danny's baseball cap into her bag. 'That's an altar of our national grief!'

With the crowd gathering, Danny steps up another tier.

'So, let's be having you, police! Where are you?'

Danny's foot slips – he nearly drops the Bullhorn, but reflexes kick in, and he grabs the ankle of the fallen soldier behind him.

'Police, where are you? Investigate! Please! *Investigate now. Investigate now.* Come on, people. *Investigate now…*'

The bin drummers bang their lids to the rhythm of Danny's chant, and it ripples across the square. He climbs another level of the monument, holding his placard aloft with precarious balance.

A police van zigzags through the square, screeching to a halt by the water fountain. Four counter-terrorism officers leap out and charge towards the monument.

'*Investigate now. Investigate now. Investigate now…*'

A taser is aimed at Danny. A voice orders him to get

down. The drummers fall silent, but Danny keeps going.

'*Investigate now. Investigate now…*'

The chant dies down. Danny speaks.

'What are you pointing that thing at me for? Your criminals are over there, mate.' He jabs a finger towards *Isabella's*. 'In there. *The Velvet Lounge*. That's where you should be aiming. Go on – *investigate now. Investigate now...*'

Like porky ninjas, the officers drop to one knee and aim their tasers.

'What do you look like?' Danny's voice echoes loudly through the megaphone, cutting through the silence of the square. They creep closer.

'Alright, alright. I'm coming down.'

It's a shaky descent now that the adrenaline has worn off, but he manages to make it down another tier.

'Come on!' one of the officers yells. 'You can jump down from there!'

'What? You're joking.' The placard slips from his hand. Danny grabs the edge of the tier above, his legs wobbling like jelly.

'Turn around! Face forward!'

'I'm trying!'

The Bullhorn smashes to the ground. The officers close in. 'Turn around! Turn around! You've got three seconds!'

Then it happens. A warm spread journeys down his leg, embarrassingly visible through the front of Danny's jeans. They taser him, two tiers above the base. It's like being shredded with a fork, and incapacitated by the sudden jolt of electricity, Danny drops to the floor, his muscles seize, then spasm wildly as he hits the floor.

When he stops twitching, the police surge forward to cuff him and drag his limp body over to the van.

Yet, through the pain of his bitten tongue, Danny smiles. Something this big can't be ignored. Something of this magnitude could make the international news.

Well, it might – if one of the Chief Constables at

Scotland Yard didn't hold a platinum membership to *The Lounge*, where a smorgasbord of elite luxuries awaits company vice presidents and chairmen.

An old boys' network of high rollers, financiers. Harrovians and Etonians. The landed gentry. Respected figures of honour, jurisdiction, and dominion: director-generals. Doctors, lawyers – the trusted professions.

People with sway.

For these people, no request has ever been too big or too small during their many years spent unwinding in *The Lounge*.

Rock oysters and caviar at three-thirty in the morning. A four-poster canopy bed relocated from the Cartesian Suite to the Piedmont on one extravagant Sunday night. A room full of monarch butterflies. A pygmy baby goat to pet.

However strange, outlandish, or whimsical, Heather has always delivered – satisfying their colourful whims and their darkest indulgences alike.

Everyone is as compromised as everyone else, and that's exactly why Danny's little "exposé" won't make it to the international news – or even the local gazette.

'So that's it? I'm free to go?' Danny's first utterance after spending a night in the cells, his urine-soaked jeans now dry. 'But I don't understand. Aren't you going to look into this? Investigate?'

The female officer opens the door. 'Mr. Finch, as we already explained, your information will be passed on to an investigating officer. It's up to them to make a judgement based on the information provided, of which there is very little.'

'Don't you want to take a statement? I've given names. Surely you want to look into this...'

'Look, I just process the paperwork.'

'Well, can I speak to an investigating officer then?' says Danny, as she herds him out into the corridor.

'No.'

'Why?'

'Because that rank isn't stationed here.'

By mid-afternoon, the onslaught from the press has already begun to sizzle:

"It was clear that the perpetrator was becoming increasingly violent. We had no other choice than to deal with the dangerous individual at a distance. It was not a decision we took lightly, but it's my job to keep the public safe."

(PC Ephgrave – Metropolitan Police)

No mention of why he was up there. Not a word about what he said through that megaphone – but plenty of quotes from the authorities and members of the public, condemning Danny's "thoughtless" and "repugnant behaviour".

They've blurred out his placard and accused him of "outraging public decency" by urinating on a protected monument.

Chaining cigarettes and searching for a scintilla of truth, Danny keeps scrolling – his left side and shoulders still sore from where they sprayed him off that memorial like a bug, his body slamming against the granite.

"Young soldiers lost their lives for this country," a Royal British Legion veteran is reported to have said after being left "visibly shaken" following yesterday's incident. *"We must remember the service of our veterans. What has happened to duty, honour, and country? May the wrath and indignation of the British public be heaped upon him. Disgusting."*

It was an accident. Those officers scared the hell out of him with that Taser. It was just something to stand on – he didn't know that it would cause so much offense. His father was in the Falklands for God's sake.

'It's still there, still in one piece.'

This time, he really thought he'd gotten somewhere. Thought he'd done it. But the truth is, most of the people chanting with him in that crowd have already forgotten the words.   Danny could have all the evidence in the world –

and still, it wouldn't be enough. People don't want to know. Can't stomach it. And he doesn't blame them.

The subject's unpalatable. Yucky. So fucking horrible that even Danny doesn't want to believe it.

And his shoulder hurts. And his head. And his acne. And he's tired.

And the comment thread keeps growing:

LostToddler, Bristol: "Get the disgusting POS to clean it with a scrubbing brush and a bucket of hot soapy water!"

Tasha33, Boston, Lincolnshire: "Utterly disgraceful when there are toilets in the square."

CaveDweller, Richmond, North Yorkshire: "I idly wonder how the Russian authorities would deal with a person urinating on a Moscow war memorial? String him up."

'POS?' ponders Danny, scrolling back up the comments. 'Prisoner of… person of… point of sale? Get the… get the disgusting…'

Piece Of Shit.

A disgusting piece of shit.

CHAPTER 15

'I don't care how you do it. Tell him if he doesn't play ball, then it'll be your sisters working *The Lounge* from now on. Or make a blackmail video – get some footage on camera, a sex tape. I've got some GHB if you need it.'

Deadened by over a decade of abuse, Heather's disturbed mind no longer shocks Yin. 'Built up an entire archive of things over the years. They work wonders for getting people to do what you want, especially when you want to... shut them up.'

But Danny's been quiet for weeks, ever since he was tasered, his contorted body splayed at the foot of the war memorial like a helpless Daddy-Longlegs.

'But that's not really your style, is it? *Mmm?*'

'If you mean drugging people with a central nervous system depressant to facilitate sexual assault and immortalising it on film... No, not really.'

Resting her arms on her leather swivel chair, Heather leans back. The void between them grows larger.

'Is that your attempt at wit? Aw, how sweet. Here—' Leaning forward, she slides a small device across her desk. 'I want you to wear this.'

Tentatively, Yin picks it up. 'A recording device?'

'So I can listen in remotely. In real-time. Make sure you're not up to anything. You're not, are you, Yin? Because you know what will happen if you are.'

Yin has seated countless girls at Lounge tables, touched up their lipstick, and coached them on how to pout and how to stand.

'Like lambs to the slaughter, they'd be in there. Can you imagine?'

Yin turns the device and looks at its underside.

'He wouldn't want that on his conscience, now, would he? Would you? How old did you say the twins were again? Thirteen? Double trouble, I'm sure.'

Yin drops the device, her deadened nerves firing, coming back to life.

Heather snatches it away. 'There's a good few years in them yet.'

Thin lips curl back over whitened teeth, exposing receding gums. Quite out of character, Heather's smile finally reaches her eyes, and they twinkle.

'You know, the new massage bed arrived today. PVC leather. Wipe clean. It would look good in the Cartesian Suite, don't you think?'

'Why don't you just kill him?' says Yin, her nostrils flaring, Heather's smile evaporating, and the pigginess returns to her eyes. 'I mean, what good is a promise? Danny doesn't owe me or my sisters any loyalty. Swearing to stay quiet doesn't guarantee anything, does it? He could still speak out at any moment.'

'Not this time. It's too messy, and completely unnecessary when we're dealing with someone like Danny. Someone with a conscience, with heartstrings. A couple of tugs on them is all this needs. I can't be bumping anyone off, not now, not when I'm reaching my second spring.'

Heather fans herself with a manila envelope.

'These are very good,' she says, tapping a finger on a small rectangular box of vitamin-infused tea bags. 'Lemon balm, sage, and peach – *Cool Moments*, they're called.'

Heather the *hag* is revolting enough without Yin having to think about her ovarian retirement. She fights to mask her disgust.

'You may think I'm a monster, Yin, but if Danny doesn't keep schtum, then it's *he* who'll be the monster. And it'll be *his* fault your sisters end up working *The Lounge*. See how that works?'

Reaching behind, Heather picks up her handbag and takes something out.

'And if you don't get him to keep schtum, then – *then* – come on, *Yin* – then…'

'Then *I'll* be the monster?'

'Give Polly a cracker! And if *I* don't get *you* to keep Danny schtum, then *I'll* be – well.'

Heather tosses a dark red booklet, its cover emblazoned with a gold emblem of Thailand, across the desk.

'Well, go on. Take it. It's yours.'

'My passport? I thought you'd burned it,' says Yin, flicking straight to the biodata page. It expires in eight months. Something falls out – a photograph of her sisters lands face up on the taupe-gray carpet tiles.

'If he buttons that lip of his, you get to go home.'

'You don't mean it.'

'So, you think you're indispensable do you? Oh, *pur-lease*. Look at your hair. It's started to thin. Fair play, you hide it well with those scraped-back buns and fluorescent wigs, but you won't be able to forever. And those ankles of yours, they're getting thick. It won't be long until you – until you look like one of those,' Heather starts to laugh, 'like one of those godawful women. You know the ones. From where you're from, always piling rice into bowls and always wearing those ridiculous hats. No teeth and a big stick!'

These past ten years have undoubtedly taken their toll. Yin picks at her bitten nails.

'Hunched over, serving drinks – can you imagine? No, no, no. *The Lounge* demands fresh blood for front-of-house. And Thai is so unimaginative for this industry these days, don't you think? We need to branch out – somewhere like Guatemala or Nicaragua. Maybe even Russia. Yes, yes, yes, a willowy, ageless blonde. There are no bald *stubbies* in Russia. Those Russian girls know how to look after themselves. And what on earth happened to your eyebrows? Is that pencil? And your skin… You know, someone the other night actually asked me if you were a ladyboy—'

'Okay, okay, okay.'

173

Yin stands and snatches the recording device from the table.

'So, how do you want me to wear this thing?'

CHAPTER 16

It's raining. It's late. Yin buzzes Danny's room again and steps back from the doorstep, wondering why a partially covered snooker table is leaning against the front of the building, getting ruined.

She knows someone's inside because she can hear a television blaring from the front room. She adjusts her bra strap, the tiny device digging into her collarbone as she holds down the unhealthy-sounding buzzer for nearly ten seconds.

Nothing.

'Hello?' she calls through the letterbox, hoping the front-room tenant will hear. 'Is anybody there? Sorry, can you let me in? Hello?'

The letterbox flaps shut. Danny stops stoking the fire and turns down the television. This is it – the moment he's been dreading for weeks: someone looking for Murphy.

'Hello?' The letter box flaps back up. 'My name is Yin. I'm here to see Danny. Please, can someone...'

Yin? The relief nearly floors him. He rushes to the door and frantically pulls her inside.

'Who's with you?' he says, bolting the door behind her.

'Oh my *God*, your hair. What have you done to your hair?'

In the last photo she saw in the paper, he'd been all legs and arms – a blur of movement. She hadn't realised he'd shaved it off. Now, faced with him, she's shocked: sunken, skittish, his wide, ringed eyes flashing with something wild.

'You alone? Who's with you?'

'No one,' she says, her tone firm, eyes locked on him. He's gained weight and he's aged dramatically, looking like a much older man. Danny watches her gaze move over him, clocking every change.

'What? What are you staring at?'

'Your hair. It looks so…'

'So what? So, I shaved it off,' says Danny, swamped by his filthy dressing gown, his hand smoothing over his bald head. Yin's eyes dance with a mix of disbelief and a spark he can't quite place.

'…so different.'

They stare at each other in silence. Yin's mind races. Where are his other arms? She can only see one pair through his dressing gown sleeves.

'Shall we go up?' Yin asks, stepping forward, oblivious to the roll of unlaid carpet at her feet. It's been there for weeks, abandoned in the hall – he hasn't had the strength or inclination to lean it back against the wall.

'Watch your step,' he warns, guiding her into the front room. 'I'm in here now.'

'Did the tenant move out then?'

'Uh… something like that.'

Luckily for Danny, Yin is too distracted by the overwhelming stench – a wildly mix of nicotine, sewage, and rank body odour – and the albatross centrepiece on the mantel, to pay much attention to his recent room relocation. He doesn't need to say another word.

'Wow,' says Yin, lightly pinching her nose as she steps over yet another roll of carpet. 'What's that smell?'

'What smell?' Danny replies, returning to stoking the fire. 'I don't smell anything.'

One of the urinals in the men's room fell off the wall last week and started leaking. Danny stuffed it with old towels, and though it's stopped, the washing machine and shower haven't worked since. He's been washing himself with a flannel at the sink and he's completely nose-blind to the smell now.

Yin moves the pizza box-turned-ashtray from the sofa to the floor and sits down, her gaze lingering on the expensive-looking flat screen amid such a bleak landscape. She pulls her shoulder bag on the sofa, the bottle of tequila clinking against her phone. She'd hoped they'd talk things out over a drink, maybe end the night with a hug – mutual forgiveness and understanding on both sides. She'd planned to tell him how she'd write to him as soon as she reached her home in Phuket, imagined him writing her back. But looking at him now – deflated and hunched, the flickering flames deepening the shadows of his pockmarked profile, his spirit gone – she doubts he could even muster up the will to lick a stamp.

'Danny, you haven't asked me why I'm here.'

A mouse darts out from the hearth. Yin lets out a short, sharp squeal, pulling her legs up onto the sofa. Danny doesn't react – he's long since gone numb to this Dickensian nightmare.

A log drops softly into the ash, landing with a muted thud. He prods at it, absentmindedly.

'That's some fancy-looking firewood you've got there,' says Yin, eyeing the glowing embers of the antique snooker table leg. The fire crackles and pops, competing softly with the low murmur from the television.

'Danny, where are your arms?'

With deliberate slowness, he lights a cigarette.

'Danny? Your arms? Where are they?'

The albatross becomes briefly shrouded in smoke as Danny exhales, his gaze fixed on the fire. 'Out of sight, out of mind,' he finally mutters, not bothering to face her. 'Keep 'em tied. Keep 'em away now.'

'Tied?'

Yin watches as they wriggle beneath his dressing gown, just above his lower back.

'But why? Why would you do such a thing?'

'Oh, calm down, woman,' says Danny, his lip curling. 'They're fine.' He flicks the butt of his cigarette into the flames. 'They just get in the way otherwise.'

'In the way? How can your own arms get in the way? Surely they must be useful? The other day in the supermarket, I dropped a jar of peanut butter right on my

177

foot because I didn't bother with a basket. My hands were full, you see.'

Browsing the supermarket aisles feels like a lifetime ago – it's been so long since he last stepped outside.

'Toilet rolls, face wash, crisps… It was a nightmare. I had to ask someone stocking the shelves to go fetch me a…'

'Okay, Yin – why are you here?'

'Because she knows you know, Danny,' says Yin, feeling the hard edge of the tequila bottle through her canvas bag. 'She knows you *know* she knows. Because of your letter. Everything you said in it… it was true.'

A strange sense of vindication washes over him, but he doesn't dwell on it for long.

'Nice place to work then, is it? Nice people?'

Meeting her gaze, he catches a flicker of shame in her eyes.

'Danny. It's not like that—'

'Good tips? Must be.'

'You think I choose to be there?'

Flashing her a narrowed-eyed glance, he lights another cigarette. Yin lowers her chin, straightens her bra strap.

'Danny, that woman is insane. You have no idea what she's capable of. Didn't the duck mean anything to you?'

Danny eyes the rubber duck on the mantelpiece.

'And going to the police isn't a good idea, Danny. It won't do anything anyway – she's too protected. You know she's bugged your room, right? Been listening in?'

'How the hell would she have done that? No one's been in here.'

'Oh, come on, Danny. Why do you think this place is full of unlaid carpet? She's tapped your phone, too.'

'You're joking.' Danny thought it was odd how his data usage suddenly increased.

'She's been listening in, Danny. Listening in on *everything*.'

He steps away from the fire and begins to pace.

Listening in on all his aborted masturbation attempts – gripping his penis half to death just to feel the faintest glimmer of sensation. Danny's libido has been non-existent these past few weeks. It vanished as quickly as it came.

'Listening in?' Danny paces faster. *Oh, the indignity.* 'What if she's listening in right now? She is, isn't she?' He pulls his phone from his dressing gown pocket and turns it off. 'I should have known,' he says, kicking the nearest roll of carpet. 'Should've *fucking* known.'

Danny stops pacing, comes over to her. 'Wait.' *Snap.* He clicks his fingers. 'When did she tap my phone? How long ago?'

'Err… I'm not sure.'

'Well, think, woman. *Think.*' He grips her shoulders firmly.

'Danny, you're scaring me.'

'Can it pick up sound?' The sound of Murphy sputtering his last breath? The sound of the spades slicing through the earth?

'Well, yes. I guess so. I don't know. Probably. Danny, let go of me.'

He releases her and steps back. She's right – maybe going to the police is not such a good idea after all. He calms down and lights a cigarette.

'Why are you protecting her like this?' he asks, sitting up at the bar.

'Protecting?'

'Yeah, protecting. Showing up here at this time of night, persuading me, getting me off her tail.'

'It's not her I'm protecting.'

'No? So, it's me is it?' He exhales. 'Do me a favour.'

'Well, yes, and…'

'Nightmares I've been having. On the rare occasions when I actually manage to sleep, that is.' His cigarette slips from his fingers and drops to the floor. He lights another.

179

'Their faces. Those girls' faces. I saw you smiling. Giving 'em sweets.'

'Danny,' says Yin, keeping her eye on the fallen cigarette, its cherry glowing bright. 'Aren't you going to pick that up?'

'Smiling and – comfortable – yeah, that's it. You looked *really* comfortable. Real…' The cigarette singes the carpet. 'Relaxed.'

'Danny!'

'Not like now,' he says, crouching down to pick up the cigarette. 'How can you stand it?' he asks her, taking a drag from what's left of the rescued butt. 'How can you work in a place like that – and do what you do?'

'I know what you must think of me, but it's more complicated than you think.'

Gripping the edge of the bar counter, Danny hauls his aching body upright. Yin watches his face twist with pain. 'Danny, you don't look well.'

'No? Don't I?' He turns his back to her, slips off his dressing gown, and drapes it over the bar. 'Yeah? Well, take a look at that, then.'

Danny unties the string around his little fellas' wrists, and they drop to his sides – limp, atrophied. Instinctively, Yin covers her mouth, confronted by the sight of his overgrown fingernails and the grime caked into the folds of skin between his forearms and elbows. 'See that! Get a load of that! Go on—' He presents them to her with an exaggerated "muscle dance" – *cha, cha, cha.*

'My God, Danny.' Yin's stomach turns as she tries to process the spectacle – the arms and hands of an old man, twisted and frail. She can hardly bear to look as he parades them across the living room in all their unkempt, mistreated glory – scratched, bruised, yellowed and purple, and with multiple cigarette burns.

'Oh, Danny. What have you done?" she says, her voice faltering. She wants to reach out, wants to comfort him, but his body odour repels her.

'What, to these?' Danny sneers. 'The arms of a sexual predator?' Spittle flecks off his bottom lip.

'Why would you harm them like that?'

'Harm *them?*' he says, stepping toward the sofa. 'They've harmed me! I'd lop the bloody things off if I had the guts, but I can't even do that, can I. I just slice 'em up now and then.'

'Danny, you're cut to ribbons. What have you done?'

'It feels good. '

Returning to the weakly flickering fire, he stokes the dwindling flames.

'You should try having these things. Maybe then you'd understand. A burden, they are. A bloody burden. Useless... Brought me nothing but misery.' He jabs at the fire, the embers crackling in response. 'Chuck us them ciggies off the mantelpiece, would you?'

'You're a chain smoker,' Yin observes, tossing them over to him, nonetheless. Danny misses. They land, spilling out onto the floor, and the tiniest flash of a smile passes between them, before Danny's jaw clenches tighter than a hermetically sealed space capsule.

Meanwhile, back in her lair, Heather tops up her cranberry soda with vodka and yawns. 'For Christ's sake, Yin. Don't drag this saga out any longer than it needs to be.'

'What did I tell you? Useless. Absolutely useless,' says Danny, the little fellas ineffectually scrabbling at the cigarettes. The old guys take charge, but every time they move, a reflex makes the little fellas flail awkwardly. Their clumsy efforts only send the cigarettes scattering further.

'*Get out of it*,' he growls, elbowing his little right hand aside as it reaches for a cigarette. It stays back a moment, then jerks forward again. 'Stay – *stay!*'

'You treat them like a dog.'

'And?' says Danny, shoving the cigarettes back into the pack as his eyes lift to meet hers. He sees the scar on her

181

neck. 'Did Shiva do that to you? You know – Shiva. The Queen of *Shiva*.'

Yin lightly touches her neck with her fingertips. 'Sheba,' she says, with a playful coyness. 'I meant *Sheba*.'

'Well, Sheba don't scare me,' says Danny, throwing his dressing gown back on loosely, the little fellas hanging rigidly at his sides.

'No?' says Yin, fingers trailing her neck, her eyes drifting. 'Last week, a girl came in... and never came out. It was like she vanished.'

She wipes her eyes and rummages in her bag. Danny watches, saying nothing.

'Here,' she says, pulling out a photograph. Danny takes it, immediately noticing the resemblance.

'Blimey,' he says.

'They're my sisters.'

'Spitting image, aren't they?'

'They're twins.'

'Nah, I meant you,' he says handing it back. 'They're the spitting image of you.'

'Heather says unless you stay quiet, she's going to traffic them over. Get them working *The Lounge*.'

Danny hands the photo back to her. She takes it, her eyes lingering for a moment before she mutters, 'At least that means I'll get to see them soon – I guess.'

Quickly, she pulls a bottle of tequila from her bag – a cheap brand she picked up from the off-license down the road – and knocks back three quick swigs. It burns like paint thinner; the grimace on her face says at much. 'And I'll be the one who has to make them "look pretty" and send them down there. Me!'

She takes another swig. Danny watches her, elbows on the bar, chin resting in his hands. Pensively, he speaks.

'So, it's okay for other girls – other people's sisters – to work there, huh?' His tone darkens. 'Just as long as it ain't *your* sisters, that makes it's okay?'

Yin's face is flushed from the alcohol, her eyes watery.

She rises unsteadily from the sofa, tequila bottle in hand, her denim skirt riding up her thigh.

'She'll do it Danny. She will. My sisters. They're just babies. Can you sleep with that on your conscience?' Gold liquid sloshes from the bottle as she points it towards him. 'Can you?'

'That's the way to do it!' says Heather, in a *Punch and Judy* voice, grating and menacing. Her eyes gleaming as she pours in more vodka. 'Now we're getting somewhere.'

Conscience? What conscience? Danny thinks, already knowing there's no way he's going to the police. For all he knows, Heather might have a full audio recording of Murphy's last breath. He's saving his own skin, but he'll spin it as if his decision is driven by far nobler reasons – eventually. For now, he'll let her talk him into it a little longer.

'All I want is my sisters to be safe. Is that really so hard to understand?'

Snatching the bottle from her, Danny drinks, and sits on the sofa beside her. The smell of cheap tequila briefly masks the stale funk of his body odour.

'My mother thinks I'm a masseuse, you know.' The detachment returns to her eyes. Danny keeps hold of the tequila, his grip tightening slightly.

'So, if I stay quiet, then…'

'Then I get to go home,' she says, turning into him, that detachment now fire. 'I get to go home, Danny.' She reclaims the bottle. 'I get to have a life again, be with my family.' She drinks. 'They need me.' She drinks. 'They need me so much.'

Leaving the sofa, Danny goes over to his albatross atop the mantel. He breathes on its beak, then buffs it with his dressing gown sleeve, his back turned to Yin.

'Danny?'

A spider crawls out from behind the massive seabird. Danny watches it for a moment before helping it onto his hand. '*Hmmm?*' he murmurs, his gaze fixed as the spider dances onto his other hand.

'So, you'll stay quiet, yeah? Do I have your word? Danny?'

Danny nods, his attention shifting to the noise of the traffic, amplified by the rain-slicked road. The sharp click of high heels on pavement and a burst of drunken laughter cut through the night air.

'I'll write you.'

'Will you?'

'Yes. I'll write you as soon as I get there.'

'Yeah, yeah, I heard you the first time.'

'You're doing the right thing,' she adds, heading for the door.

'Yeah?'

'Thank you. Thank you for saving my sisters.'

'Whatever.'

'You should let some light into this room,' she says, turning to leave. Danny knows she won't be able to reach that top bolt and, with a reluctant sigh, follows her out.

'Here, you'll never reach that,' he says, a waft of his body odour escaping from his dressing gown, enclosing her in the hallway. When the door opens, she can't slip out fast enough – but turns back with a smile.

'That denim rara thing you're wearing,' he says flatly, half behind the door.

'Yeah? What about it?'

'Pull it down. It's halfway up your arse.'

Those are his parting words before he quickly slides both bolts across and double-locks the door. Back in the front room, he turns the television back up and shuts the world out once again.

CHAPTER 17

It's Danny's fortieth birthday – although he doesn't know it.

A month has passed since Yin's visit, with each day blending into the next. It's now late October, but Danny has no need for dates, or days, or even time itself.

His wrists are sore from developing a habit of grinding them against the rough string he uses to tie them behind his back. Half the time, he doesn't even realise he's doing it. It happens mostly when he's staring blankly through the television, day or night. He knows it's weird. He's doing it now. A quiet, compulsive ritual. A peculiar kind of self-harm, but one that brings a strange sense of release.

The frayed string snaps, and the little fellas are released. That was the last of the reel; what's left around his wrists isn't enough for a re-tie. But they must be restrained – otherwise they'll drift back towards his belly again, seeking warmth, seeking comfort. And he can't bear that. Their touch repulses him, even now, with the sharp nip in the air that's crept in mid-way through the season of mists and mellow fruitfulness. Danny's felt it once or twice, on the rare occasions he's stepped outside for a smoke. But why bother, when he can smoke indoors and ignore the garden's fiery show of autumn altogether?

Down in the cellar, searching for more string, Danny spots a roll of gaffer tape. He picks at the stubborn end, then heads back up to the front room, a thought creeping into his mind. If he wraps it tightly enough, would he cut off the little fellas' blood supply? Maybe then they'd drop off – redundant things that they've become.

All the muscle Danny worked so hard to build has withered away. His biceps sag, flapping like stretch-marked wings. The takeaway pizzas have given him a belly and a double chin. Danny can now demolish an extra-large in under twenty minutes.

'*Get out of it,*' he snarls, as the little fellas' fingers brush against his lower back. His right old guy keeps doggedly picking at the stubborn tape, though, in a twisted way, he's grateful for the distraction.

He's been hearing this taunting voice, relentlessly negative. At first, he was convinced it was Murphy, then he thought it was Gramps from beyond the grave, but it's neither. It's coming from inside him, inside his head. It tells him that pretty soon, someone's going to come a-knocking for Murphy, convincing him that "Sheba" heard everything – and that she's probably listening in on him right now. Danny knows he should just toss his smartphone away, smash it with a hammer – but it's his only window to the world. It's as if his whole existence has been hijacked by fear – fear of Murphy, fear of the future, fear of himself.

For this reason, Danny plays the pepperoni game, throwing up and catching discs well into the early hours, fixated on beating his personal best of fourteen in a row.

'Yes,' Danny mutters, finally freeing the tape by the glow of the television. But the victory is snatched when the voice returns:

You left them to stagnate, didn't you, it says. Held them back. It was you. You didn't even try. I saw you – picking your nose and scratching your arse with them. Flicking through the channels, slurping endless cups of sugary tea. Boozing. Brilliant. Well done, mate. Give the man a hand.

Danny can almost hear the applause as he gnaws at the industrial-strength tape with his teeth.

Don't tell me. It's there again. Can't even be arsed to go upstairs for a pair of scissors? No ambition. No drive. No confidence. No guts. That's always been your problem. Forty years old – and look at you. Look at how you're living!

'Thirty-nine,' Danny tells the voice, hauling himself up by the banister.

Wasted on you, those arms. They'd make anyone else's life easier, but somehow, they've made yours harder. How's that even possible?

Oh yeah. I forgot – because it's you.

Hunched at the end of his bed, hacking at the thick adhesive tape with scissors, Danny gets himself into a sticky tangle. Somehow, the tape has fused to the back of his old right hand like a waxing strip – and he knows there's only one way it's coming off.

'Christ almighty!' he yells, looking down at the glossy black hair stuck to the tape, the raw bald patch left behind on his hand. The voice laughs:

Look at you. You could win the lottery and still end up more penniless than before.

Danny rubs his burning hand.

If you fell in a barrel full of fucking tits, you'd come out sucking your thumb – all four of them!

'Stop. Just stop!' Danny binds his wrists with tape as tightly as he can. 'Just fuck off.'

A missing person's report will be filed sooner or later, you know. Or there'll be a knock at the door. Didn't you think about that, did you? Course you didn't. You'd trip over a cordless phone. You'd get fired from a blow job!

'Shut up!'

People will put two and two together eventually. Idiot. Divvy boy. Stupid idiot. Murphy's face on a milk carton soon enough. They got CCTV in that DIY store, you know. Pay by card, did you? They'll have all your track data – card number, expiration date, cardholder name. Did you even check the carrier bags for a receipt? You know, the ones you put over his fucking head!

Danny wraps another layer.

Knock, knock.

Danny rolls his eyes, but with his wrists numbing and starting to tingle, he gives in to the tiresome voice.

'Who's there?'

Dunno. The police, most likely, ha, ha, ha, ha, ha.

'Oh, will you just stop? Just stop, okay?'

You returned a doughnut because it had a hole in it - ha ha ha ha ha ha…

With his circulation slowly strangled, the voice finally recedes.

Fireworks explode in the park, muffled and distant. *It isn't Guy Fawke's yet, is it?* thinks Danny, looking up through the skylight. Halloween's still a long way off.

All the snooker table legs are reduced to ash. The boiler's fucked. Danny pulls his oversized blue puffer coat from the wardrobe, slips it on, and heads back down to the front room, the glow of the television waiting for him.

Flicking through the channels, Danny wishes Babe Station would start sooner. There's nothing on. There never is, yet up and down he scrolls, searching for something, like staring into an empty fridge hoping for something tasty to jump out. Staring continually into that abyss with a mix of desperation, boredom and hunger, until...

You land on one of those excruciatingly long, celebrity countdown shows like: *Top 100 Highest Paid Celebs* and get swept away by the overstimulating opening credits.

With the heaviest of sighs, Danny tries to get comfortable. He's in for the long-haul with this one.

Like a trainwreck that's impossible to look away from, Danny's made it to the ad-break before celebrity sixty-two.

'Why must the adverts always come on so *bloody* loud?' he grumbles, turning the volume down. That's when he hears it – a scratching noise. The mouse had been back the other night, nibbling on some leftover pizza, leaving a trail of droppings in its wake. Danny, careful not to startle it with the rustling of his puffer coat, lights a cigarette and, using the flashlight on his phone, goes to investigate.

Something scuttles behind the bar. Danny shines his phone.

'Little bleeder' he says, discovering another trail. The ad-break ends, and he rustles back to the sofa.

By celebrity thirty-six, Danny is half-asleep when he hears it again – only louder this time. Whatever it is sounds bigger than a mouse. Rats, maybe. Foxes, even. He mutes the television, grabs his phone, and follows the sound out into the garden, the flashlight guiding him down the outside steps that lead to the cellar.

The sound seems to be coming from behind a row of metal kegs in the corner. Danny leans back against the damp wall, grabs one of the spades he used to dig Murphy's grave, and aims his light into the shadows, illuminating an enormous, silver-silken cobweb. If he clangs the kegs with the spade, with any luck, whatever it is will bolt straight out into the garden.

There it is again – only this time breathier, almost like a ghostly moan. The air shifts. There's a definite presence.

'Murphy?'

Bracing himself, Danny's grip on the spade tightens. As he steps forward, one of the metal kegs moves a couple of inches, scraping against the concrete floor.

'Quit playing Murphy. You hear me?'

It moves again, this time with a sharp, sucking breath. Danny's eyes flick to the open cellar door and Murphy's grave beyond it.

'Who's there? Murphy? I'm warning you,' says Danny, raising the spade and swinging it against the stack of empty kegs. One topples and rolls away, revealing the source of the ghostly moan – a young woman with scraggy, bleached hair, curled up and hugging her knees to her chest. She looks harmless enough.

'Oh, Jesus. Thank God. For a minute there, I thought you were… I really thought you might be…'

Murphy's vengeful spirit rising from the dead?

The blonde waif thumps her ankle with a clenched fist, biting her bottom lip hard.

'You alright?' Danny asks.

'Pins and needles,' she says, the crawling sensation now at its peak. She keeps on thumping to get the blood flowing again. 'Sorry. I'd get up if I could—'

'*Get up, Lil.*' A deep gruff voice – unfamiliar and close.

189

'Who's with you? Who's there?' Danny sweeps his phone torch.

'*Shut up, Welbs,*' hisses the waif, elbowing the shadowy figure beside her.

'Come on, stand up. The pair of you. Come on—'

'I *am* trying. My foot's still asleep.'

'Well, *his* isn't. Come on. Get up.'

The creature beside her, slowly rises, shielding his eyes from Danny's torch light. 'I'm Welby.' he mutters. He's at least twice her age, tanned from either dirt or the sun. It's hard to tell.

'How the hell did the both of you get in?' They make a swampy pair. 'Wait a minute... how many more of you are there?'

'There's no more. Just us,' Lil says, steadying herself on the keg and finally managing to stand. She points towards the window.

'Sorry, matey,' says Welby, his voice thick with a West Country accent, something Danny notices immediately.

'Yeah, sorry. We didn't break in, honest. It was already open. Tell him, Welbs.' Welby grunts in agreement. 'We were going to sleep rough again, but then Welbs spotted this place, and...'

'Jesus,' says Danny. 'Your accent's even stronger than *his.*'

'No, it ain't. His yap's from bloody Somerset. Even *I* can't make sense of half the words he says.'

Welby starts mumbling – something about Cheddar Gorge. Danny furrows his brow, trying to make sense of it.

'See? Listen to that yap.'

For the first time in months, Danny laughs, and all the tension built up over these hellish months suddenly discharges through his body.

'Can I use your toilet?' Lil asks, crossing her legs and bouncing behind the keg. 'Then we'll go. I promise.'

'You'll have to use the men's, I'm afraid,' says Danny,

rustling them through to the house. 'I've been doing a bit of tinkering, and now, well, the plumbing's screwed. Down the corridor, first door on your left. Or feel free to use the one on the top floor—'

'No, no, the men's is fine,' says Lil, close behind, her voice tight with urgency. 'Excuse me.' She quickly scoots past.

'I'm afraid the boiler's fucked! But if you fancy a wash at the sink, I can do a quick kettle for you! Get you a flannel?' Danny calls after her, holding the men's door open – ever the consummate host.

'No, no. You're alright!' she calls back, locking the cubicle door.

'The boiler?' says Welby. 'What's the matter with it?'

'Me, that's what the matter is. I've been meddling.'

'Straight up there, is it?' says Welby, looking up the stairwell. 'I can have a look if you like.'

'Here—' Unsettled by Welby's sudden show of hospitality, Danny places a hand on his shoulder. 'Wait a minute. You don't happen to fit carpets as well, do you?' he adds, straightening his posture with fresh concern that Lil might be bugging the men's toilets.

'No. Why?'

'It's just that you're being... overly friendly, that's all.' Danny folds his puffy arms across his chest, leaning against the banister with a wary glance.

'*Me*, overly friendly? You just offered my girlfriend a flannel for a strip-wash at the sink. Now, do you want hot water or not?'

'Lived in a fair few squats over the years,' says Welby, reaching behind the boiler. 'It's amazing what skills you pick up in the community. There it is,' he says, flicking a switch and glancing back at Danny. The boiler hums to life. 'It's back on now.'

'Really? As quick as that? That's impressive. What was the problem with it?'

'Someone had turned it off, that's all.'

'Like I say – meddling.'

'Welbs?' Lil calls from the bottom of the stairs. 'Where are you?'

'Hear that?' says Welby.

'Yeah, she said...'

'Not her – *that*. That gurgling coming through the pipes? That's your radiators coming back on.'

'Welbs!'

'Wait a minute!'

'Come on. We've gotta go!'

'Blimey. Got some pair of lungs on her, hasn't she?'

'Yeah – "Foghorn Lil", I calls her,' Welby says with a look of mischief.

'*Welby!*'

'Anyway, thanks for the warm.'

'Leaving so soon?' Danny says as Welby turns on the stair. 'At least let me thank you, with a nice cup of tea? Warm yourselves up a bit more first, before going back out – into the bitter cold, the wet.'

'Go on, go through,' says Danny, ushering them into the front room. But just before he follows them in, he notices a red letter marked "URGENT" in the front door post basket. 'Go on. Make yourselves comfortable,' he adds, seeing the letter's for the attention of Murphy. 'A nice hot cup of tea. How do you take it? Milk? Sugar?'

While Lil and Welby warm themselves by the radiator behind the sofa, Danny opens the letter. It's a utility bill – *a final demand*, no less. It hadn't even crossed his mind to put the bills in his name now that Murphy's not around.

But he doesn't want to think about that now, not when he has guests – two people who are a lot worse off than him, by the looks of it, and two people who don't seem to have a clue who he is.

As the kettle boils, he rips up the letter and tosses it in the bin.

'Fancy a pizza?' he says, taking the teas through. 'It's

just that I usually order around now. The deep-pan pepperoni's out of this world. Proper Italian style.'

'What's that snooker table doing out there?' Lil asks. 'Sorry, but we had a look at it before we climbed over the wall. It's getting wrecked out there.'

'No, yeah, I know. I tried bringing it in, but as you can see, I didn't get very far.' Danny slurps his tea as the rain hammers hard against the bay window.

'Well, you got us now, ain't ya? Come on.' Lil puts her tea down. 'Welbs?'

'So that's three large pepperoni, one large Hawaiian – easy on the pineapple – two litres of Coke, one garlic bread – extra cheese – and, oh, two packs of cigarettes. And remember the safe code, okay? Smashing. Great. Bye.'

'Well, I think we'll have earned this pizza when it arrives,' says Danny, proudly smiling at the snooker table in the middle of the room, where it will remain on its side for the foreseeable. 'Teamwork.'

'Nice seagull,' says Lil, with a look of confusion.

'Seagull? That's an albatross, I'll have you know.'

'Yeah, you get 'em down Plymouth. Noisy buggers.'

'What, albatrosses?'

'No, seagulls.'

'Got a spoon, matey?' mumbles Welby, from behind the snooker table, where he seems to have "set up camp."

'Welbs!' snaps Lil.

'What? I've gotta cook up, don't I.'

'Cook what? The pizza?'

'Oh, leave it a while, Welbs, yeah? You don't need a spoon.'

'No, it's alright. I've got loads – although I've never heard of anyone eating pizza with a spoon before,' says Danny, his naïve smile fading into embarrassment as he watches Welby pull a roll of tin foil from a black carrier bag. 'Oh – *I see.*'

'See, he don't mind, do ya, matey?'

'No, not at all,' says Danny, quickly fetching him a teaspoon from the kitchen. 'Cook up 'til your heart's content. I don't mind. Go ahead.'

The idea of a stranger shooting up heroin in someone's living room, would probably horrify most. But loneliness can have a peculiar effect on people. Danny comes back through, awkwardly moving around the table to get a closer look, as if Welby were some kind of live art installation.

'Want a picture?' says Welby, taking the spoon and glaring up at him from the floor, like a dog just before it attacks – and for a second, Danny thinks he might. But he's saved by the insane scream of the intercom, like metal scraping against metal. Lil and Welby cover their ears, while Danny, with finger raised, takes a moment to decipher the static screech.

'Aren't you gonna get that?' Lil says, crouching like she's in the midst of a dawn raid.

'Yep. Just a sec,' says Danny, waiting for the familiar *duff-duffs* of the long-running British soap opera's theme tune.

'Eastenders?' says Lil, recognising the rhythm.

'That'll be the pizza. They're quick, you know.'

'So,' asks Lil, her mouth full of pizza, 'how long you been squatting here?'

'Sorry?' responds Danny.

'We've squatted in loads of places, ain't we Welbs?' Welby doesn't respond. 'But nothing like this.' Captivated by the smoothness of the bar counter, Lil swivels on the bar stool.

Squatting? Danny isn't sure why she's drawn that conclusion. He's always been a reliable tenant, never missed a payment. So what if there are a few mice, a few snails crawling up the walls, a bit of mould, and the constant smell of drains. It's hardly what you'd call squalor – is it?

'Us squatters gots to stick together, you know,' she says, peeling another slice from the box. 'Me and Welbs, we was squatting in this place in Hackney, but it had nothing on this. Like a castle this is.' Tilting back, she folds the pizza slice into her tiny mouth. 'And you're the king!' An olive drops and lands on the bar.

But these words fill him with such a sense of belonging that he gives her an answer.

'Ten years I've been squatting here. Ten good years.'

'Ten years! You're a real vet then.'

'Vet?' says Danny, lighting himself a cigarette.

'Yeah – veteran squatter. Welbs is one too. Been squatting for *years*, Welby has, but I'm still a newbie.'

'Don't worry. I'll take you under my wing,' says Danny, propping up the bar and glancing over at the albatross. 'Stay if you want. Welby too, of course.'

'We had this huge squat rave in Hackney, mental it was – wait a minute, you what?' Lil hops off the stool. 'Do you mean it? Do you really mean it? Stay? Stay here?'

Silently nodding, Danny smiles, throws up a pepperoni disc and catches it in his mouth.

'Nice one brother. Nice one! Cheers.' Lil raises her slice to him, then salutes her fellow comrade. 'So, raves. You had many?'

'Yeah. Well, no. Not really. I mean, not for a while.'

'You should have seen our last place,' says Lil, hopping back on the stool. 'Acid DJs on one floor, punk bands on another. Welby's well into his techno, ain't ya, Welbs?' No answer. 'Hundreds of us there were, all raving away. Mad it was. I can't *stand* all that commercial rave bollocks, can you?'

'No, yeah. No, I know. Can't *stand* it. Yeah, I hate all that commercial *shite*.'

The weight of stolen valour forces Danny out into the kitchen. 'Fancy a brew?' he calls through to the bar, only to realise Lil has followed him out.

'Squatters' rights are human rights,' she says, giving him an emphatic nudge as he fills the kettle.

'Absolutely. "Squatters rights are human rights,"' parrots Danny, throwing up a peace sign – then turning to face the sink and cringe.

But despite the cringe, he feels part of something – part of a movement, part of Lil and Welby's little world – and they sip Murphy's whisky with Coke, smoking at the bar.

'Aren't you hot in that puffer coat? It's roasting in here,' says Lil, removing her multi-coloured chunk-knit cardigan. 'You must be sweating your bollocks off in that.'

'Nah. No. I'm a cold fish, me.'

Helping herself to another of Danny's cigarettes, Lil surveys the room, her eyes suddenly fixing on the far corner.

'No way!'

'What?'

'That! The jukebox.' Rushing over, an unlit cigarette dangling between her fingers, she embraces it like a long lost friend.

'Oh – that. Put it on if you want,' he says, turning the radiator down.

And while Welby lies smacked out within the confines of the snooker table, Lil dances to songs Danny's never heard, breathing life once again through the barren walls.

'I forget everything when I'm dancing,' she says, bumping into the snooker table. Welby gives an unhealthy moan. 'Oh, *shut up*,' she snaps, giving the table a kick and spilling some of her drink.

'Is he alright in there?' Danny asks, peering around the table and seeing Welby's eyes blissfully rolling in his head.

'Yeah. He's fine. Come on – *dance*.'

'No way.'

Narrowing her eyes, she steps closer to Danny, studying his face from both sides. 'Wait a minute…'

This is it. She's finally twigged.

'What's your name? You never said.'

'Didn't I?'

'No. You didn't. Wait—' Jumping back on the stool she points her finger at him. 'Don't tell me. I've got psychic powers, you see. I'm getting a… G? Gary?'

'Gary? James?'

'No.'

'Not James?' She closes her eyes. 'I'm getting a D… Dave?'

'You're hardly Mystic Meg, are you?'

'Who?'

'Never mind. Before your time.'

'Well, go on then, what is it?'

'Daniel,' he spurts, instantly regretting not having made something up. He should have agreed to Dave, but he's no good when he's put on the spot, especially when he's tipsy.

'Daniel? Really?' says Lil, lolloping back over to the jukebox, Murphy's whisky having taken hold.

'Yes! It's on here. I love this song,' she declares, her words punctuated by a hiccup.

'No,' says Danny. 'No please—'

But then it starts – the Elton John song Mairead used to sing to him as a baby. Lil makes him listen, reciting every word with heartfelt precision. Before he know it, tears well up, and he starts bloody crying.

'You alright?'

'No, yeah. It's just the smoke. It's a bit smoky in here.'

Walking away from the jukebox, gruffly sniffing and hating himself for letting any emotion slip through, he abruptly calls it a night.

'Help yourself to towels in the airing cupboard,' he says, his voice tight. 'Night.'

'Yeah, night,' says Lil, left wondering what she might have done to upset him.

CHAPTER 18

'So, who's this Murphy then?'

Coffee splurts from Danny's mouth, and he recovers with a cough.

'What? Who?' he stammers, hastily setting down his mug on the walnut finish of the snooker table.

'Murphy. You were calling to him down in the cellar. Who is he?'

Scratching his face, the rustle of his puffer coat loud in the silence, amplifying his jittery unease, Danny tries to think.

'Was he a squatter as well then?'

'Err... yeah. Yeah, he was.' Danny fidgets with his sleeve. 'Only... that wasn't his name. That's not what I said.'

'Sounded like it to me. You were yelling it at the top of your lungs, large as life.'

'No, no, I was yelling – *Puffy*,' says Danny, drawing inspiration from his coat.

'Puffy?'

'Well, it was more like, *Purfy*, 'cause he was... he was Welsh, you see. From the *Valleys*.'

'What sort of name is *Pervy*? Even if you are from the *Valleys*.'

'No, *Purfy*, like that, see? You must have misheard.' Danny takes a big slurp of coffee. 'I thought it was him down there.'

'Where is he then, this, *Purfy*?' Lil asks, looking up to the ceiling. 'Is he still here?'

'No, God no. He left weeks ago.' Slurp. 'A good few weeks now.' Another slurp. 'We had a falling out – then he said he had to' – slurp – 'move on.'

Wandering over to the bar, Danny peels a cold slice of pizza from the box. 'Want some? It's better cold, if you ask me—'

'Move on? Us squatters have got to stay together. Stronger in numbers, ain't we. You never know, he might come back,' says Lil, with a smile.

'Does Welby want some pizza?'

'Welbs? – *Welby*! Daniel's asking if you want some pizza. *Welby*!?'

And life goes on like this. A little trio Danny likes to think of as "us squatters." Welby stays a permanent, near-mute fixture, comfortably numb within his snooker cave, while Lil comes and goes as she pleases, often late into the night. Danny expects she's "on the game," but he never confronts her about it. They eat a lot of pizza, smoke a lot of cigarettes, exhaust every song on the jukebox, and drink Murphy's booze dry. Welby shoots a lot of heroin. Danny's absurd puffer coat never comes off, and the little fellas remain unseen, so much so that Danny almost forgets they exist at all, in his world of denial, where he's content playing the pepperoni game with Lil, convinced that one day he'll beat her top score of twenty. The headaches and worries about his future fade, along with the steadily dwindling shoebox of cash under his bed.

One more reminder through the door and the gas and electric will be cut off. Danny could pay what's outstanding, even set up a direct debit, but is paranoid about leaving a trail. It's turned so cold that the radiators don't make much of a difference anyway. Even on full blast Danny and Lil can still see their breath in the air.

'It's bloody freezing in here,' says Lil, her bum against the radiator, eyeing Danny's puffer coat which no longer seems so absurd. 'Shouldn't we burn some logs? Get the fire going?'

'Logs? What logs?' *And soon, we won't have electricity either if I don't pay that bill.* Danny imagines what it'd be like to suddenly be plunged into total darkness. Surroundings are bleak enough.

'The logs in the log store. Down in the cellar, dummy.'

'Really?' It seems the antique snooker table legs died in vain. 'Oh, cool. Yeah – of course. The log store.'

'Ha! Another thrashing. That's twenty-one you've got to beat now, matey,' says Lil, smugly reclining on Murphy's sofa and taking a hero's drag on her cigarette.

'I don't know how you do it, with that little mouth of yours,' says Danny, stoking the fire, staring into the ambient light of the flames.

'How old are you?' she asks, over the crackle of the burning logs.

'Older than I look, probably. Older than you.'

'About – fifty?'

Eyebrow raised, Danny turns from the fire, hoping that she's joking. Unfortunately, her face tells him she's not.

'But you look good for it. For fifty, I mean. Bloody good,' she blurts, seeing that she's struck a nerve.

'Thanks,' he says, turning back, the blood rushing to his face.

A whole decade more. During this morning's ablutions, Danny realised he'd missed his fortieth birthday, and fearing she might go even higher, he quickly says, 'Yeah. Fifty. Spot on.'

'There's a box of Christmas decorations down in the cellar, you know.'

'And?' answers Danny flatly. Unsurprisingly, Christmas isn't his favourite time of year.

'I'll go get them. This place could use some cheering up.'

'Yippee! Just one more sleep!' he bites, watching her bounce off to fetch them.

There's an energy shift. A mismatch in mood, and he blames Lil for spoiling it. They were having a nice, relaxing time just now – peaceful. Ambient. 'Maybe I *am* getting old,' he mutters, jabbing at the fire. He decides he'll sleep through Christmas Day, claiming that he's sick – though he likely will be. The mere thought of a glass bauble makes his stomach turn.

'You left the door open again and let all the warm out,' he says to Lil, as she comes back through with the box.

'Oh, sorry. Didn't think. I'm too excited! There are some silver pinecones in here.'

'Yeah. *Triffic.*'

'They're a bit musty, mind,' she says, blowing off the dust. 'But look what else I found—'

Preparing himself to be decidedly underwhelmed, he watches as she pulls a dartboard from the side of the box. 'Oh, goody,' he says, throwing down another log.

'But I could only find one dart,' says Lil, rummaging through the box.

'I guess the tournament's off then? What a shame.'

'No. We'll just have to share it, that's all.'

'We? As in you and me? I take it Welby's sitting this one out. Let's ask him, shall we?' Danny says, tapping the snooker table with the fire poker. Welby moans like a drain. 'I think that was a no. And anyway, what about my albatross?'

'What about it?'

'I'm not having you sticking her with that dart.'

'*Her?*'

'And besides, we don't have an oche. You can't play darts without an oche.'

'A what?'

'The line you stand behind when you throw,' says Danny, marking an imaginary line with his poker.

'A line?'

'Oh, it doesn't matter. There ain't enough room, alright? With all this bloody carpet lying about, we'll break our bloody necks.'

'There is if we push the sofa back—'

'Just leave it Lil.'

'Oh, lighten up. It's Christmas Eve.'

'Lighten up? What, with Welby smacked out of his head behind there?'

Lil sticks the dart into a roll of carpet leaning by the radiator. 'I'm trying to have fun, that's all. We've got to do something. We can't just sit here and—'

'Why not? Who says we have to do anything? It's just another day.'

'How about I make us a dinner. A proper, traditional Christmas dinner. With all the trimmings. Turkey with stuffing. Cranberry sauce. Yorkshire puds. Pigs in blankets! Stuffing, plenty of stuffing. Parsnips. Peas…'

'You'll be hard pressed finding all that lot this time on Christmas Eve. The shops shut in an hour,' he says, plucking the dart from the carpet roll. 'I'm going to bed.'

'Mince pies. You like a mince pie, don't you, Welbs? Welby? *Welby*!'

~

'You hardly touched my dinner,' says Lil, draping a piece of red tinsel around the albatross' neck.

'Take it off,' says Danny, looking on disapprovingly from the bar.

Amy Winehouse's *Back to Black* rolls on repeat for the second time. 'Oh, not this again. Put Boney M back on.'

'No. I like it.' *It's full of regret and wallowing, perfect on a day like this.*

'You never even tried my red wine gravy. I spent ages on that. Followed a recipe and everything,' sulks Lil, confused. 'You could have at least tried it. Even Welbs tried it.'

'What – *Turkey Twizzlers*?'

'Well, I had to improvise, didn't I. There wasn't much on the shelves.'

'Well, I did say…'

Defiantly, Lil continues to dress the seabird.

'Take it off.'

'What?' Lil shakes the end of the tinsel. 'This? Why? It's shiny. It's festive. A little Christmas boa. It suits him.'

'*Her*.'

Danny marches over, whisks it from her hand, and throws it in the fire. The tinsel sizzles and disintegrates into nothingness. She looks up at Danny, a pitiful expression on her face.

'Look, I'm sorry, okay? Christmas just isn't my favourite time of year, that's all. I'm going for a lie down.'

'What? On Christmas Day?'

'Lil, I'm tired.'

'Alright, grandad!' yells Lil as he rustles up the stairs.

But heavy footsteps soon return, and he bursts back in. 'What did you just say about my grandad?'

'You what? I didn't say anything.'

'Don't you *ever* mention him again. You hear me?'

'Merry Christmas!' she shouts, waiting for his bedroom door to slam. It does.

~

'Welby!'

It's almost noon when Danny is jolted awake by Lil, screaming Welby's name.

'You're fucked now, aren't you. Proper *fucked*,' she rages, with menacing zeal, and although Danny's in no mood for a show down, he puts on his puffer jacket and goes down to investigate.

Slurring, her words thick with alcohol, Danny hears her ramble something about Welby's leg behind the door, though he can't quite make it out. Then, a strange smell hits him – chemical, like burning rubber.

Too strong to ignore, he kicks the door open, the sting of acrid smoke hitting his eyes.

'Fucking hell!' he wails, swatting the suffocating fumes away with the nearest pizza box. 'What the fuck's going on? What the fuck you got burning in the fireplace?'

Swivelling on the bar stool, Lil cackles watching Welby retract his head inside the neck of his jumper like a tortoise.

Rushing through to the kitchen, shielding his air-ways with the pizza box, Danny fills the washing-up bowl with water. 'Jesus Christ,' he says, dousing the flames and only intensifying the smell.

'What the fuck is burning? Say something one of you!'

'It's my leg,' sputters Welby, his voice muffled by his jumper. 'The stupid cow threw it in the fire.'

'Your leg?' coughs Danny, his eyes drawn to Welby, where he can just make out, through the smoke, a fleshy stump below his knee. Glancing back at the fire, Danny now sees what looks like a prosthetic leg. Covering his mouth, he approaches, prodding it with the fire poker. The toes have melted away. 'You've only got one leg? She threw your prosthetic leg in the fire?'

Danny steps back, his mind struggling to process.

'You threw his fucking leg in the fire?' he says, looking at Lil, now slumped over the bar. 'Why did you do that? What the hell is wrong with you? The whole place could have gone up! I can't believe this.'

Danny collapses on the sofa.

'This is – this is too much. All this time? All this time you've only had one leg? How's he going to walk, Lil?'

'Walk?' Lil's head lifts a couple of inches from the bar top. 'I picked up his gear for him again last night – *lazy git*,' Lil slurs.

'And just look at my bird. Look what you've done to her.' The albatross is charred black. 'Look what you've done!'

'She don't care, matey,' says Welby, dragged back down by his weight as he struggles to get up. 'She'll pass out any second anyway – *lightweight*.'

'So, how did you – you know…' says Danny, helping him up on to the sofa, and looking down at Welby's stump. Welby gives it a little waggle.

'A dirty hit. Got infected. Had to be amputated.'

Free to move, the little fellas sympathetically jerk

beneath Danny's coat. At night, he removes the tape, otherwise he can't sleep on his back.

'Injected into my ankle, didn't I. The gear must have been cut with glass or something – God knows what – but it wasn't long before the gangrene set in.'

Danny's never heard Welby speak at such length, and much like the *Ancient Mariner* captivating the Wedding-Guest, he finds himself compelled to listen.

'You should have seen it – abscesses everywhere. Next thing I know, I'm waking up in intensive care with a blown capillary and an ulcer the size of a bloody mango.'

'And all this, from a "dirty hit"?' says Danny. A "dirty hit" – one in each arm – followed by a double amputation. Danny wonders if Welby still has the dealer's number.

'That's right, all from this dirty hit – and then, *bang*!' Welby punctuates his words with a sharp smack on the sofa arm, making Danny jolt.

'What?' says Danny. 'You got shot?'

'No. Then the mango burst. Bloody hell, the pain.'

Danny lights two cigarettes: one for Welby, one for himself, and they ash onto the floor.

'What about the gangrene. What was that like?

'Fucking awful. The stink! Foul-smelling. Discharge. Pain. Pus. Thought I was dying, matey. Went into septic shock a couple of times.'

'Fucking hell. What about the amputation. Did it hurt?'

'Nah. Didn't feel a thing. Had some phantom limb pain afterwards, though, like, and my stitches got infected. But I'd take that over the pain of going cold turkey any day of the week. That's what's coming next – cold turkey. I'm not going anywhere without me leg. Stuck here like a pudding. Can I cadge another ciggie?'

Danny lights him another. Shakily, Welby takes it from him.

'I miss it, you know, my leg. Took it for granted. Had this big dragon tattoo on my calf. Designed it myself.'

Welby stops talking and flicks his rapidly smoked cigarette onto his smouldering prosthetic.

'Still,' he resumes. 'Could be worse. Could've been me arm. Or both arms. Can you imagine that?'

'Yeah,' says Danny. 'Yeah, I can.'

CHAPTER 19

Danny's bidding on a leg for Welby: an *OttoBock Pro-Flex* above knee bionic prosthesis with foot. He's been two days without one now, and Lil and Welby's arguing has gone nuclear.

It's high time they left. Danny wants them out. He's supported them for far too long, and if Lil's new trainers and the wad of cash he saw her stuff into her bra tonight are anything to go by, her freeloading is taking the piss.

The safe code buzzes through on the intercom while Danny and Welby sit by the fire watching *The Weakest Link*. Earlier, Danny cleared the leg out of the crate while Lil hovered, helping herself to his cigarettes and sneering. Sense urges him to listen to the buzzer a little longer before answering – though from the abstract rhythm, he already knows who it is.

'Get that for us, Welbs,' he jokes. Welby doesn't crack a smile. With a reluctant sigh, Danny heads to the door.

'Here—' Lil storms in, all elbows and teeth, tossing a small baggie of white powder heroin down at Welby. Cornered in his snooker cave, he looks at it, then at her. 'Go on, then. Take it. You was begging me for it this morning.'

Bum-shuffling towards the baggie, Welby brushes it with his fingertips. It's just out of reach. Lil falls back on the sofa with a self-satisfied smirk, pulling a bag of *Cheetos* from her handbag and munching on them like popcorn. She watches as Welby grunts and stretches for the bag. Just as he's about to grab it, she kicks it towards the door, throws her head back, and laughs, radioactive orange cheese puffs clinging to her gums.

'*Cheetos*?' says Danny, observing the cruel scene from the bar. 'Where d'you get them?' The old-skool snack is one of Danny's favourites.

As Welby begins to drag himself towards the door,

Danny notices the relish painted across Lil's face. 'Oh, just give it to him, will you?' he snaps.

'No,' she says, wiping her cheesy fingers on the sofa and digging out the remote control wedged between the seat cushions. 'You give it him if you're so bothered – *bloody junkie.*'

While Lil flicks through the channels, Danny strides over and snatches it from her.

'Oi! Give that back.'

'Wash your hands if you want to use my remote. Getting your cheesy fingers all over it.' Wiping the buttons with a cloth, he resumes his seat at the bar. 'And besides, we were watching that, weren't we, Welbs?'

Acknowledging Danny with a grunt, Welby continues to shuffle and drag his arse as Danny flicks back to their gameshow.

'Alright,' Lil says, exaggeratedly licking her fingers like a giant cat before wiping them on the sofa again. 'Keep your hair on, *baldie.*'

Watching her from the corner of his eye, Danny refuses to bite.

Reaching the finish line, Welby grabs the bag. Lil throws a *Cheeto* at his head to mark his victory, which he picks up and eats, too fixated on the bag for Lil's cruelty to register. It's a sorry sight.

But not as sorry as Danny's beloved albatross. Its once brilliant white plumage is now a carcinogenic grey, like wet asphalt. Its creamy yellow beak was black this morning, until he gave it a spit and polish.

Danny goes over to give it another buff.

'*You are the weakest link. Goodbye,*' says Lil, as Danny rustles behind the snooker table, perfectly in sync with another disgraced contestant being ejected from the show and forced to do the walk of shame. But again, he isn't lured. He ignores her and instead watches as the *Mariner* searches for a vein, recalling their conversation from the other night.

The gameshow ends in silence, and as Danny heads back upstairs to check on his leg bid, Lil lobs a *Cheeto* at the back of his head and misses. Oblivious, he leaves the room.

Approaching the stairwell, Danny spots a letter in the post-basket. Sifting it out from the stack of takeaway flyers he can already see that it's another reminder. It's time Lil started paying something towards the bills.

'It's only fair,' he says, eyeing her brand-new fluorescent trainers. 'You're obviously earning.' She pulls forty-quid from her bra, and they say no more about it.

By the time Danny reaches his room, Lil and Welby are at each other's throats again. Maybe his demand for cash triggered something – he can't tell, and he doesn't want to. The sooner Welby gets another leg, the better.

Trying to block out their argument drifting up the stairs, he checks the *OttoBock Pro-Flex*. He has a good feeling about this – after all, how many people bid on things like this?

A remarkable number, from the looks of things. Turns out bionic legs can fetch a pretty penny. Danny's been outbid. It went for nearly two-and-a-half grand in the end.

The yelling cranks up a notch. Danny's heart sinks. Will they ever leave?

Trying a different approach, he starts an internet search for prosthetic legs. "Prosthetics." "Prostheses."

'Osseointegration limb replacement?' How can finding a prosthetic leg be this complicated? Determined he'll get somewhere soon, he presses on.

'One-to-one visits. In-person custom fittings. Lower-limb prosthetics. Joint and foot components. Orthopaedic sockets and axials. Residual limb interfaces and their therapeutic benefits.' Lying back on his bed, he keeps scrolling. 'Intrinsic stump pain and what it feels like to wear too few ply socks – or too many? Lower-limb donation, limb transplantation. Hand and upper-limb

209

transplant services...'

But then, things get interesting.

A news story about an amputee named Sital – a smiling young woman with somebody else's arms successfully transplanted onto her. Danny is immediately drawn to her picture.

There's a noticeable difference in skin tone, and the donor's arms and hands are too large for Sital's frame. The fingernails are painted pink, and a gold bracelet dangles low on one wrist. Zooming in on the article, Danny tunes out the distant battle cry from downstairs.

"*He was a tall man with long, spindly fingers,*" Sital's mother is reported to have said about the donor. Sital now has the hands and arms of a man, and she doesn't mind at all. In fact, she's overjoyed with the result.

'Daniel!'

With jutting jaw, Danny opens his room door. 'What?' he calls down over the banister.

'Welby needs the toilet!'

'What, again? Can't you take him this time? Surely it's your turn? I'm in the middle of something up here!'

'He wants you – not me.'

'Right. That's it.'

Just when things couldn't get any more ridiculous, Danny marches downstairs, ready to escort a one-legged heroin addict to the toilet.

'It really is like having a couple of toddlers,' he mutters, bursting in the room. 'Honestly.' Since the fire, Danny's seriously considered installing baby monitors just for peace of mind. 'Come on, matey,' he says, pulling Welby up from the floor.

The toilet flushes.

'Finished,' calls Welby from inside the cubicle, Danny's cue to help him back out.

'Anything else I can do for you, sir?' says Danny, guiding Welby back through to the front room. 'A foot massage? A soothing lullaby, perhaps? A finger puppet show? Or a game of bloody peek-a-boo?'

'Welby, your flies are undone.' Lil says, sprawled on the sofa, tossing *Cheetos* into her mouth. 'His flies are undone. Here, watch this,' says Lil, preparing for another toss. 'I'm on number nine already.'

'Can't you see I'm busy,' Danny snaps, struggling with the rusty zipper. 'Jesus, how old are these jeans?'

'Fancy a quick game?'

'Maybe later, Lil. Got more important things to be doing right now.'

As Danny heads towards the door, Lil launches another *Cheeto* at the back of his head. This time, it lands, nestling itself into the neck of his puffer coat. Danny feels it, then shuts the door behind him with a sharp thud.

'Ten!' Lil shouts.

Dislodging the *Cheeto* from his neck, Danny eats it with a loud crunch behind the door for Lil's benefit.

Indian families, for cultural reasons, are often reluctant for the hands of loved ones to be donated after death. That's what makes finding a donor the greatest challenge – more so than the advanced surgery itself. And Sital had been waiting so long for a perfect match that, in the end, she didn't care whether the hands matched her skin tone, gender, or age. Any hands would do. And when a match was finally found, she saw them as a gift from God.

At first, Sital's new hands underwent a lot of changes – something to do with melanin stimulation in the skin and the lack of testosterone. But in time, they became less hairy, slimmer, and the skin lightened in tone, gradually matching her own.

After removing his puffer coat, Danny peels this morning's gaffer tape from his wrists.

It's time he confronted them.

Even in their unloved, unkempt, tattooed state, Danny thinks his arms and hands are a far better match for her than the ones she ended up with. Picking at the dirt beneath his fingernails, he notices the cigarette burn he gave himself – right in the middle of his "MUM" tattoo, just before Christmas – is healing nicely.

According to Dr. Agarwal, the lead surgeon who masterminded Sital's transplant, the entire procedure took thirteen hours and involved a team of twenty.

Boney M suddenly blasts from the jukebox.

'Boney *fucking* M.'

Yet again, Danny finds himself out on the landing. 'Turn it down! Please?'

The volume decreases slightly.

Apparently, the ideal donor for an amputee is a living one – a "live-to-live transplant," they call it. But due to ethical constraints, this has only ever been performed once, in Vietnam. The live donor had been crushed in a factory accident. His arm became gangrenous and had to be amputated to save his life. Luckily, the hand was uninjured and ended up being the perfect match for another man, whose hand had been lost in a truck collision.

Being a live doner would be a lot easier than injecting a dirty hit. Besides, he knows he's too squeamish for all that gangrene and ulcer stuff. Danny doubts he'll ever eat another mango again.

It seems that people all over the world are crying out for limb donors.

Looking down at his little arms, Danny is shocked by the state they're in – so stiff and weakened, they're almost cadaverous. The lack of movement, the cigarette burns, the cuts, the bruises. They're in no shape to be considered a suitable donor for anyone.

'*Twenty-two – twenty-three…*'

Fifty push-ups used to be a breeze – he'd finish in no time and spring back up, ready for squat lunges. Yet here he is, gasping for breath, barely halfway through. Giving up, he collapses back onto his bed.

Boney M has stopped and things have been eerily quiet

for a while. Worried it's the calm before the storm, Danny heads downstairs to check on them.

'Lil? Welby?'

They've gone.

'They've gone. They've fucking gone.' How Welby managed to walk out the door, Danny doesn't know. They never go anywhere together. 'Lil? Welby?' It's too good to be true. 'They've gone.'

Setting himself up at the bar, Danny continues his research by the warmth of the fire. A few minutes later, he helps himself to one of Lil's avocados seeing that she's gone, and then scours the internet for email addresses, names, university boards, and hospitals – anything he can find. Charities, donor selection trusts. He's knows he's going to have to cast his net wide to get noticed.

But what if nobody wants the hands and arms of someone like Danny Finch? The hands of a sexual predator. A violent druggie. A raving looney. Would Sital have minded?

The intercom blasts out a beat-deaf attempt at the safe code, making him jump and knock the avocado stone off his plate before it rolls to the floor. 'Lil.' He knew it was too good to be true. Unable to see where the avocado stone rolled, he leaves it and goes to the door.

'Ah – Oh, how I've missed you,' exclaims Danny, spotting Lil's finger lingering on the buzzer. He glances down. 'Welby?'

'Move out the way, then. Let him through,' says Lil, wheeling Welby through to the front room.

'How did you... Where did you get that?'

'I remembered this matey of mine, who got some crutches from a charity shop once, so I thought I'd hop down the high street and see what I could find. Turns out, they was giving this away behind *Scope*. It'd only end up in landfill otherwise, the lady said.'

Wheeling himself over to the sofa, Welby cracks open a

can of full-strength cider.

'Yeah, Welbs is well chuffed with it, ain't you, my soldier.' Lil plants a wet one on Welby's cheek and drapes herself over him. 'My brave little soldier.'

'You've made up, I see? How long's it gonna last this time – five minutes? Maybe ten? When's the wedding? Shall I get a hat?'

'Shut up,' says Lil. 'You're only jealous.'

'Fancy a can?' offers Welby.

'Err, no thanks,' says Danny, gathering up his research material from the bar. 'You're alright. I was just going back upstairs anyway.'

As Danny leaves the room, his foot knocks the avocado stone, sending it rolling across the floor until it comes to rest beside Lil's bag. She glances down.

'Oi, have you eaten my avocado?'

'Leave it, Lil,' says Welby, keeping the peace.

'*Shut up*, Welby. That was *my* avocado.'

'Like you were gonna eat it anyway. You had crisps for dinner last night,' he adds.

Danny's footsteps retreat quickly up the stairs, and by the time he reaches his room, the wedding's already off.

It seems that even a homeless, one-legged heroin addict is more capable than Danny – a man with two legs and four arms. A homeless, one-legged squatter, who can fix boilers, design dragon tattoos – and get the girl. A wheelchair, of *course*. Why couldn't Danny have thought of that?

Refusing to let Welby's resourcefulness get the better of him, Danny decides to match his resolve.

Just as Danny's ready to hit send on his live-to-live donor application, he spots a text box prompting him to attach pictures – at least five: side angles, front and back views, close-ups, shoulders, fingernails. His little fellas aren't exactly what you'd call photo-ready, so he saves his progress and heads for a shower.

Scrubbing and clipping his nails, Boney M blasts back

up the stairs at full volume – Lil's petty vengeance for the avocado.

'You'll have to do better than that, love,' he mutters to his reflection in the steamed-up mirror. Truth is, he's always rather liked Boney M. If she really wanted to wind him up, she should have put Elton John back on.

Stripped down to his vest, he sways to the driving beat, bathroom door propped open to let the condensation escape. The extractor fan's in even worse shape than the intercom.

Avocado stone clenched tightly in her fist, Lil creeps up the stairs, a neat pile of nail clippings accumulating on top of the toilet cistern. Pausing halfway up the top floor staircase, she watches Danny, his nails flying in all directions, his four jagged elbows moving to the music.

Are her eyes playing tricks on her? Gripping the banister, she lowers herself and peers through the stair spindles. Illusion or reality? Widening her eyes, the line blurs, leaving her unsure. Creeping up on the top step, she calls his name, but the music drowns her out.

If the mirror weren't so fogged up, he'd see her reflection, hand pressed tightly over her mouth. He doesn't hear her sharp gasp, nor the sound of the avocado slipping from her grasp and tumbling down the exposed wooden steps, each bounce swallowed by the music.

Knocked for six, Lil races down the stairs, her feet barely grazing the steps. Bursting into the front room, she snatches the needle from Welby's hand. 'Come on, Welby. We're leaving,' she commands, her eyes blazing.

'What you doing? Give me that—'

'We're getting out of here *now*.' Lil says, bagging up Welby's drug trappings as fast as her trembling hands will allow.

'Lil? You're shaking.'

'I said, let's *go*,' she says, wheeling him out from behind the snooker table.

'Why? It's nice here.'

'Believe me, it isn't.'

'What? What's happened?'

'You wouldn't believe me if I told you. Now quick, *before he comes down.*'

'Oh, Lil, come on. I know he's a bit of a miserable fucker, but we've stayed with far worse. Surely we can—'

'No,' she snaps through gritted teeth. 'We should never have come here.' She clutches her chest. It's gone tight.

'Lil, you alright?'

'Do I look alright?' she screams over the booming beat of Boney M.

'All this over an avocado. Here – you haven't killed him, have you? Knocked him out with that stone? He ain't... dead, is he?'

'Of *course* not! Now get your stuff together!'

'Well, gimme that needle back then.' Welby reaches for his carrier bag. Lil dangles it like a carrot, and he wheels towards it, looking back at his snooker den, knowing it's the last time he'll ever see it.

'Lil, you gonna tell me what's happened?'

'I'll tell you on the way,' she says, wheeling him towards the door.

The thud of the front door echoes through the walls. Danny stops clipping, throws on his puffer coat, and heads downstairs.

The doormat halts the avocado stone's trajectory. He picks it up, steps into the front room to turn off the jukebox and hears Lil and Welby arguing in the distance. Welby's foils and detritus have been cleared from his drug den. Lifting the bin liner curtain, he spots them, their belongings hanging off Welby's wheelchair. Lil stops under a streetlight to light one of Danny's cigarettes.

Pressing the bin liner back into place, Danny rolls the avocado stone between his fingers. He'd have eaten it a lot sooner if he'd known it would have had such an impact.

CHAPTER 20

The rag-and-bone man took the snooker table away three months ago – the same day Danny submitted his donor application. He's heard nothing back and doubts he ever will. Still, it was a nice dream while it lasted, as delusional as it was.

The job at the postal sorting office that he applied to two weeks never bothered getting back to him either. Is a polite rejection really too much to ask? Just a quick call to say they won't be taking him forward, or that they'll keep him on file – hardly chasing rainbows. If he had the guts, he'd call the bakery, see if Gerry might take him back. He might have to if another opportunity doesn't present itself soon. That shoebox of fifties won't last forever.

But things are looking up in other ways. Danny's no longer "sailing at half-mast," and he "shook hands with the milkman" for the first time in months this morning. The spring weather has helped – he's up with the lark these days, doing his floor exercises in the garden, and sipping green tea with a slice of lemon like some born-again yogi.

Danny's phone rings.

'Maybe, just maybe...' The sorting office.

With eight fingers crossed, he takes the call.

'Hello?'

'Hello. Am I speaking with a Mr. Finch?' asks a calm and authoritative voice.

'Sp... speaking.' *Just give me a trial, man, and you'll see what a whizz I can be. Hand-sorting the mail like—*

'No need to be nervous, Mr. Finch. This is Dr. Dupree from the Donor and Transplant Department at St. Barts. I'm calling regarding your application – and I'm pleased to say the news is good. Your test results look extremely promising, and we believe we may have found the perfect match.'

A surreal hush settles over the scene.

'Mr. Finch?'

'Sss... sorry. Really? *Really*? I don't... I don't... *really*? My identity hasn't put people off?'

'No, no, Mr. Finch. Without arms and hands, these people are unable to work, feed their families, or have any quality of life at all. You could be a genocidal maniac, and it wouldn't make the slightest bit of difference to the majority of recipients on our books.'

'Oh – good?'

'Good *indeed*. But I'm afraid the operation carries significant risks.'

'Oh?'

'Yes, even when a perfect match *is* found, there's always a chance of post-amputation infection, which could lead to sepsis, or even death during the operation itself. But I wouldn't worry about that now.'

'Oh,' says Danny, recalling a particularly vivid nightmare from last week. 'Right.'

Deadened and blue, he saw them laid out on a bed of ice, ready to be discarded onto a heap of decaying organs and body parts by a man in a white coat. The operation had been unsuccessful. The little fellas had been rejected. 'Where are you taking them?' Danny screamed, only to be told by a faceless man in white that they were to be incinerated immediately.

'Mr. Finch? Are you there?'

'Yes.' Hanging on by a thread. 'Please, go on.'

'If you'd like to proceed to the next stage, we'd be happy to invite you in this afternoon at three o'clock to run some tests, further analysis, and check you over.'

'To*day*?'

'It's essential that we get the ball rolling as soon as possible. Timing with a procedure of such magnitude is critical. Unless, of course, you'd prefer us to withdraw your application? We can always—keep you on file.'

'No, no. I'll be there. Three o'clock. I'll be there.'

~

'Just a little higher for me, Mr. Finch. *That's* it.'

Dupree lets go of Danny's left little fella. 'Lovely stuff. Now, just pop yourself back behind that curtain, and one of the nurses will be with you shortly.'

The curtain is drawn back, catching Danny off guard. He was just drifting off.

'Close the door behind you, would you, Forbes?'

'What's all… What's all this about?' asks Danny, watching as Dupree enters, followed by a team of nurses and endocrine specialists.

'Mr. Finch. I'm afraid there's been an unexpected turn of events. We're keeping you in overnight.'

'Overnight? Why? What's happening?'

'It seems you have an imbalance.'

'An imbalance? But I excelled on the balance test. You said so yourself – didn't wobble an inch.' Two nurses begin placing electrodes on Danny's hairy torso. 'You said my dynamic gait index was quite something. Over two minutes I held that last position for—'

'Mr. Finch, do you have a history of steroid abuse?' Dupree looks down at his clipboard.

'Steroids? Roids? Me? No. No way.'

'Testosterone injections, that sort of thing?'

'Tost – tostesterone? You havin' a laugh?'

'If you wish to be a successful donor, I'm afraid your integrity is paramount. Full disclosure is essential if we are to proceed.'

'You calling me a liar?'

'It's just that we usually only find such levels in gym-addicts, bodybuilders, power athletes, fitness fanatics,' says Dupree, clutching the clip board with a knowing smile. 'Such levels suggest someone who may have injected in the past few months.'

Scrutinising faces surround him. Danny shifts his gaze

219

towards the window.

'Come, come now. Don't be shy. There's no stigma these days. Have you injected anything at all? You can tell us.'

'Well, I – I was having these… I mean, I was given these, these vitamin injections. B-shots, I think they're called, or something.'

'Or… something?'

'He told me I was B-12 deficient.'

'He?'

'The doctor. He said I needed 'em. All the stars take 'em, Guy said.'

'Guy?'

'Yeah, Guy – my personal trainer.'

'I see. And you rapidly began gaining muscle after taking these – "vitamin injections"?'

Danny exhibits all the hallmarks of someone who has dabbled with "vitamin injections" – the acne, tissue swelling around the nipples, changes in libido, headaches, anxiety, hair loss.

Unable to shake the image of Guy's minty gum-chewing face from his mind, Danny gets the awful feeling he's been duped. 'I should have known something was up,' he says, glancing down at his groin. 'Or down.'

'We'd like to keep you in a little longer.'

'How long?'

'Just until your normal, healthy hormone levels are restored. We'd like to begin an intense course of hormone replacement therapy. You'll start feeling more alert, motivated, energetic. The treatment includes a series of tablets which mimic the luteinising hormone, followed by derma gel and patches under the skin. We will then closely monitor your LH receptors in the brain and keep an eye on any signs of primary, secondary, and tertiary hypogandism…'

'Vitamin injections. That's what they told me they were.'

'You'll be perfectly safe in our hands. Now, if you could stand please. We'd like to take some more hand span measurements. Turn around Mr. Finch. That's it, all the way around. Now, spread your fingers as wide as they will go. A little more… Lovely stuff. Keep your feet wide apart, and aaarms *up*…'

Prodded and pulled, arms up, arms down. It's like being back in wardrobe, trying on that hideous collection of sleeveless leather jackets.

'How much longer' – Danny yawns, 'do I have to hold my arms out like this?'

'Oh, nearly done. Out to the sides. That's it, like a bird. Stretch them *riiight* out for me – as far as they will go.'

Like a bird, like an albatross, sleeping on the wing, Danny locks his arms and surrenders to yet another stranger in a white coat.

CHAPTER 21

The aerial sunset view from the Boeing 777 window is spectacular. Fluffy, mountainous clouds, ablaze as the sun's rays slice through like the fingers of God.

But unable to handle the light exposure, as beautiful as it is, Danny pulls down the window blind and reclines in his first-class seat – a luxury afforded gifted by the generosity of a wealthy Indian family.

'May I tempt you with a little more from the cheese board, sir?'

'Seconds?' says Danny, turning his attention to the cheese board, apricot and violet sunset hues still simmering behind his eyelids. 'What's that runny one there?'

'That's the Normandy Camembert, sir.'

'Ah, the Normandy camembert,' says the gentleman seated over the aisle, lowering his newspaper to glance over approvingly. 'An excellent choice. Such heavenly, sweet notes, and that *divine*, buttery texture.' He inhales through his nose as Danny slathers a thick, creamy slab of camembert over the remnants of his truffled brioche – the last thing that will pass his lips before tomorrow's surgery.

The last time Danny dared to eat such a pungent cheese on public transport, the uproar was so relentless that a guard had to move him to another carriage. But then again, that wasn't first-class. Up here, it seems, they can't get enough of it.

'Such pungency, such depth. Divine, *divine*,' the gentleman says, lifting his newspaper back up.

Once Danny's hormone levels were restored, things moved quickly. A twenty-two-year-old man named Surinder, who suffered a severe upper-limb crush two years ago, is set to become the new owner of Danny's arms.

Donor: 4726 is all that Surinder and his family know

222

him as. Not "that bloke from the scratch card adverts" or the "drug addled, sexual marauder who made women paralysed with fear," as one headline proclaimed. And that's exactly how Danny wants it – anonymous.

It's for Surinder's own good. Knowing the truth would only give him nightmares. Hasn't the man suffered enough?

But Danny can know anything and everything about Surinder and his family, who have provided him with a robust, gloss-laminated information pack, which he's looking forward to reading after his second cheese course.

It was a plane crash. Surinder was lucky to have survived. The overhead lockers folded in on themselves, crashing down and squeezing him like a sandwich toaster. So severe were his injuries that he was assigned a mangled extremity severity score (MESS) of nine.

The Air India Boeing 777 drops. The butter knife falls from the side tray table, and things gets bumpy. Danny feels the strain against his seatbelt, which he's had fastened since take off.

'Ladies and gentlemen, we're experiencing some light turbulence,' the captain announces. The little fellas tense up beneath their first-class snuggle blanket. 'Please return to your seats and fasten your seatbelts.'

Danny looks up at the overhead locker, then over to the *Connoisseur de Fromage*, who has assumed the brace position, his giant pink newspaper over his head.

The erratic atmospheric change passes, and the comforting low-pitched hum is restored inside the cabin. *Mr. Cheese* coughs gruffly, snaps his newspaper back up, and garbles something about the dollar index, while Danny steadies his finger and resumes his reading place.

All limb salvage attempts failed. In the end, emergency amputation was Surinder's last chance.

Overindulgence in the cheese board has taken its toll. Danny pulls his curtain across and settles in for a doze.

Due to a tailwind over the Persian Gulf, the turbulent flight AI8152 lands early. The little fellas tuck themselves in behind Danny's rucksack and is swiftly escorted to a taxi, bound for the Amrita Institute – the very same place Sital's surgery was performed.

Family photos of the driver's family, along with a lifetime of collected trinkets, smother the dashboard.

'Is that the Crazy Frog?' asks Danny, recognising the Swedish CGI-animated amphibian dangling on a keyring and swinging from the rearview mirror. 'Is he blue? I never noticed he was blue.'

'Yes, blue.'

It's funny what the mind focuses on before undergoing life-changing surgery.

'*De ding, ding, ding, ding, ding, ding, ding. De ding, ding, ding, ding, ding, ding, ding...*' goes the driver.

'*A ring-ding, ding, ding, ding, a ring, ring, ring...*' follows Danny.

Gowned up on a gurney, Danny is wheeled into theatre, holding onto a small, gold-rimmed card featuring a picture of a four-armed Indian god, with an inscription on the reverse: "*Vishnu – the Hindu god of protection – the preserver.*"

'I'm afraid you can't take that with you,' says the female nurse, parking the gurney and prising the card from Danny's hand.

'But it's from Surinder. He asked one of the hospital staff to pass it on to me. For good luck.'

The nurse pins it to the wall opposite Danny, and he relaxes.

A formidable-looking man walks past the rectangular window to Danny's right. It's Sital's surgeon. Danny recognises his face from the picture in the paper – smooth and round, although now a little plumper.

'Where's Surinder?' asks Danny, sitting up on the gurney as soon as Dr. Agarwal walks in. 'Is he already in theatre? Is he next door?'

'No, no. Stop that now,' says the doctor, wagging his finger and smiling as he comes behind Danny's surgical-capped head. 'I want you to focus on your breath.' A machine on Danny's left pulses a slow, staccato beep. 'Please, try to relax. Try to *Relax*.' The doctor massages Danny's temples while a man in scrubs unravels two transparent tubes at the back of the room.

A latex gloved hand presses on Danny's rising chest. Another machine beeps: four beeps then two rests – four beeps, two rests – *1, 2, 3, 4 - - 1, 2, 3, 4* – while Danny is hooked up to electrodes. The anaesthesia syringe driver is inserted into his hand, and he looks ahead at Vishnu until his eyes begin to feel heavy and everything slows. Echoey, dreamy voices speaking an unfamiliar language meld into one, and the room, along with Vishnu, disappears.

'*10...9...8...7...6...5...4...3...2...1*...Danny?   Can you hear me, Danny?'

Paralysis is preventing him from responding. His face is set like stone. He can hear him, along with the infernal beeping of machines. A contraption covers his airways, and a tube is fed down his throat. His body is limp. His eyelids don't flicker. His heartbeat slows, and he sinks deeper.

'Skalpel dayavayi.' It's Dr. Agarwal's voice. 'Skalpel dayavayi,' he repeats, and Danny is lucidly reminded of the time when the dentist didn't administer enough novocaine. A particularly painful experience where he ended up begging for more. But it will kick in soon enough, Danny is sure. The great doctor who masterminded Sital's success wouldn't make a mistake like that.

Then why can he hear fluid whooshing through his veins? He tries to speak, bang his foot against the gurney, anything to get someone's attention, but the room seems oblivious to his implorations for mercy.

After a quick polish of the scalpel, Dr. Agarwal goes in with the first incision. The sharp stab of cold steel slices through his left little armpit, and he feels every stretch, hears it – the microscopic separation of tissue and sinew, every drag. A flap of skin falls to one side, and a hook-like instrument is inserted. The infernal machines start to race. Danny wills his body to thrash and writhe, but it remains cemented to the gurney.

Every nerve, every fibre vibrates with liquid fire at each cut, until Danny is no longer human.

Finally, an anaesthesiologist adjusts Danny's IV, and his veins flush with fluid. The beat of his heart slows a little more. The pain is dulled, but he's still conscious.

Everyone claps as his left little fella is raised in the air, placed on a tray of ice, and immediately taken over to Surinder's side. Agarwal stitches Danny's shoulder – a mere tickle in comparison to the butchery he's just endured.

But there's no time for respite. A fresh incision is made on Danny's right side.

He can taste the shape of his heart. He can feel its sound. He's become sensation itself, trapped in a vacuum where only agony and eternal torment can exist. He doesn't want to be inside this *thing* anymore, this body, and he feels himself slipping away – going, going, going…

The anaesthetist team had undershot. They failed to account for the additional veins in Danny's extra arms. Anaesthesia awareness they call it. Danny was awake the whole time and is now at risk of post-operative blood clots.

They wheel him out to the emergency wing, and as stupefied and disorientated as he is, he wants answers.

'I'm afraid we know surprisingly little about how anaesthesia works. Even the world of science doesn't have all the answers. Think of it more as an art than an exact science, okay?'

'Okay?'

Dr. Agarwal's annoyingly round, plump face beams down at Danny.

'Okay?' he repeats, his tongue lolling out the side of his mouth, impeding his speech. Since surgery, he has been unable to put it back in. 'I'm gonna punch you,' he mumbles.

'There's no need to worry. We expect you to heal remarkably well,' says the smug, smiling orb. 'It's important that you get as much rest as you can.'

Lunging forward in a restless, disturbed fervour, Danny rasps, 'They've gone.'

'Your stitches – *please*, you must be careful,' Agarwal pushes him back down. 'You're not in your right mind.'

Danny takes a swing at him but misses, crying out in pain.

'You mustn't exert yourself – nurse!'

'Where are they?'

'*Nurse!*'

'What have you done with them?'

'Please. You must stay calm—'

'Couldn't wait to rip 'em off me, could you. Where are they? Give them back.'

Much like grieving a death, the permanence of their parting has yet to sink in.

'Where are they?'

'My arms. What have you done with them?' Another swing. Closer this time.

In time, he will adjust. And although the doctor assures him that his reaction is perfectly normal, the sudden loss is profound.

'Nurse! *Please!* Come quickly. Surgical wound dehiscence.'

Danny's stiches have burst.

CHAPTER 22

Staring down at the cream, padded wedding album on the low-level coffee table, Danny sits motionless and mute

'Aren't you going to open it?' asks Dr. LaPage, Danny's current psychiatrist, standing over by the window, gazing out across the carpark. She had been hoping to wrap up today's session early. The dinner reservation she made should have been for six people, not five, and Mama Rosa's isn't the kind of place that usually accommodates last-minute changes.

The rectangular clock above the door ticks loudly, filling the void.

'Well, why don't you take it home with you then, have a proper look, in private,' she says, sitting down in the lime sedan opposite him. 'You said you couldn't wait for it to arrive in our last session.'

Tick, tock. Void, void.

The Liebermanns will have to make their own way there. Why did she offer to pick them up? There was never enough time. If she does her makeup in the car and has that can of hairspray still in the glovebox, she'll manage – she touches her earlobes, and she stiffens. Her pearl earrings. They're not there. They were there after this morning's spin class. Or were they?

Tick, tock, tick, tock.

Edging forward on the faux suede couch, Danny tugs at an insert poking out from the top of the album.

LaPage's hands fall from her naked earlobes and she moves towards her desk. 'Well, that looks like a good place to start,' she says, opening a drawer in search of her earrings. 'Why don't you read it out,' she adds, closing the drawer rather brusquely, silently mourning their loss. Saltwater pearls. Akoya oysters. A present from her late aunt.

'Shall I read it? Read it out?'

At last, Danny speaks, his speech slow and laboured, as it has been ever since the amputation.

'Why not,' she says, conscious not to overdo the mock enthusiasm. 'Please. I'm all — ears.' She'll look dead without those pearls.

'Dear Donor: 4726. My brother, ever present in my heart, and always with me on the happiest day of my life. To you I will be eternally grateful. I owe you my life. Your brother, Surinder.' Danny flips the album over. 'Oh, look. It's old Vishnu again. Surinder must have stuck him on for me.'

'Good old Vishnu,' she says, checking her wrist for her Piaget watch. It's there, thank God. At least she didn't leave *that* in the gym. But time is pressing. She'd better call the Liebermanns first, and *then* the restaurant.

'The happy couple. Just look at 'em.'

Red and white confetti rains down on bride and groom, and over the wedding guests, strategically staggered on the marble staircase behind. Surinder is wearing a gold embroidered suit accompanied by a red silk scarf. The little fellas' hands shoot out from bright white cuffs.

Danny holds up the photo album for LaPage who tilts her head and flashes a sympathy smile, massaging her wrist, certain the watch strap wasn't this tight this morning. *Water retention*, she thinks, glancing at her wall calendar.

Danny brings the album closer to his eyes and sees a gold wedding band on Surinder's finger. A finger that spent many an hour exploring the caves of — *Mount Nostrilous*.

Another minute gone, LaPage re-crosses her shapely legs, and notices a ladder in her tights

'Is it *my* finger or *his* finger? Man — it's weird, you know. Looking at it, seeing it like this, like that,' says Danny, turning the album like a steering wheel.

'Well, Danny. I think you've made another

breakthrough today. I'd like to pick this up in next week's session,' she says, hastily stuffing the wedding album into a carrier bag for him, and looking over at her bureau, almost certain there's a spare pair of barely blacks hiding in there somewhere. 'Same time next week?'

The bus decants Danny at his stop and pulls away with a pneumatic *phhsst*, and with the rubber end of his walking stick pressed firmly against the wet pavement, he limps to the pharmacy.

It wasn't long after the transplant that Surinder decided to blindfold himself. He wanted to *feel* with his new hands and has shared every incremental development in his frequent letters to Donor: 4726. And he was off to a flying start – until his immunosuppressive drugs had to be changed. They weren't working, but eventually, he responded positively to the anti-rejection medication. This rejection was a mighty, personal blow to Danny, who spent the best part of a year believing that the little fellas were seeking revenge for having been given up. How else could the agony he sustained on that operating table be explained? It had to be the universe's way of telling him he was making a terrible mistake. Maybe even his Gramps decreed it.

That's when Danny hit rock bottom.

But it was nothing a high dose antipsychotic couldn't fix. In a matter of weeks, he was back to being the unfeeling, unthinking jelly that his therapists had all worked so hard on helping him become. And while Surinder was learning how to live with arms and hands all over again, Danny was unlearning what it had been like to have existed with those uncanny extremities – and let go.

At first, Danny wasn't sure he'd be able to do it, nor were the doctors. They even discussed the possibility of finding Danny a donor himself due to the chronic phantom limb sensations, and the overwhelming loss Danny was experiencing.

But he's done grieving now, made his peace. They visit

him in his dreams now and then, but in his waking life, he hardly thinks of them at all – a major milestone, the doctors tell him.

The shop doorbell sounds as Danny enters the pharmacy. A few people turn as he fumbles in his pocket for his prescription and joins the end of the queue. They've put him on so many things these past three years, he couldn't tell you what.

When Surinder's family found out what happened that day in theatre, they were mortified. Surinder suffered terribly with survivor guilt, even needing therapy himself for a while, but this was appeased by giving Danny the best recovery and treatment plan his family's riches could buy, as well securing him a modest bungalow.

The bungalow has been placed in a trust because Surinder is the legal owner. Danny doesn't care that it's not in his name. What difference does it make? It's an honour. Danny's just grateful to be a beneficiary, living out his days until one day, he dies peacefully in his sleep.

The pharmacist hands Danny the meds, which he has no intention of taking, and he heads home.

The kettle boils. Danny flicks through the wedding album. Surinder looks as though he was born with the things. The proportions are perfect. He says he even likes the tattoos – says they make him feel like he's rebelling against his privilege, embracing British subculture. But what does he make of the cigarette burns, the scars?

Surinder's next letter should be arriving in the next couple of days, a handwritten one with the aid of a special stencil this time, rather than typed up in his usual two finger "hunt and peck" style. In his last letter, he shared a memory of how his favourite schoolteacher used to praise him for his confident, flowing script.

Approaching his twenty-sixth year, Surinder is a well-read young man. Much of what he communicates in his letters goes way over Danny's head. The Romantic poets.

Dickens. Shakespeare. Danny could never stand all that at school. But Surinder's mad on them, and with Danny being English, he assumes that he must be equally enamoured, in the same way Danny thinks all Indians love Bollywood – Surinder doesn't.

"How splendid it must be in England, where people are so accustomed to such beauty," said Surinder in a recent letter. Danny prefers to stick to subjects he knows about, like koi carp, railway strikes, or the weather.

After knocking back his tea dregs, Danny pushes his prescription to the back of the plate cupboard, along with the rest of them. LaPage, of course, knows nothing about this, Danny having gotten his act down to a tee, knowing just what to say and what not to say. The nightmares, too, he doesn't mention them.

Or what happened on the forty-three bus the other week.

When he's off his meds, everything's heightened, likes he's living in widescreen technicolour and surround-sound. It's painful and raw, and he sometimes wakes up screaming in the middle of the night – a gauge that lets him know he's not dead, and there are rare joyous moments of beauty and wonderment too, rich with emotion. It makes all the darkness and unpredictable mood swings seem worthwhile.

But Danny's a ticking timebomb. There's no knowing when he'll blow. That's what happened on the bus – he blew.

It started before Danny had even sat down.

They were talking, this Indian couple sitting near the front. Triggered by their native tongue, Danny was transported back to the nightmare of the operating table, and he told them in no uncertain terms to "pack it in," to "shut up," at the top of his lungs, with his hands over his ears. They stopped immediately, bringing their shopping bags up on to their laps. But Danny just kept on at them, 'Speak English! Speak English!'

Now, Danny doesn't have a racist bone in his body, but that's not how it looked, especially to the driver, who was of Asian descent, or to the other passengers. A baby started crying, and the driver stopped the bus and called the depot for backup.

Danny's therapist can never know about this, nor Surinder.

They *can* know about the bumblebee he brought back to life with diluted sugar water on a teaspoon, though.

'Sucked it right up, he did, with his little… his little…'

'Proboscis?' said LaPage.

'Yeah. That's it, with his… *probiscus.*'

Danny wouldn't have been capable of such acts of kindness numbed out on his meds. He wouldn't have noticed the poor thing circling about on the floor, its waterlogged wings buzzing away in desperation. He would have stared straight through it.

Surinder was so touched by the story that his next correspondence was typed up on bright yellow paper, with a cartoon bumblebee design around the border of each page. Danny cried when he saw it – another thing that never happens when he's on his meds.

Tick – tock – tick – tock…

CHAPTER 23

'Pull your knickers up, make yourself decent, and give us your name—'

'Fuck off, I'm busy.'

The punter scarpers. The much younger and fitter officer runs after him.

'That's £30 you just cost me!'

'Again?' sighs Constable McCann, the remaining officer, turning away to give the familiar pavement princess some dignity while she pulls up her skinny jeans. 'Why are we doing this again, *hmm*? You know soliciting in a public place is against the law.'

''Coz I'm a thick bastard, aren't I.'

The officer takes a seat inside the bus shelter. 'Come on. Let's have a chat. Come on. Take a seat.'

Reluctantly, she steps out from behind the shelter. 'Oh, it's you,' she says, recognising him from last time. 'Soft touch.' As far as coppers go, he's a pretty decent guy and let her off last time – but will he again? 'Look, I'm not hurting anyone. What's the problem?'

'Oh, come on, Lil. You know it's my job to step in when I see something like this. There's a youth club just over the road. Suppose some of the kiddies saw you, eh?'

'Yeah, and what am I supposed to do? I need to eat. I need to survive.'

'When was the last time you ate?' Lil looks noticeably thinner than when he last caught her. 'Can you even remember?'

'Yeah!'

'Look, sit down, will you? Here—' The white-haired, heavyset officer pulls a Mars Bar from his pocket and hands it to her.

Hungrily, she looks at it.

'Go on, take it. You'll be doing me a favour. If my wife knew about my nightly Mars Bar intake, she'd have my guts for garters. I'm on a diet… well, meant to be.'

'Thanks,' she says, opening it with her teeth.

'Look, I'm not here to make life harder for you. But having sex out here – especially in a bus stop – it puts you in a vulnerable position. You've been warned before.'

'You think I don't know that?' she says, chocolate and caramel sticking to her teeth. 'What you gonna do? Fine me?'

'No, I'm not looking to fine you. What I'd rather do is refer you to some support services. There's a group in town that helps people in your situation – housing support, addiction services, whatever you might need.'

'And what happens if I say no? They don't help people like me. You're gonna arrest me, aren't you?'

'Not tonight, no. I'd rather not see you here again, though. Next time, it could be different.'

'You said that last time,' she says, stretching out her legs and crossing them over at the ankle. '*Soft touch.*'

'So you'd rather I was like most coppers, do you?' The privilege of an early retirement on the cards has certainly had a mellowing effect on Constable McCann. 'Still knocking around with your mate, Welby?'

'No.'

'Well, good. He's no good for you. He's trouble that one, mark my words, he's—'

'He's dead.'

'Oh – I'm sorry. I'm very sorry to hear that. A fateful misadventure, I take it?'

'Yeah, his parachute didn't open.'

'A skydiving accident?'

'No, of *course* not. It was the brown, weren't it. Poor bugger. Where's *your* mate, anyway?' she says after finishing the last bite of Mars Bar and screwing up the wrapper and tosses it in the bin. 'You think he got him?'

'No. Probably not. Probably just buying time. Probably been lured by a saveloy in that chippy on the corner. How he maintains that washboard stomach of his I'll never know. Why don't you go and warm yourself up with some chips? Generous portions in there. A rare thing these days.'

'What, and have your mate nick me in there? In front of everyone?'

'He won't. Look – take this.' The good officer pulls out a fiver. 'Take care of yourself. I mean it. And... let's not meet like this again, alright?'

The fiver between her fingers drops to the floor. The officer stamps on it before the wind can blow it away.

'Lil? Did you hear me?'

'Fuck.' Frozen like a statue, Lil stares ahead at the notice board inside the bus shelter.

'Missed the last night bus? I distinctly remember this happening last time. Come on, get in the car. I'll take you back – Lil? *Helloo*?'

'I used to live there, you know,' she says, her eyes glued on the missing persons poster behind the notice window. 'Well, squatted there. They've done it up now, though. Some Irish-themed pub. Brendan *Murphy*. Well, I never.'

MISSING: HELP FIND BRENDAN MURPHY!

Also goes by: Murphy or Murph/ Age 76/ Blue eyes/ Reddish-grey hair/ 5'7"/ 200 pounds/ Last seen on August 6th, 2022, captured on CCTV outside Ladbrokes, Ealing Broadway, wearing blue jeans and green Celtic FC top.

For any information that can help us find him, please contact his brother

(056 456-8976)

#HELPFINDBRENDANMURPHY

(photo taken 1998)

'Know him, did you?'

'No. He told me his name was Puffy,' she says, picking

caramel out of her teeth. 'But these letters would come –
you know, reminders, final demands – for a Murphy, a Mr.
Brendan Murphy. He kept ripping 'em up and putting
them in the bin. Told me he was Welsh.'

'Who did?'

'You wouldn't believe me if I told you.'

'Try me.'

'All scratched up they were. All withered and scabby.
Kept 'em away, he did. Kept 'em hidden. All that time.
Never said a word. No one believed me. Not even Welby.'

'Listen, Lil—'

'All pale and dead-looking, they were.' Her eyes seem
fastened to some distant star. 'Dead and ghostly. I thought
they were wax at first, but when I saw 'em move...' She
shudders. Facing Constable McCann, she adds, 'It was like
they was on the brink between life and death. I remember
he always had this bump round his lower back, but I
thought nothing of it at the time. Just thought he had bad
posture, you know – a herniated disc or something, but no,
no, no. It weren't that. It was *them.*' Her voice drops. 'He
can't have liked 'em, can't have wanted 'em. Looked like
he'd tried to hack 'em off hisself – had a good old go like.
Must've had a complex.'

'A killer with a complex is often a deadly combination.'

'Killer?'

'Lil – would you be willing to come down to the station
and give a formal statement about what you saw?'

That faraway distance hardens to steel. 'Why? So you
can nick me? No way.'

'I promise you won't get nicked. You could really help
us with this investigation.'

'No. No way.'

'Okay. Have it your way. Looks like a long wait,' he
says, squinting at the bus timetable. 'Four hours twenty
minutes to be exact.'

He walks to the kerb and opens his car door. 'Oh well.

Cheerio.'

'Oi, where you going?'

'To the station. Might pick something up on the way – ooh, I don't know, some KFC, or a cheeky McDonalds?'

'What about your diet – fat bastard?'

'Sure I can't tempt you?' he says, once in the driving seat with the window halfway down. The engine hums.

Too proud to ask about that fiver, Lil pulls her bomber jacket tighter around her tiny frame.

'Lil – based on the information you've just shared, this could open up a whole new line of enquiry.' Opening the glove box, he pulls out a bag of *Pickled Onion Monster Munch.* 'Not for the faint of heart, these. Vinegar so strong they should be outlawed – *Yeehaw!*'

With a slight tug, the bag gives way with a pop.

'Yeah? And what would your wife say?' she says, jumping in the back, and lunging forward to snatch the packet of maize snacks from his hands. 'I'm a *Cheetos* girl myself.'

She pulls the door closed, sealing them in a haze of sharp, tangy pickled onion scent. 'So, what is it you want to know?'

~

'It seems that Finch and this Murphy had some kind of a falling out. All this time we've been looking for a man with four arms, when he's been walking around like the rest of us. It's the perfect cover for his crime. How could we have been so stupid?'

Constable McCann pushes through the double-swing doors and trails after Constable "Washboard" Dakine, through to the briefing room.

'But how can someone get rid of their own arms?' asks Constable Dakine, glancing up at the shift rota pinned to the corkboard.

'Quite easily when you've got another pair,' says McCann, over by the coffee station. 'Want one?'

'Nah,' says Dakine, dragging one of the stackable chairs out from the U-shaped seating arrangement and dropping into it. 'When'd you say the girl saw him last?'

'Summer, just gone.'

'Where?'

'Outside the precinct. Said he walked past, while she was begging – threw a couple of quid her way but didn't recognise her. Said he was walking with a stick. And definitely – only one pair of arms.'

The kettle boils. McCann fiddles with a leftover shortbread biscuit still inside its plastic wrapping. After reading the calorific content on the back, he puts it straight down again.

'But how can she be sure? These modern chest-binders can do wonders, you know. Contoured stitching. Bonded edges…'

'Oh yeah?' says McCann, lifting the kettle with eyebrow raised.

'Who's to say he wasn't simply hiding them again. Compressed them. Flattened them down.'

'In a white vest and knee-length shorts?' Resisting the sugar bowl, McCann takes his coffee and pulls out a chair opposite Dakine.

'Seamless she said. Smooth as a baby's bum. I'm telling you, he did the old man over.' McCann takes a sip of instant coffee and grimaces.

'But how did he do it?'

'Well, that's what we've got to find out. He was obviously covering something up because he told the girl Murphy was Welsh. The contractors who did the pub renovation said they found this creepy pub sign displaying the image of a four-armed man inside some kind of ritual circle, which might hint at the occult. "The Finch's Arms," it said on it, so we know he had designs on the place…'

'No, I mean, how did he do it? Did he chop his left one off first with his right hand, then use his left hand to chop off the other one? And seamless, you say? So now our killer's an expert in needlework? Seems a bit far-fetched to me.'

'That, Dakine, I don't know. But what I do know is that it's time we started looking a bit closer to home. That girl's lucky she got out while she did. She could very well have been his next victim.'

CHAPTER 24

Tired of being unable to match Surinder's level of depth in his letters, Danny's joining the library. He's made a list of all the books one might expect someone to have read at his age. He's set himself a realistic reading target: one book every three months.

Inspecting the spines of the books, Danny locates shelf address: EH-537. It's thicker than he'd hoped, but the cover's a lot racier than he expected, featuring a naked woman, reclining back with her hands behind her head, eyes closed. Danny checks whether he's got the right book and is pleased to see that he has.

'Just the one book today, sir? You know you can borrow up to eight at a time,' says the long-haired young man in a burgundy pullover at the circulation desk.

'Just the one.' Danny slides his book through.

'Do you have any proof of address? You won't be able to join without it, I'm afraid.'

'I know, I know.' Danny slides his utility bill through, then his picture is taken and he's issued with a library card.

'Jesus – you're no David Bailey,' he tells the man, eyeing the photo on his newly printed library card. The light catches his receded forehead, making it look enormous. 'I look like a ghost. Don't give up the day job, yeah?'

Sliding the card and utility bill safely inside the book, he exits through the double-doors, now a member of Ealing Road Library.

LaPage set him a therapy task to "try something new" each weekend. Last week he made a pasta sauce from scratch: tomato and roasted red pepper, jarred and labelled.

'Well done, Danny. That's wonderful,' LaPage said, when he handed her a jar.

The week before that, he was tasked with writing a

poem – about himself. Deciding to keep it short, he chose a limerick, but the only word he could find to rhyme with Danny was inappropriate, so he shortened his name to Dan:

There once was a man called Dan,
Who never had much of a tan.
He sat in the sun,
And burned his bum,
And cooled it under a fan.

LaPage told him he'd missed the point. He hadn't. He knew exactly what it was she was trying to draw out of him, and it wasn't humour. After a cheeky grin and a few self-deprecating words, he thought he'd gotten away with it, but she re-set the task and is still waiting for his second attempt. He'll call himself Daniel this time. *There once was a man called Daniel, who dated a cocker-spaniel…*

'I'm trying something new this weekend, actually,' she told him during their session. 'Mandarin Chinese.'

But Danny was too preoccupied with the past for her words to have registered and stared straight through her. *What were their names? Selby? Selby and…Will? Was it? Will and Selby?*

'Danny?' LaPage said, with a clap of her hands. Slack-jawed and open-mouthed, he turned to face her. 'Danny, I was just saying how I'll be giving Mandarin Chinese a try. Tonight. Straight after our session. I've signed up to a six-week course.'

'Six weeks?' Danny replied, straightening himself up on the couch. 'I've been trying to stay off the takeaways myself. I've been eating a lot of pasta though. A *lot* of pasta. I eat a lot of pasta now.'

"Trying something new" is important to Surinder, so he'll get around to writing the stupid poem at some point and continue "trying something new" on the weekend, and next weekend, and every bloody weekend after that.

The library's not far from the precinct, or The Finch's Arms – only it's not called that. It never was. It's called

"The Irish Bar" now. Someone took it over, did it up while he was in rehab. New roof. New windows. Knocked the whole place through. Black serviettes with green leprechauns on them. Harps and shamrocks. Tacky. Cheap. But the *Guinness* is good.

With his book under his arm, Danny waits to cross the road, gazing across at the pub. It's all a bit of a blur when he thinks back to that place, that time. *Selby? Selby and Will?*

The opening time tang of cleaning products and pulled-through beer welcomes him in.

It's not how he would have decked the place out. They've gone for that cliché, Irish theme, with *Mna* and *Fir* in black lettering above the toilet door. And his carpet's gone. But the hearth is still there, with the biggest flat screen he's ever seen wall-mounted above it, playing the news – something about the young royals.

'You waiting?' asks the fresh-faced barman. There's a different face behind the bar every time he comes in.

'No,' says Danny. The place is near-empty. 'I'm just standing here for my health.'

The trauma of the amputation has left Danny with a hardened edge, and his narkiness goes unappreciated by the barman, staring humourlessly. 'Usual?' he asks.

A dog noisily laps water from a bowl in the snug area while Danny's pint is pulled. Following his ears, Danny turns to see a man in black combat trousers and a black roll-neck sweater, with a large dog – possibly an Alsatian. They make eye contact, all three of them, and Danny takes his pint, whistling the theme from *Mission Impossible* on his way past through to the garden.

A young couple seated in the wooden, sheltered smoking area talk loudly. 'Mind if I...' says Danny, clearing his throat and tapping his walking stick against the decking, taking the couple by surprise. The desired effect is achieved as they scoot along to the other end of the bench, waiting for some words of gratitude from the old man now

243

making himself comfortable.

He gives none.

It's heavy going this book – not the relatable page-turner its title led him to believe. Long sentences make Danny lose his thread, reminding him why he hasn't bothered to pick up a book in years. It's a hard slog.

A pigeon flies down on the lawn, offering the perfect distraction.

It's on Murphy's grave. Time and trauma may have skewed his memory, but he still knows exactly where he buried him – could even give you the precise coordinates, probably. *A little more to the right, maybe, by the potted shrubs, or over there, by the rhododendrons, perhaps.*

There was blood, he knows that, and a lot of hands thrashing about. There was a struggle, some kind of a fight, but whatever it was, Danny knows he would never have killed him in cold blood. Self-defence, yes, or a mercy killing – very likely. Danny can't stand to see anyone suffer.

But what does it matter? That's all in the past, buried somewhere over there, never to be unearthed.

The pigeon beats its wings and flies off.

After half a page, Danny tunes into the discussion the couple next to him is having.

It's getting pretty heated. Bickering and strained voices. *She* thinks the pub was called *The Sun Inn* before it became *The Irish Bar*, but *he* insists it wasn't. Back and forth, back and forth.

'The Finch's Arms,' bursts Danny, snapping his hardback shut and placing it down before knocking back his pint and awkwardly squeezing himself out of the tight space. 'The Finch's Arms,' he reiterates, slowly standing. 'A real nice boozer. A proper boozer.'

It was only ever *The Tavern* in its heyday. It's potential as "The Finch's Arms" was never realised. Yet somewhere in his addled mind, he made it – he really made it – and breathed new life through the walls. There was a snooker table, and people dancing, doing things like the jive, the jitterbug. There was drinking and fighting, and lots of it.

'It was real. A real old-fashioned boozer. They had to put sawdust on the floor to soak up all the blood there was that much. The place was more like a boxing ring, really.' The couple look up at him cagily. 'Big fella used to run it. *Huge* he was. Four arms he had. Hands like spades on the end of every one of 'em. "Finch the Fist" they called him. A different girl hanging off each arm. No one ever gave "Finch the Fist" any trouble. They wouldn't dare. And there he'd be, larger than life, lifting blokes in the air four fists at a time. Knocking 'em back, knocking 'em back. Of course, all this was before your time.'

Pushing his stick forward, Danny turns to go.

'Finch? That bloke with four arms? Didn't he end up inside?' the boyfriend asks. 'Weird, lanky-looking thing, with a big nose, like a beak?'

'No, that was just a myth.' adds the girlfriend. 'Some old legend.'

Their words stop Danny dead in his tracks.

'No, it was real. He was institutionalised. Complete psycho.'

Back and forth, back and forth they go as Danny makes his way to the men's, confused as to why he spun the couple his tall story. He just gets carried away sometimes, that's all, wrapped up in the roguish grandeur, starting to believe his own distorted delusions. And yes, it's probably clinical, but what harm's it doing? He can dream, can't he? How else is he supposed to escape the nightmare he's lived through? One last dream where he feels like a somebody, not a nobody – at least for a couple of minutes.

Tom Cruise and his dog are waiting outside the men's when Danny comes out. The dog's whining, straining at the leash and lunging toward the garden.

'I'd take him outside if I were you,' says Danny. 'Unless of course he knows how to use a urinal. Clever dogs,

Alsatians. Excuse me.'

Offering another rendition of *Mission Impossible*, Danny squeezes past, whistling all the way out the pub, and is across the other side of the road before the couple in the smoking area notice he's left his book.

'*A Farewell to Arms*. Oh yeah, I remember that,' says the boyfriend, picking it up.

'No, you don't. You don't read.'

'We did it in school.'

'You never.'

'We did. Straight up.'

'Oh yeah? What's it about then?'

They hand the book in at the bar, putting an end to their squabbling, and head back out towards the garden.

'Sorry,' the barman says. 'I'm afraid the garden's closed.'

'Closed? It was open just a second ago.'

'Well, it's closed now. Until further notice. Sorry.'

It's not until Danny is almost home that he realises he's forgotten his book. The incurrence of a library fine this early in the reading game would be a true mark of failure, and by misplacing the book and his library card, he'd have the perfect excuse to abandon his road to intellectual betterment. What would Surinder say? But more pressing is the thought of that couple opening the book and finding his library card – with that hideous picture. Like a superconducting magnet, it pulls him back to the pub.

The place has filled up considerably in the short time he's been gone. Scanning the room, Danny's eyes fix on two distinct men wearing Northface: one in a hoodie, the other a jacket, both with neat, well-groomed hairstyles, loitering by the fruit machine.

'Is there a match on or something?' Danny asks them, and they nod. 'Oh,' he says, not at all interested in who's playing, and heads for the garden, navigating with his stick.

'You can't go out there!' accosts the barman. 'Garden's closed!'

'I won't be a second.' Danny keeps walking. 'I'm just getting my—'

'I *said* the garden's closed.' The barman points at a freshly posted sign behind the bar and reads aloud: "GARDEN CLOSED UNTIL FURTHER NOTICE."'

'Alright, keep your hair on. I only want my book. My book's out there.'

'Book? Oh, hang on a second.' The barman moves along the bar and comes back in a flash. 'This one?'

Holding up the book, Danny's library card slips out, landing face-up on the bar. Seeing the photo, the barman smirks.

'Careful.' Danny swipes up his card. 'Do you mind?' he says, snatching the book from the barman's hand with such vigour that the utility bill he repurposed as a bookmark also falls out, no longer marking his page.

'You live at The Bungalows then?'

'God, you youngsters. Very nosy, aren't you?' says Danny, whipping the letter off the bar, realising that the barman must have clocked his address. 'Lost my place now.'

The news plays on the flat screen to the side of the bar. Danny watches and places his bookmark back where it was – the second page of chapter one.

'My nan lives at number twelve, that's all. The lady with the deaf cat?'

'Yeah? Well, that bloody thing keeps shitting on my flowerbeds,' says Danny, not taking his eyes off the screen. The barman sneaks another look at Danny's photo ID, resting flat on top of his book on the bar. He remembers his nan mentioning something about a "miserable old bugger" relocating cat shit into her front garden. He reads Danny's name, then reaches behind the Drambuie and peach schnapps for something.

'Danny Finch?' says the barman, pulling out a small, fat, pink envelope with Danny's name written on it. No address. No postmark.

'What's it to you?'

'Someone left this for you, that's all.' The barman hands it to him. A dog starts barking from the garden.

'What's this?'

'A woman came in. Small. Short.'

'Small?'

'Yeah, I dunno. I mean – I wasn't here. Excuse me—'

'What woman?' asks Danny, as the barman heads out to the garden, leaving Danny alone with the mysterious envelope for a moment. He considers opening it – but something holds him back. He's not sure what.

When the barman returns, he looks disturbed.

'You alright? You look like you've seen a ghost.'

'Yeah. Fine. I'm fine,' he says, dragging a heavy, dark-wood barstool over and placing it against the door to the garden. 'Garden's closed, people!' he announces. 'Nobody goes out there. Nobody. The garden is strictly off-limits. Closed. Sorry.'

As the barman comes back behind the bar, Danny sees him cover his mouth, turn, and gag before addressing the bottleneck of punters that's formed in his absence.

'Who's next?' he asks, voice strained but steady.

'Heavy night was it?' quips Danny, while the barman pulls a pint. 'Look at you, you're shaking. You youngsters. Can't handle your drink, that's your problem. Anyway, this woman. Small was she?'

The barman moves along to the busiest part of the bar. 'Next please!' The dog continues to bark, deep and strong.

'Petite? Pretty?'

'Who? *Double or single, mate?*'

'The woman,' says Danny, craning his neck. 'The woman who came in.'

'Like I said, I don't know. *Ice and lemon?*'

'What's that dog doing out there?' The bark has an intense, resonant quality that puts Danny on edge. 'I thought the garden was closed.'

'It is. *Next please!*'

'*Conservative MP, Edward Ashworth, has been charged with the rape of a fifteen-year-old girl, inside private members club, Isabella's. Ashworth will remain in police custody until a court hearing can…*'

'Turn it up, turn it up,' says Danny urgently to the barman, while the dog works itself up into a frenzy. 'Please, turn it up.'

'With pleasure,' says the barman, cranking up the volume, only too happy to drown out both Danny and the dog.

'*Ashworth met the girl at a house party in Camden three months prior to his arrest. The MP for Islington South forced the girl to drink gin and watch pornography before being driven in a black Phantom to the famous Mayfair club. The body of media buyer Jeremy Quimby, RipCurl Entertainment's former head of creative diversity programming, was found hanging inside the bedroom of Ashworth's Islington flat following the charge, and police have confirmed that the death will be treated as suspicious…*'

'Put the match on!' a punter in a red and white scarf, excitedly demands as the face of a curly-haired man fills the screen.

'*…evidence of foul play was discovered at the scene. A post-mortem examination will follow, and an investigation remains ongoing. Officers are appealing for anyone with information to come forward—*'

Everybody cheers as the *Match of the Day* theme comes on – everyone except Danny, who's fighting his way out through the now-rammed exit with his stick, his head reeling, forgetting his book for a second time.

Jem is dead?

Looking down at the envelope pinched tightly between his fingers, Danny has a strong feeling who the letter is from, and the lack of a postmark can only mean one thing: she's back in the country.

Jem is dead and… and… Lin? Lil? Lin is back?

Ready to fight for justice now that *Isabella's* has made

the news. All out in the open – finally. Once and for all. *Together.* Justice for those girls. Their memory has remained clear as crystal, no matter what life has thrown at him.

Flinging his stick down, Danny hobbles as fast as he can through to the kitchen and flicks on the radio. News about the *Isabella's* case is all over the airwaves. Bringing the brandy down from on top of the fridge, he pours himself a drink, knocks it back, and opens the letter:

Dear Daniel,

I didn't know how else to find you, but I saw you in the papers and recognised the pub from the pictures. I know that was a long time ago, but I gave this letter to a member of the bar staff, and they said they would look out for you. A long shot, I know, and even as I write, I don't believe that this letter will ever find you, and by the time it does, it will probably be too late anyway. You could be in another country for all I know, and the way the press hounded you, who could blame you? For what it's worth, I've got cancer – of the liver, unsurprisingly. It's terminal. I want you to know that I'm sorry.

Danny pours another brandy.

Son, I'm sorry. You were not to blame for Gramps' death. It wasn't your fault. If you can ever find it in your heart to forgive me…

Redemption.

A lifetime of guilt lifts from his shoulders. As tears roll fast down hollowed cheeks, the doorbell rings.

'Mum?' he says, wiping his eyes, his feet pointed towards the door.

Behind the frosted glass, Danny can make out two blurred figures, both male. Crestfallen, he opens the door and, after a few seconds, recognises them from the pub.

'Oh, it's you. Over by the fruit machine? Didn't fancy sticking around to watch the match, then?'

Their eyes scan Danny's frame, wondering if he's stuffed them up his jumper, and unsure whether they needed to bring that second pair of cuffs after all.

'Danny Finch?' one of them asks.

'A Farewell to Arms?'

They stare at him, confusion evident.

'I'm sorry?' says the other one.

'The book? I left it in the pub. I assume that's why you're here?'

As Danny looks to see if either of them has hold of it, their hands rise, and they flash their police badges.

'We were hoping you could come down to the station and help us with our enquiries.'

'Enquiries?' Danny stares down at their footwear. 'Oh, I see! Plain clothes policemen.' He could curse himself for not having spotted it sooner. It's so obvious to him now. The brown hiking boots. Both wearing *Northface*. The incredibly neat haircuts. 'Certainly, officers. Certainly. In fact, I was going to pop down later today – help you fill in any gaps.'

'Were you now?' The officers exchange a glance.

'Yeah,' says Danny, bringing down his best jacket from the coat rack. 'I think an occasion like this demands my finest tweed, don't you, boys? Sorry – officers.' He slips the jacket on. 'I can't believe he's dead. I never warmed to the bloke, though – had that really punchable face. Smug as hell.'

'That's very interesting.'

'I'm sure you'll be able to tell us plenty more down at the station.'

'Oh, yes. Plenty.'

Picking up his stick, Danny locks the door behind him.

'No, he wasn't my cup of tea, not at all. But still... nasty business, death. But you've got to go somehow, I suppose. Awaits us all.'

The officers hadn't expected him to be so forthcoming.

They follow him to their unmarked police car, parked outside Danny's white picket fence, the deaf cat crouched beside the marigolds, digging the earth with deliberate motion.

The End

Laz Newton

ACKNOWLEDGEMENTS

Thanks to my partner Tim and my good friend Helen for always being brutally honest.

ABOUT THE AUTHOR

Originally from Basildon, Essex, Laz now lives in Rutland, England, with her partner, Tim, and two rescue border collies. She loves playing the handpan in the forest, going for long walks, and people-watching from coffee shop windows.

Finch's Arms is her debut novel, and she is currently working on a thriller titled *Marzipan*, about a man who spends his retirement pretending to be deaf.

OTHER TITLES FROM
BURTON MAYERS BOOKS:

WOMEN'S
PRIZE
LONGLISTED
DISCOVERIES

NO OIL
PAINTING

YOU'RE ONLY AS OLD AS YOU FEEL.
NOT THE ART THAT YOU STEAL...

GENEVIEVE MARENGHI

NOTES: